death

Medallion Press, Inc.
Printed in USA

"Mary Ann Mitchell's book is a story about fallible people making the best decisions they can in a dark and dreary world that's only a short drive away from anywhere we live. It is the dark journey into this reality that makes this book truly worth reading, and heeding. For the demons and drives that plague the protagonists in SIREN'S CALL remind us of their very real presence whenever we flip open a newspaper or turn on the TV."

—*Thor the Barbarian*

"Mitchell's fine prose and characters should keep your interest until the good ending."

—*The Horror Fiction Review*

Published 2007 by Medallion Press, Inc.

The MEDALLION PRESS LOGO
is a registered tradmark of Medallion Press, Inc.

Typeset in Adobe Jenson Pro
Printed in the United States of America
10-digit ISBN: 1-93228158-4-8
13-digit ISBN: 978-1932815-84-9

10 9 8 7 6 5 4 3 2 1
First Edition

DEDICATION:

To John, with love.

prologue

GENTLY THE OLD WOMAN BRUSHED THE DAMP RAG across the dying woman's forehead. The bed linen was wet with sweat and bile. The candle's wick on the windowsill burned low. The room was chillier than it ought to have been for one so ill, but there was no money for fuel, no money for a physician, only the arduous wait for death that hung in the air.

"How is she, Maria?" asked the priest.

Maria touched an index finger to her lips and softly walked across the room to join the priest at the threshold.

"She is much worse. I feared you might not come."

The priest looked into Maria's bloodshot eyes and saw the agony she suffered from carrying this dying woman's soul on her conscience. Too young to fear his superiors, the priest had come when Maria's grandson had brought her plea. He looked to the bed and saw Susanna tossing in an uneasy sleep.

"Bring the candle closer to the bed. I have brought the Host, if she is able to repudiate her past and consign her soul to the Lord."

When he reached the head of the bed, Susanna's eyes opened. Even in her feverish turmoil she could sense this man of God.

"Why are you here?" she asked.

The priest awkwardly looked to Maria.

Embarrassed, Maria lowered her head and admitted that Susanna had not asked to see him.

"That is not what your grandson led me to believe."

"She has tried to turn her life about, Father."

"Many times, from what I've heard, but she forever found herself wandering from one man's bed to another."

"What could she do? She has no father, and her family has disowned her. She depended on men to survive."

"She would have been better off dead." The priest's voice was charged with indignation. "Why waste my time here, when I could be serving a Christian family?"

"But, Father, often you have preached that we all are God's children. Isn't Susanna entitled to have the hand of God resting on her brow?"

"I am worth nothing, Maria." Susanna attempted to raise her head from the pillow but fell back. "A child who kills a parent will never be called to the presence of any God. I am resigned to the contempt my body will receive after I die. You are a wondrous woman to stay by me and listen to my contrite rambling. However, I cannot set my hopes in a religion that is foreign to me."

Maria rushed to the side of the bed. "It does not matter whether he is dressed as a priest or a rabbi. They both carry the Lord with them."

"Maria, that is slanderous. There is only one God. And He recognizes only His own papal religion."

Maria turned quickly toward the priest.

"And He is the God who would torture a people for being different. There is no sin on Susanna's soul except for the desire to live that has driven her to this ignoble deathbed."

"She admits she killed her own father, Maria. What do you expect me to do for one such as she?"

"Susanna did not kill her father with her own hand."

"No, her lover did that for her by informing the Inquisitor. The wench's lover related seeing her father heading the table of a family seder. You know that the Edict of Faith requires that a Christian report the name of the home that celebrates the Feast of Unleavened Bread. She knew the law, but allowed her baser drives to overcome even her love of family."

"She did not expect him . . ."

"Stop, Maria. The priest is right. I sinned dreadfully against my own, and I have not paid enough for the evil I brought upon our house."

"Repent, Susanna. Repent and die in peace," begged Maria.

"Peace. I don't deserve peace. I should have been the one placed on the rack, not my father. My body should have been singed by the flames that licked my father's flesh. Instead, the Inquisitor deemed to take all that I had and set me free in the streets. I have slept on cobblestones, and when it rained I sought shelter in doorways and taverns and, yes . . ." Her voice lowered, and her eyes met the priest's. ". . . in the beds of men both kind and brutal."

"Repent, Susanna, while the Lord's representative stands before you." Maria fell to her knees by the side of the bed, holding Susanna's skeletal hand tightly. Susanna's flesh sagged and paled as the hour of death approached.

"For you, dear woman, I would seek forgiveness if I felt in any way worthy. Your kindness and attention deserve more than what I am capable of giving to you."

"Do it for your child, Susanna."

"My daughter is a stranger to me. Shortly after I had birthed her in a convent, I fled. She does not know who her mother is, and that is for the best. She must never know that my Jewish blood flows through her veins. Safe within the arms of the sisterhood she will live out her life, not knowing man and the terrible yearning he can spark in her flesh."

"She has a daughter?" the priest asked.

"Susanna was barely two months with child when the Inquisition took away her father. That may be one reason why her life was spared."

"Where is the girl now?"

Fear roared into Susanna's eyes as she looked between the priest and Maria.

"We do not know," mumbled Maria. "It has been more than seventeen years. The child is now an adult. Perhaps she remained in the convent. Perhaps she left and married and had her own babies." Maria shrugged.

"If you have any idea where the daughter is, you should call for her now so that she and her mother can make amends. Susanna does not have many more hours to atone for the evils she has set in motion."

Jumping to her feet, Maria let go of Susanna's hand.

"The evils, Father, were set in motion by the men who called for the Inquisition. Not by simple souls who were caught up in the confusion." She turned to face the priest. "Even you know, Father, that many died so that others could abscond with the wealth that the victims left behind. This is not a battle for souls, but a war of greed."

"Silence. If someone should hear, you would be reported to the Inquisitor."

"I have no wealth. I merely comfort those who are leaving this world. And sometimes I envy them when they finally close their eyes. Instead of finding peace, I cleanse the corpse and help families to bury those they love. Do you know the number of tears I have seen? The number of children left stunned and often homeless because of death?" Her voice faltered. "What am I saying? Of course, you see the same hideous repetition as I do." Maria got down on her knees and kissed the hem of the priest's cassock. "Forgive me, Father. You are here because you understand the anguish. I should never have spoken in such a way."

The priest's hand shook slightly as he reached for the top of Maria's head.

"I will stay until the end and require no false contriteness."

Maria smiled up at the priest, but became alarmed when she heard the wheezing breath of her patient.

"There is one more favor I must ask, Maria." Susanna's voice cracked as she spoke.

Leaning over the bed, Maria promised that she would fulfill this last request.

"You must take my head to the Inquisitor. Ask him to place it above the front-door lintel of what was once my family home. Let everyone see my shame, and let the vermin eat my flesh. And when there is nothing but skull, let it stand as a reminder of the lowly life I brought upon myself."

Maria began to shake her head, but Susanna would not allow her to speak.

"See to it, Father, for I fear Maria may weaken and bury me whole. Someday my daughter may walk past my skull and condemn the life that forced her into such a cruel world."

chapter 1

TERESA HESITATED BEFORE WALKING DOWN THE dark cobblestone street. She brushed her dark hair back from her face and wished she had thought of wearing a shawl to cover her head and shoulders. A mild chill made her shiver. Her arms were bare and bore the woven tattoo from the basket she had been carrying. The basket now lay at her feet, filled with the sweets and meats Sister Agatha had packed for the newly widowed wife of an admitted heretic.

How was she supposed to locate the home of the widow in the darkness before her? Her green eyes could see only shadowy forms crowding the street. Teresa crossed herself and took a deep breath. As she bent to lift the basket, a small animal ran past, almost touching her skirt. A rat nosing its way closer to the banquet that rested at her feet? she wondered. Swiftly she lifted the basket into her arms and took slow, careful steps down the street.

The street was known as *La Calle de la Muerte*, the

Street of Death. Many *conversos*, Jews who had convert-ed to the Roman Catholic faith, had lived on this street. Most were now dead due to the efficiency of the Inqui-sition. Whispers floated through the air on this street, whispers of the dead carried by the wind to the ears of family who were left behind. The cries of children suf-fering hunger and isolation rang through the street by day, and only in the quiet of night could the whispers lul-laby their babes to sleep. Gossip spoke of widows being embraced in their beds by ghostly arms that felt familiar, and children smiled in their sleep as if a loving father had tousled their hair.

She listened intently, hoping that she would not hear the specters that mourned their former lives. Her eyes were opened so wide they ached. Another small animal crossed her path. She hoped it was not a black cat.

The fourth door on the right should have a simple handmade crucifix attached to it. This would be the house where she would leave the burden she now carried.

The moon lent enough light that she could see on the ground a crucifix obviously fallen from an old bare wooden door. Perhaps many of the houses had crucifixes, she thought while edging closer to the door. Through a side window she could see several candles burning, shed-ding a glow on a pair of sleeping children.

Teresa rapped lightly on the door. She could hear a chair being moved, and soon a graceful woman stood in the open doorway. The woman's eyes were swollen from tears but still carried the glint of pride. Her high cheekbones were set on a lean face. Her skin looked so smooth and pale that Teresa wondered if this woman actually belonged on this poverty-ridden street.

"Señora Esther?"

The woman nodded her head, and Teresa stretched her arms out, offering the overflowing basket to her. As the woman reached to accept the gift, Teresa saw how weathered the woman's hands looked. Calluses and bruises marred the flesh. An open wound crisscrossed the back of one hand. Teresa sensed that the woman had noticed her gaze when Señora Esther almost pulled her hands back, but reason quickly made her change her mind and take the basket.

"Would you like to come in?"

"No, I see that your children are sleeping, and I do not wish to disturb them."

"Thank you. This is the first night they have managed to nod off. Children heal more quickly than we do, don't they?"

Teresa nodded her head, thanking God she had never known what it was like to lose a parent or go hungry in the middle of the night.

"You should also try to sleep."

"I have his clothes laid out on the bed. I will bring them to the convent soon. I just can't . . ." The widow's voice cracked.

"There is no hurry. Sister Agatha wished to ensure the children weren't going hungry."

"Thank her for me." Embarrassed, the widow tilted

her head down toward the basket.

Teresa squatted to lift the crucifix off the ground. When she stood she saw Señora Esther's complexion turn ashen.

"I did not realize it had fallen from the door," the mother said, reaching out with one hand for the cross.

"I'm sure it was the wind. Let me help you reattach it."

Together they fumbled with the crucifix, one shaking with fear and the other embarrassed to have caused such emotion.

Finished, Señora Esther turned with pleading eyes to Teresa.

"You'll not tell anyone about finding the crucifix on the ground, will you?"

Trying hard to bring peace to the mother, Teresa clasped hands with the woman and swore she would not.

With a parting blessing, Teresa turned away from the door as it softly closed.

She looked straight ahead and saw that she was being watched by one of the dead. A skull loomed directly above the door on the opposite side of the street. An iron lantern with a thick candle had been placed next to the skull.

Susanna Diego's skull, she remembered. Everyone spoke of the woman who had brought disaster on her own family. If the night were quiet enough, Susanna's cries and screams could be heard begging for forgiveness, begging for the life of her father as she had done in life, when the flames had lit the brush surrounding her father's stake.

Teresa thought she heard soft crying, as of a spirit

mourning. "Child." The air seemed to catch the softly spoken word, but no other living person was near. She looked up at the skull and pitied the woman who had brought the Inquisition's curse on her family.

As she moved closer to the skull, she spied a tear. Could it really be a tear? Teresa wondered, slipping down over the grayish-white bone that had been aging there for several years. Teresa reached her hands out, palms upward, and felt the beginnings of a long-needed rain. Again she cursed the fact that she had forgotten a shawl and turned to hurry up the cobblestone street back to the convent.

chapter 2

"I MUST HAVE SOMEONE WITH EXPERIENCE, NOT an orphan child no one else needs."

Teresa heard the loud masculine voice as she opened the door to the convent. She saw Sister Agatha standing in the doorway of the parlor, facing a pacing male who was smartly dressed.

"She has had much experience here at the convent caring for the other sisters when they have been ill. She knows well how to give comfort to the dying," said Sister Agatha.

"Death! My father will survive this illness, Sister, and outlive you by many a year."

"I did not mean to offend. Only I wanted to assure you that if the situation worsened, Teresa would know what to do."

"But she is merely a child."

"No, I beg your pardon, Señor Velez, she is a woman of twenty. Already many other women of that age would be raising their own brood."

"And why isn't she? Has she taken vows? Has she

even experienced life beyond your shuttered doors and windows?"

"Yes, she is often our link to the outside, running messages and bartering for food."

Teresa closed the door softly behind her, all the while trying to decide whether she should inform Sister Agatha of her return. The man's voice coming from the parlor sounded angry and rough. His speech indicated he was well educated, but he obviously did not know how to speak to those who labored for the Lord. Not wanting to embarrass Sister Agatha, Teresa crossed the hall to the staircase.

"Teresa has not taken vows and will not. Her life will be dedicated to the needy and unhealthy such as your father."

"My father has all his needs met, Sister. He doesn't need pity from the Church."

"Ah, but he does need someone to care for him while he is laid low by the sickness."

"I do not want a peasant looking in on him. I want someone who is of a higher status."

"Is that why you expect one of the sisters to go with you to your manse?"

"I expect it because my father is Señor Roberto Velez, confidant of the bishop, who is your superior."

"We all know that your father has done much for the Church since his conversion. His money has filled the bellies of many starving families. That is why I am willing to allow Teresa to live with your family. We will miss her. I hoped you might recognize our own sacrifice in giving her to you."

"Where is this Teresa now?" he asked.

"Here," Teresa answered, coming into view of the parlor. She curtsied, keeping her head down, afraid to meet this man's glare.

"You are back, my child." Sister Agatha put her arms about Teresa's shoulders and pulled her to the center of the room. "You are wet."

"A light rain. I am not soaked to the skin. A fitting rain to ease the discomfort the heat has caused this past week."

"Perhaps you should run upstairs and change before meeting with Señor Velez."

"I do not have the time to wait, Sister. A brief conversation with Teresa now will not harm her health, I'm sure."

"Perhaps that is the kind of attitude that led to your father's bedridden state," replied Sister Agatha.

"It is all right. I will stand by the fire while we talk." Teresa moved to the strong fire in the fireplace. The days had been hot, but evenings chilled homes quickly when the sun descended. She watched a burst of sparks explode as one of the logs fell forward.

"I would prefer that you face me," he said.

She turned slowly but kept her head bent toward the floor.

"Look at me, woman." The gruff voice frightened Teresa. Most of the men she had dealings with were men of the cloth who spoke with patience.

She raised her head and found herself staring into

dark, ominous eyes. His cheekbones accentuated his gaunt but handsome features. A dark hue settled on the skin just below his eyes. This man had not slept well in days.

"Teresa, this is Señor Luis Velez. His father is Roberto Velez, one of our most generous sponsors."

The man threw back his shoulders and stood taller. He had to be at least six foot two or three, Teresa thought. The lace at his throat was delicate and finely crafted.

"It is a pleasure to meet you, Señor Velez. I have heard much about your father and am sorry to hear that he is ill."

"How do you know my father is sick?"

"I couldn't help but hear the conversation you and Sister Agatha were having when I came in."

"In other words, you were eavesdropping." The sarcastic tone of his voice hurt and made her blush.

"I have been taught better manners than some," she said, proudly returning Señor Velez's glare.

He ignored her comment.

"Come, tell me how a woman such as yourself finds contentment in a convent." He backed away from Teresa to take a better overall look at her body.

Conscious of the dampness of her clothes, she turned back toward the fire. Her breasts seemed to be swelling against the white cotton of her blouse. She folded her arms and wished she had taken Sister Agatha's advice and changed.

"I was born in this convent, Señor Velez, and have always considered it to be a blessing."

"Born to one of the nuns?"

"No! My mother was a misguided woman who allowed herself to be tricked by a man's charm."

"And she left you here?"

"What else could she do? The sisters have taken good care of me, and I pray every day that my mother's soul was eventually saved."

"Not likely."

Anger caught in Teresa's throat, but before she could say anything, they were interrupted by Sister Agatha.

"I must insist you allow Teresa some time to warm herself and change her clothes. If she becomes ill, there will be no one else to send to care for your father."

Teresa sensed the man turning away from her, and with relief she hurried toward the doorway. She stopped just outside the room.

"Does Señor Velez still have need of my services?" she asked.

There were a few moments of silence. She did not know whether the man had nodded in assent or whether Sister Agatha had made the choice for him, but the sister instructed Teresa to be up and ready to leave by eight the next morning. Her heart fluttered with excitement. She should fear this assignment, she knew; instead she felt a strange desire for this new adventure.

chapter 3

TERESA PACKED HER FEW BELONGINGS BEFORE retiring for the night. Her narrow bed didn't seem as inviting as on most other nights after she had spent a full day running errands, cleaning, and caring for the ill. The muslin sheets were too cold and the wool blanket much too scratchy, but she shut her eyes tightly and prayed that sleep would finally come.

Deep in the night, Sister Agatha knocked softly on the door to Teresa's small room, and she responded immediately, relieved that she had something to distract her from the boredom of a sleepless night.

"I'm sorry to wake you, Teresa." The nun held a black rosary in her hands.

"I wasn't sleeping." Teresa pulled a shawl around her shoulders and invited the nun into the room. "I'm a bit nervous about joining the Velez household."

"Don't allow Luis Velez to intimidate you. He is spoiled and very full of himself, but he is also afraid of losing his father, which makes him even more disagreeable."

"Is his father dying?"

"From what little I have heard, I believe so. The doctors are probably bleeding him into the grave."

"Then they must be told to stop."

"It is not your place, Teresa, to advise on how to treat the sick. Besides, no one will pay any heed. If it is time for Roberto Velez to die, then it is up to the Lord."

Teresa made the sign of the cross and bowed her head.

"We have told you little about your mother." The nun hesitated when she saw Teresa eagerly look up. The hope in Teresa's eyes brought sorrow to the nun's heart. "And I will not break the promise I made to your mother to keep her name a secret from you. She didn't want you to carry about the stigma from the circumstance of your birth. However, I can tell you she loved you and would be proud of how you've grown." Sister Agatha brushed a few strands of hair out of Teresa's eyes. "You look so sleepy."

"But I can't sleep. I do and I don't want to leave here. There is too much confusion inside my head for me to sleep. I keep hoping I won't fail the trust you have in me. Señor Velez is an important and influential man."

"Yes. His main power rests in the wealth he has accumulated."

"My clothes . . ."

Sister Agatha reached out and pressed several fingers against Teresa's lips.

"You are not going to a ball. You are serving an invalid. You are a handmaid to the dying."

"Señor Velez's son does not agree with you. He

expects his father to have a full recovery. How shall I deal with his disappointment if he is wrong?"

"Gently. Neither the father nor the son is cruel. You will not come to harm, if that is what worries you."

Teresa nodded her head.

"We will all miss you, Teresa."

"When Señor is better, or called to the Lord, won't I return here to the convent?"

"I have a premonition that your life here may be drawing to a close. But don't look so sad. There is much for you to do outside these walls. Of course, if need be, we will always accept you back."

"Why didn't my mother choose to stay at the convent? Couldn't she have joined the order?"

"That was impossible."

"Because of me?"

Sister Agatha turned from Teresa and caught sight of the package Teresa had prepared for her trip.

"Your mother came here to have you. She didn't want to stay. She wanted a good home for her child, a safe home during these violent and uneasy times. I came to you at this late hour because I've been praying in the chapel, asking God whether I have taken the proper action in sending you away. You've played an important role in our lives ever since we heard your first cry. We actually bickered over who would change you or feed you. Sister Lucia refused to give up your 2AM feeding, and most of the other nuns resented that. Sometimes you have been a disruption, but overall you've been a blessing." Sister

Agatha faced Teresa and placed the rosary she had in her hands around the young woman's neck. "Keep these with you. My own mother gave them to me when I entered the order, and now I want you to have them."

"But I'm leaving the convent."

"All the more reason you should have them."

"I'll use them every night." Teresa's fingers played with the beads. "I shall always include each of you in my prayers, for this is the only family I have."

chapter 4

AFTER SISTER AGATHA LEFT, TERESA NODDED off with the rosary threaded through her fingers. Upon awakening she rubbed the night sand from her eyes and wrapped the rosary beads inside a clean handkerchief, slipping it neatly inside the bundle she had prepared the night before.

She ate her morning meal with the nuns as usual, but when she tried to assist in taking away the dishes, Sister Agatha stopped her.

"There is no time for cleanup; Señor Luis Velez will be here any minute." As Teresa followed Sister Agatha out of the room, each of the other nuns came forward to hug her. Having taken the vow of poverty, the nuns had no parting gifts for her, but they had something worth far more: love in their hearts for the wee babe that had grown into such a beauty. Most of the nuns brushed tears from their eyes, except for Sister Roberta who sobbed passionately on Teresa's shoulder.

"Sister Roberta, you are going to make the girl late."

Sister Agatha, with a stern expression, briskly chased the older nun away. "I believe you have kitchen duty this morning, Sister, and I see several tables still covered with the remains of breakfast."

Like a child, Sister Roberta used one of her sleeves to dry her face.

"Promise you'll be back for a visit, Teresa. And don't wait too long, or I'll be forced to walk the distance from here to Señor Velez's home. My poor legs are way too crippled with arthritis to comfortably make it."

"You must continue with the exercises I taught you." Teresa found herself pulled along to the front door of the convent with Sister Agatha in the lead.

Teresa saw the bundle filled with her possessions waiting on the nearby window ledge.

"Are you sure you remembered to pack everything?" Sister Agatha asked.

Teresa nodded, afraid that the lump in her throat would break into a sob if she opened her mouth.

"Señor Luis Velez is not such a monster as he appeared yesterday. He is young and unsure of himself and overcompensates by being rude. On the other hand, his father is a delight. He is charming, generous, and well educated, especially in the doctrines of our religion. He traveled a great deal and missed out on a large portion of family life, I'm afraid. His wife died a few years ago, and his health has steadily worsened since then. I believe he blames himself for not showing more interest and affection to her when she lived. But success in business does not always allow one to cater to the family."

"Then his son must not have seen much of him."

"On the contrary, the two have traveled together a great deal. Perhaps as a small child Luis Velez did not see much of his father, but once the boy finished his education, father and son were inseparable."

The sound of a coach approached the convent door. Sister Agatha and Teresa stood still, almost holding their breaths until the coach stopped.

"That must be Señor Velez. Hurry, grab your bundle." Sister Agatha threw wide the convent door and stared at a shabbily dressed coachman.

"Are you Sister Teresa?" the man asked. He didn't appear to be an old man, but the lines on his face were deep, and the hair on his head was sparse. In his hands he held an old cap that looked older than him.

"No." Sister Agatha hurried Teresa to the door. "Where is Señor Velez?"

"I'm here by myself, Sister. But don't worry. I know the way home just like an old mongrel."

Teresa smiled and threw her arms around Sister Agatha. "Don't worry, I'll be fine."

"The least he could have done is made sure of your safety."

"Safety? Sister, hardly anything happens on the road between here and the Velez manse. Even the Inquisitor travels this road lightly, with just a few guards." The coachman's round eyes seemed honest enough, and his broad body gave some hope that he could battle at least a single highwayman.

Teresa knew that several attempts had been made on the life of the local Inquisitor, and because of that at least ten people had been either burned at the stake or sent off to the New World. She crossed the threshold and waited for the man to open the coach door.

"Aren't you going to wear your habit, Sister?" he asked.

"I'm not a nun."

The coachman's nose twitched. He probably wondered why she had been locked up in such a place. Had her sin been all that grave?

"Take special care of Teresa," called Sister Agatha. "We prize her skills working with the ill, and we have raised her from a baby."

One of the nun's own bastards, his leer communicated. He opened the coach door and helped Teresa slip inside. The coachman closed the door so softly that Teresa feared it would not stay shut during the rough ride. She pulled the door closer to her but found that it held fast. Her eyes shifted to Sister Agatha, who numbly watched as the coachman prepared to leave. Teresa waved at the nun, but all Sister Agatha could do was swallow hard and draw her lips into a tight line.

The jolt of the coach awakened Teresa's mind to the reality of the situation. For the first time she would not sleep on her cot. She would not be protected behind the thick convent walls or awaken to the sound of the sisters chanting in the chapel.

She wanted to shove the coach's door open and run

to Sister Agatha, but as she looked back she saw Sister Agatha already shutting the convent door. The peeling paint zigzagged across the wooden door, and the weather-aged crucifix hung tiredly under the morning sun.

Teresa leaned back in her seat and hugged her bundle to her breasts. The roomy inside of the coach smelled of wet dog fur, and paw prints marred the velvet cloth of the seat. Did the coachman have a pet? She had seen dogs sitting up next to coachmen before, but never inside such an expensive carriage. She shook her head and wondered whether the paw prints could be cleaned off before the up-pity Señor Luis Velez took his next ride. He'd certainly not tolerate such behavior from a servant.

She enjoyed the ride, especially since she had the in-side of the coach to herself. Strained conversation could wait until she arrived at the Velez home.

Several children ran up to the coach, thinking she might be a fancy lady with sweets or a bit of charity to give. Disappointment crossed their faces when they rec-ognized the coach's occupant. Not that they weren't fond of her, but most could do with a few scraps of food. She waved, and they responded in kind, broad grins finally cheering the expressions on their faces. Several cried out for a ride, chasing the coach for several feet, but the driver sped up and quickly left them behind.

"Nasty old man," she grumbled.

Finally she caught sight of the Velez manse. She couldn't believe just one family lived in a home that size. Of course, servants also abided there to wait on the

Velez's needs. She herself was about to become one of those servants, but, no, for her it wasn't the same. She served God. She would bring God's mercy into the senior Velez's sickroom.

When the coach stopped, she waited eagerly for the driver to open the door. He offered her his hand to steady her step down.

No one opened the mansion door or stood outside to greet her.

"Is anyone at home?" she asked the driver.

"They're all in there, just too lazy to open the door." He walked up to the mansion door and pounded with his fist.

Several minutes later the door swung open.

"Jose, we have a door knocker. Must you always forget that?" A tall man with a neck the size of a bulldog's filled the entrance. His clothes were clean and loosely tailored, allowing room for his muscles to flex with each confident movement he made.

"Why is it you turn deaf whenever I pull up?"

"It is difficult to hear from inside the house, unlike the barn where you spend most of your time."

Teresa stepped forward, hoping to avert an argument.

"Is Señor Luis Velez at home?"

"We're not giving alms today, child. Come back on Wednesday, when the bishop will be visiting. It's the best time to catch the masters in a generous mood."

"She's going to be caring for the senior Velez, Gaspar."

"She's much too young," said Gaspar, still guarding the door against intruders.

"I don't believe that is a decision for you to make. Please tell Señor Luis Velez that Teresa is here." The coachman rubbed his nose with the back of his hand.

Gaspar almost closed the door in their faces, but Jose set his foot in the doorway.

"She's no beggar. I've just fetched her from the convent. Let her wait inside."

Teresa smiled a thank you at Jose and stepped across the threshold. She paused for a moment and then turned back to Jose.

In a low voice she whispered, "The coach smells of wet dog fur and there are paw prints on the seat. Perhaps you should avoid taking your dog for rides."

"Not my dog. The hound belongs to the master's son. It's a wonder you didn't catch fleas while in there."

An itch tickled her right side, but she ignored it and moved gracefully into the hallway.

chapter 5

"DID YOU HAVE A COMFORTABLE TRIP?" LUIS Velez queried.

"Yes, your driver was helpful."

"Helpful? Jose? He must have been waylaid on the way to the convent. I'm sure some highwayman must have brought you here." Luis had been in the room for at least five minutes and had paced the floor the whole time.

A shame, Teresa thought, looking down at the richly colored Persian rug. No doubt he'll wear a hole in the fabric before the interview is over.

Her eyes glanced about the room, making note of the white marble mantle on the fireplace and the decorative screen that stretched across the hearth. The furniture looked expensive but bachelor-worn. From the array of hairs on the settee, she assumed the dog had also been there. Near the double doors hung an incredibly beautiful portrait. The fineness of the strokes and the rich color of the textures brought the pale woman to life.

"That's my mother," Luis said.

"She certainly was beautiful."

"Mother wasn't ugly, but the artist did his best to enhance her features and complexion. Mother was an invalid, and her face often showed the weariness of her illness."

"I'm sorry."

"About my mother? She's been dead for years and is finally at peace."

"But you must miss her."

His muscles stiffened, making it more noticeable how his clothes hugged his body. Obviously he had his garments expertly tailored. The boots he wore were almost new, the richness of the calfskin still shiny and unmarred.

Ignoring her comment, he informed Teresa that she would not be meeting the senior Velez until the next day.

"The doctor came earlier this morning and gave Father an elixir to make him sleep. He had a very bad night, you see."

"Was he in pain?"

"Always in pain, but last night he couldn't close his eyes. Every time I looked in on him I found him staring at the ceiling. Granted, the frescos on the vaulted ceiling of his bedroom are marvelous, but I don't believe he was engrossed in the art."

"Has the doctor given you a diagnosis?" Teresa caught herself fidgeting with the lace on her skirt. Immediately she folded her hands into a tight ball.

"The doctor has mentioned several possibilities but refuses to commit to one."

"Is the doctor bleeding your father?"

"Bleeding him? He has practically drained my father of every drop. The bleeding has stopped upon my request."

Teresa nodded her head.

"You approve?"

"Señor Velez, I'm not trying to treat your father myself, but since I will be caring for him on a daily basis, I wanted some idea of what I should and should not be doing."

He stopped his pacing to stare down at the seated Teresa.

"Have many of the nuns died under your care?"

Her clenched hands ached under the strain of his questioning.

"Not a one."

"You have never seen death, then?"

"I didn't say that. Most people in Spain have seen death, unfortunately. It even intrudes upon our holidays in the guise of the *auto da fe*."

"Ah, but the Inquisitor puts on his show for the king's and our personal entertainment. Do you begrudge the peons a little show? Or perhaps you do not agree with the Inquisition's task?"

"I'm a servant of God. I don't question the work of the Church."

"But you do question the final results, don't you?"

"May I ask why you are so obsessed with the workings of the Church? Are you hiding something, Señor Velez? I believe your father converted some years ago. I assume you were brought up studying the dogma of the Church."

"This conversation has deteriorated into jibes and threats. Perhaps it means that it is time for you to be shown to your room. Come, let me introduce you to Carmen." Luis calmly ended the pointed conversation and led Teresa from the sitting room.

The poorly lit hallway crouched down upon the two figures hovering in an almost ominous quiet. The very end of the hall opened onto a huge kitchen. A rotund woman tapped her foot on the flagstone floor as she stirred the contents of a large pot. A fine mist rose from the pot, filling the room with a succulent beefy odor.

Jose skulked away from the table when he spied Luis. He had just made it to the back door of the kitchen when the rotund woman called out his name.

"Yes, Señora Toledo?" he answered.

"Where are you going?"

"Back to the barn to see after the horses."

"They don't get lonely, but I do." The woman looked up from her pot to scowl at the driver.

"Señora, I think the master wishes to speak with you." Jose managed to direct her eyes toward Teresa and Luis.

"Oh, very sorry, Señor."

"That's all right, Carmen. Although you should keep your mating games out of the kitchen."

Carmen's cheeks blushed, but Teresa couldn't help but notice the annoyance in the woman's eyes.

Jose quietly exited, closing the door softly behind him.

"This is Teresa, Carmen. She will be taking care of Father while he is ill." He turned to Teresa. "Are there any special meals you would like to prepare for Father, or is what the doctor ordered fine?"

Carmen missed the sarcasm in Luis's voice and began protesting.

"Enough," he said. "The meals will continue as before." His curt voice stopped Carmen in mid-sentence. "I would like you to show Teresa to a room. I'm sure you can take care of making her feel at home."

"How long will she be staying?" Carmen asked in a whisper, as if Teresa couldn't hear.

"Until my father regains his strength. You have quite enough to do in the kitchen and overseeing the other servants. I thought it best to bring someone in who could sit with Father most of the day."

"Of course. I'll find her a room."

He nodded to both women and left the kitchen.

"Are you the one they said would be coming from the convent?"

"Yes, but I'm not a nun. The nuns raised and educated me."

"And your poor mother?"

"I never knew her."

Carmen's eyebrows lifted, but she didn't ask anything else. Instead she gave the daily schedule to Teresa, informing the girl that no one was allowed in the kitchen during the evening.

"There would be nothing left for breakfast if I allowed the sluggards who work here to eat whenever they wanted."

"It's possible I may need to retrieve something for the

senior Velez in the evening."

"True. He doesn't eat according to schedule anymore. Some days he barely touches his food. Just don't let Jose or one of the other outside hands use the kitchen at night. I feed them enough during the day and at regular meals." Carmen gave the stew a few stirs before placing the spoon on a small plate next to the stove. "I'll take you up to your room. Do you have any baggage?"

"I left my bundle near the front door."

"Fine. Go get it. I'll meet you at the back stairs."

Teresa's bundle sat where she had left it. No one had touched it. Gaspar had sniffed at the sight of it and raised his nose into the air.

Her sandals clicked against the marble of the foyer. A faint pink ribbon wound through the flooring, contrasting with the brighter pink walls.

Several minutes later she climbed the back stairs with Carmen. The cook's thighs could be heard chafing against each other with each step she climbed. She held a candlestick in her right hand and gripped the banister in the other. Her breathing became more ragged and noisier the higher they rose. In the dim light the walls looked beige with occasional handprints adding decoration. Chips of paint had been swept up against the floorboard, a careless job that had apparently been the rule for some time as demonstrated by the amount of dust collecting there. Just when Teresa thought they had reached the top, Carmen opened another door, which led up yet another flight of stairs.

"Does anyone else have a room this far up?" Teresa asked.

"No. The garret is the only place we have for you right now. But there is a wall that separates the garret in two so you won't have to be bothered by all the clutter. We don't use the garret very much anymore. The masters don't collect much in the way of household goods."

Carmen opened the garret door, and both women were blinded by the blaze of the afternoon sun coming in through the large window. Carmen, knowing her way, moved to her right and opened what Teresa thought was a closet.

"This is your room."

Teresa peeked inside and saw a small cot that might have originally been for a child, and a stained chamber pot. A tiny window over the bed let in a narrow shaft of daylight.

"If you want to put a religious picture or a crucifix on the wall, you may. The sheets are dusty but clean." Carmen smashed the palms of her hands down on the pale yellow quilt. A flutter of dust motes spread out in the air above the cot. "I'll bring you up a pillow before bedtime. Do you use a mirror?"

"Of course."

"Wasn't sure, since you've been used to living in a convent. I'll fetch one from Hilaria. She must have a half dozen by now. Always primping. I think she's set her eye for the young master. Not that she'll ever get him. Maybe in bed, but not in marriage." With great difficulty Carmen squatted down to remove a wooden box from under the cot. "By the looks of your bundle you'll only need this for your personal things." She opened the box, and Teresa was relieved to see it empty, with a clean lining.

"Señora Toledo, do you think I may use some of the cleaning materials to tidy up in here?"

"Ask Gaspar, he keeps a lock on everything."

chapter 6

GASPAR HAD BEEN HARD TO FIND, BUT GENEROUS with the cleaning supplies. By bedtime the tiny room in the garret looked clean and cozy. Sweat layered Teresa's body, but at least she would be able to sleep after the exhausting workout.

A hand lightly knocked before opening the door. A young woman of approximately Teresa's age stood in the doorway, holding two pillows. A mirror lay atop the pillows, reflecting light onto the woman's face.

"I brought you two pillows since you have to sleep up here." She made a face and shook her head. "There are one or two free rooms in the servants' area. I don't know why Señora Toledo insisted on putting you up here. No one has roomed here since they took Catrin away."

"Took her away?"

"She went balmy. That's why they made her sleep up here. No one trusted her in the middle of the night. She liked to handle knives. Thought she was helping Cook. Never hurt anyone, though. There were stories that she used to speak to the mistress of the house."

"What's wrong with that?"

"The mistress is dead. She never spoke to her while the mistress was alive. She would have been dismissed. I guess she figured death was an equalizer, or at least, what could the mistress do?"

Teresa reached out for the pillows and mirror.

"Thank you for bringing these up. I was afraid Señora Toledo would forget."

"They had to drag Catrin out of this room. I'd sure go willingly. Of course, not if I thought the Inquisitor wanted to speak with me."

"What happened to her?"

The woman shrugged.

"My name is Teresa." She laid the pillows and mirror on the bed.

"Oh, never put a mirror on the bed! My grandma told me it brought bad luck. This room has enough bad luck attached to it." The woman lifted the mirror and looked around for a place to lay it. "Let's just put it in this corner, and when you need it, you can pick it up. Cook doesn't approve of putting holes in the wall for mirrors. She believes it encourages vanity."

"Are you Hilaria?"

"Yes. Did Señora Toledo tell you about me?"

"She mentioned that you might have an extra mirror."

"I don't think you'll be here long."

"Excuse me?"

"The senior Velez is not doing well. I've peeked in

while he was sleeping, and he makes these terrible rasping noises when he breathes. He sleeps practically sitting up."

"Has he been sick long?"

"After his wife died, he lost interest in caring for himself. He came down with colds and stomachaches. Finally, three months ago, he took to his bed and stayed there. He doesn't even try walking in the garden."

"He must have loved his wife very much."

Hilaria nodded her head. "But he had other women. Couldn't blame him. After birthing Señor Luis, she gradually lost the ability to walk. By the time her son was six, she had to be carried from one place to another. None of us knew what was wrong with her."

"Hilaria!" A hoarse voice called from the bottom of the stairs.

"I have to go. It's bedtime, and I share a room with Señora Toledo. She has to be up early for breakfast, and she doesn't trust me roaming around at night." Hilaria looked around the room. "It could be worse for you."

"Hilaria, do you hear me!?"

Teresa and Hilaria looked at each other and muffled their laughter.

Teresa still had a smile when she snuffed out the candle beside her cot.

Her head sunk comfortably into the down of the pillow. A light lavender scent emitted from the pillow, and she turned on her side to better lull herself into sleep. Her eyes half-closed as she remembered the events of the day. Her body relaxed as she drifted off to sleep.

A scratching sound forced her eyes open. The noise continued for a few more seconds until she heard the click of paws scrambling across the wooden floor of the garret.

Roof rats, she thought.

Soon she heard the scratching at the door to her room. Lighting the candle, she got out of bed and looked around for something to chase the rats away, but soon quiet returned, and she decided to go back to bed and tell Gaspar about the vermin in the morning.

However, seconds later the scratching returned as she sat down. She rose, went to the door, and slowly opened it. Infested with worthless heirlooms, the garret appeared devoid of life. Her bare feet inched their way into the center of the garret, specks of dirt collecting on the soles of her feet. The moon was nearly full, aiding the candle in illuminating the piles of debris stretched across the floor. A broom handle with a few threads of hay attached leaned against an old trunk. She grabbed the broom and guided herself to where the scratching noise persisted. Holding the broom in front of her like a saber, she edged her way around the trunk to bash the rats.

Her scream pierced the walls and flooring as she peered down at a mongrel with sharp teeth and bulging eyes. Blood dripped from its jaws; flesh lay on its tongue. She backed away, almost dropping the candle and the broom. She and the mongrel stood frozen, staring at each other, until the garret door burst open.

"My Lord, what is happening in here?"

From nowhere Luis suddenly stood behind her.

"Careful, there's a beast in here," she said, hurrying to safety behind Luis.

The "beast" came from behind the trunk with a wagging tail.

"That's Spider. Why is he up here?"

Teresa turned to Luis. "I have the same question."

Luis hadn't bothered to throw on a shirt, and under the light of the moon and the candle, his muscles stood out in sharp definition. A slight bit of hair powdered his chest. She was afraid to look any farther down his body.

"Come here, Spider." The dog ran over to his master and jumped up on the material covering his master's legs.

"I heard a scratching noise and thought there were rats."

Luis wiped the dog's mouth and looked behind the chest.

"Looks like there was at least one," he answered. "But it's dead now. Good boy." Luis petted the mongrel.

"You mean he's more of a hero than a fiend?" she said.

"What are you doing sleeping up here, anyway?"

"Señora Toledo assigned this room to me."

"She shouldn't have. This room is not to be used. She knows that. The Inquisitor wants it left empty."

"Because of Catrin?"

"Señora Toledo told you?"

"No." Teresa didn't want to get Hilaria in trouble. "I heard some of the staff talking about her. They said she went mad."

"I'm waking Señora Toledo if she isn't already up. She'll find you another room."

Shortly after he left with Spider, an apologetic Señora Toledo entered the garret.

"We have one room at the very end of the servants' hallway we can give you. It's small, and I thought you'd prefer your privacy up here."

"But you said there wasn't another place for me to stay."

"I was merely seeing to your comfort. The young master wants you moved now. Please get all your things together and follow me. I'll send Gaspar up to deal with the remains of that rat."

It turned out that the new room was larger than the last and had more conveniences, including a real bed and a full-sized standing mirror. The old dresser had some dust on the top surface, but otherwise it looked clean inside. A small throw rug lay beside the single bed.

"I'm sure I'll be happier here, Señora Toledo."

"Not once the snoring starts next door."

"It'll be better than listening to rats."

"The dog didn't belong up there. The young master gives the mongrel too much freedom."

"I'm not here to replace you, Señora Toledo. I shan't be cooking or supervising the staff. My only function will be to nurse the senior Velez," Teresa said in an attempt to win over the cook.

"I was doing that well enough before you arrived. He doesn't like having company. He prefers to brood in that bed."

"Then I'll make sure he has the privacy to brood. I can sit very still."

chapter 7

TERESA FELL INTO BED AND WAS NOT CONSCIOUS of anything until the next morning, when Hilaria burst into the room.

"I see you got your room changed."

"Thanks to a dog named Spider."

"He's a sweetheart."

"He didn't look sweet when I first saw him last night."

"You have powerful lungs. You'll need them in this house."

"Why, do horrors frequently show up in the middle of the night?"

"No, only occasionally, but you'll find it difficult to talk over everyone else's voice at the breakfast table. Is it true you're a bastard?"

Teresa had started to pull back her blanket when she stopped.

"Who told you that?"

"Señora Toledo. You were raised in a convent, weren't you?"

"Yes." Teresa laid the blanket back on the bed and stood. "But I know practically nothing about my parents."

"You could even belong to one of the nuns."

"My mother left me with the sisters because she couldn't afford to keep me."

"But they've never told you anything about your mother."

"I doubt they knew much about her."

"A woman drops a baby and abandons it. Sounds like she might have been a professional, if you know what I mean?"

"I pray for my mother every night. She had to be in great distress to do what she did."

"I suppose going to the sisters is better than visiting some old witch for herbs to expel the baby. Certainly you must agree with that."

"Why don't you have a room of your own?" asked Teresa.

"Cook doesn't trust me to roam around at night. Thinks I'll end up in the wrong part of the house. Like Señor Luis Velez's room." Hilaria smiled, the idea obviously enticing. "Besides, when I first arrived there were no free rooms." Hilaria reached out to feel the fabric of Teresa's clothes.

"May I have some privacy to dress?"

Miffed, Hilaria left the room without saying anything in response.

Most of the staff had finished breakfast by the time Teresa entered the kitchen. Jose still lingered, picking his teeth and watching Señora Toledo's round bottom.

"We let you sleep late this morning because of the

incident last night, but we expect you to be down for breakfast an hour earlier than today." Señora Toledo barely looked at Teresa.

"What incident?" asked Jose.

Hilaria was in the process of sopping up some milk with a ragged piece of brown bread, but she stopped and giggled.

"Am I the only one who doesn't know?" Jose threw his toothpick on the floor and sat up straight.

A wiry girl of not more than fifteen slurped down her porridge before speaking. "I don't know what happened, either, although I did hear an awful scream."

"Was someone hurt?" Jose plopped his cap on his head, ready to take the lead in coming to a belated rescue.

"Merely Spider having some fun with Teresa." Hilaria's eyes sparkled a glassy blue. Her complexion, lighter than the others, had the reddish tint of sunburn. "Señora Toledo tried to stick Teresa in the haunted room."

"Nonsense. That room is fine. A lot of prattle about spirits and devils." The cook banged one of her pans down on the wooden table, her glare directed at Hilaria.

"Sure, go tell the Inquisitor it's nonsense and join Catrin in the dungeon."

"Why did you put her up there?" Jose asked.

"Because I wanted to." The cook lifted the pot, and Jose decide to rise and get out of her way.

"What did Catrin do here?" asked Teresa.

"Went around spooking everyone. Lighting candles, preparing herbs, cutting her own flesh for fresh blood to put in her brews." Hilaria reached for another slice of bread, and Señora Toledo slapped her hand.

"She was a witch?"

"She claimed not to be, but most others had a different opinion. The Inquisitor took her away to quiet the neighborhood. I heard him tell Master Luis that she was insane."

"I feel sorry for her." Teresa wore the rosary Sister Agatha had given her under her blouse. Her hand automatically searched for the feel of the cross under the material.

"Rumor is, she's the bastard child of the senior Velez." Hilaria peered directly at Teresa. "That's why she's insane, because she's cursed. His wife put a curse on the girl before she died. Nobody is sure who Catrin's mother was. One day she appeared on the doorstep seeking a job. Had no references, but that didn't stop the senior Velez from hiring her. I guess he has a soft spot for bastards."

"Watch your language, Hilaria."

"But, Señora Toledo, those were your very words to me last night." Hilaria scowled. "More likely she was his mistress, anyway."

The wiry girl slipped off her seat. Her dark hair was pushed back under a cap, revealing strong features and round, expressive brown eyes. The palms of her hands were large, but her fingers looked unusually short.

"Shall we start the laundry, Hilaria?" The girl's softly spoken words cracked the silence of the room.

"Better than being stuck in that smelly sickroom upstairs," Hilaria said, glancing at Teresa.

"One day one of the masters will hear you, and you'll be out on the street," warned the cook.

45

"Like Teresa's mother?"

Hilaria and the wiry girl exited the kitchen. Both looked back at Teresa when they reached the doorway.

"I wasn't introduced to your friend, Hilaria."

"Juana, meet the new nursemaid, Teresa."

The girl shyly nodded, then immediately left the room with Hilaria giggling behind her.

"You'd best be seeing to the horses, Jose," said Señora Toledo.

"Already have. I think I have a lot to catch up on right here," he said.

"Jose can't resist pretty girls, can you?" Señora Toledo nudged Jose's arm. "The young master asked that I find some kitchen work for you, Teresa. He's busy and can't take the time to introduce you to his father right now."

"The girl isn't meant for kitchen work," Jose protested.

"I'm actually quite used to cleaning in the kitchen. I usually did the morning cleanup at the convent. Although I am disappointed in not meeting Señor Roberto Velez. I understand he can be charming."

"The old master used to have a great sense of humor. However, I'm told that changed when he took to his bed." Jose's eyes wandered toward the cook.

"You've evidently helped to care for him, Señora Toledo. How has he been recently?"

"Pale and quiet."

"And she should know pale and quiet." Jose laughed as he pulled out a chair to wile the morning away in the company of females.

chapter 8

Spider crawled under the desk chair on which Luis sat. The dog's long hairy legs skidded on the tiles as he crammed himself into such a tiny space, but this did not distract the young man from the reading material sitting before him on the desk. He had been unable to get a complete list of the Inquisitor's accusations against Catrin. The girl had been more frightened than mad when the Inquisition's soldiers came to take her away to the Inquisitor's home, which currently was being used as a prison. Rumors indicated that the temporary home of the Inquisitor was overflowing with prisoners. Many neighbors claimed that screams could be heard at all hours. Does the Inquisitor ever sleep? the people asked each other.

He sleeps, thought Luis, more soundly than he should, given the amount of torture that took place inside the prison walls. The papacy required that no blood be shed during the "questioning" of the heretics. Instead, many gruesome tortures had been implemented that left no outward signs but broke both bones and spirits.

The manse that the Inquisitor used had belonged to a *converso* who dropped his guard and fell in with a Jewish family that seduced him back into his old faith. Many of his neighbors came forward to testify against the man while eyeing his wealth, but the Inquisitor gained the most when he declared the Church the inheritor of the manse.

Now the dungeon of the manse echoed with the sounds of chains, the yanking of pulleys, the splashing of water, and the groans and cries of human voices. Those who were finally freed from the dungeon showed signs of rat bites and lice.

It should be stopped, thought Luis. But how? The monarchy and the Inquisitor remained unified; not even the pope had the power to curb the terrible poison the Spanish Inquisition sowed.

Catrin, how can I help you when I know so little about your past?

He continued to read the report given him by hired spies, but none of it made sense. The Inquisitor did not accuse her of witchcraft, as Luis's own servants had done. The Inquisitor talked of her ability to speak in tongues and call out to the devil. As far as Luis could tell from the report, she had not yet been tortured. She had been locked away for five months and had finally been called in front of the Lord's Inquisitors and asked to confess. The confused girl babbled, and it was ordered that she be taken to the Chamber of Torments. There she was shown the various equipment that could be used to force the truth from her. However, upon seeing a poor man hanging by distorted arms from a beam she fainted and was taken back to her cell.

Who are you, Catrin, and why has this senseless scourge fallen across your shadow?

His own father turned away when Luis mentioned her name. The old man's pale complexion grew whiter, and his eyes slid closed against the vision of her. Luis dared not push for an answer because he feared driving his father into an eternity of sleep.

Luis pushed the papers away, allowing one page to fall to the floor. Spider whimpered and reached out a paw to snag the paper.

"No, boy. This isn't for you to play with," he said, lifting the page and returning it to the desk. He noted that the scribble on this paper did not match the handwriting on the other pages. The writer obviously had been rushed, careless, more concerned with getting the information down on the page than with how it looked. He attempted to read the scrawl, but no matter how hard he squinted or changed the direction of light falling on the page, he could not make out the words. Either the person had not been literate or had been too weak to round their letters properly.

He didn't have time now to pore over the bad penmanship. Later in the evening, after dinner, he would sit down with a glass of port and try again to decipher what the person had tried to communicate. Now he had to introduce Teresa to his father.

He hoped Teresa wouldn't be shocked by what she saw or give any clue to his father as to how grave he looked. He resented the sisters for sending a child. He needed a woman who had toiled with the remnants of the plague and with the afterbirth of babies, but most of all he needed a woman who had the wisdom to guide the dying.

Luis's throat tightened, and his hands gripped the arms of his chair tightly. He had sworn to himself that he would not consider death to be an option. His father would triumph over this illness, just as he had over the political corruption that continually challenged each and every *converso*.

He swept back his chair, catching one of Spider's paws in the sudden movement. The dog yelped.

He reached down and brushed the dog's forehead before checking to make sure the paw had not been seriously damaged. As he made the inspection the dog slapped a wet kiss on Luis's cheek.

"Just getting even, aren't you, Spider?"

The dog seemed to grin under its shiny eyes.

chapter 9

Teresa found it difficult to keep pace with Luis. His long strides took the steps two at a time, and her ankle-length skirt twisted about her ankles. She noticed that he looked more rested, his clothes less formal than when she had met him at the convent. His boots were mud-stained, the leather bleached out. How could he dare to wear such things inside the house when they were meant for outdoors? she wondered. Ah, but then she remembered that there was no mistress of the house. Two males were in charge, and one was sickly and confined to his room. The young master could run around the house naked if he wanted. Perhaps that would pose problems for some, but not for Hilaria. Teresa said a quick Act of Contrition to repent for her unkind thought.

At the top of the stairs, she gazed down the hall at a large number of closed doors. She swallowed, hoping she would be able to find her way back to the sickroom on her own.

"He's feeling better today," Luis said.

"The doctor's elixir worked, then."

"Something worked. Perhaps it was prayer." Luis looked down at her. "Have you been praying, Teresa?"

"If you mean for your father's health, I've probably not been praying more than you."

"I find prayer difficult these days."

"That is when you most need it."

Luis turned away and continued down the hall. He finally stopped at a mahogany double door. He rapped lightly before opening the doors.

Teresa staggered backward from the smell emanating from the room. Someone had attempted to drown sickness with strong cologne.

"He must have a difficult time breathing," she said, barely catching her own breath.

"The servants bring fresh flowers every day, and he prefers the windows shut."

Luis walked into the room without any trepidation, and she followed cautiously.

The canopied bed sat in the middle of the room away from the stone walls. The burgundy velvet overhang touched the floor, framing an etched scene of a satyr and nymph on the footboard. She couldn't be sure, but the satyr didn't look like he was playing with a flute.

"Father, are you awake?" Luis's low voice sounded gentle.

"Enough with sleep. I've had too much damn sleep. I'm missing too much of what is going on around me." The aged voice crackled like fire.

"The sisters have sent someone to care for you. Her

name is Teresa." He pulled her closer to him in order for his father to be able to see her.

"Good afternoon, Señor."

"Afternoon? Already?" Teresa saw a skeletal head turn toward the window. The brow had a jumble of lines that arched with the raising of his right eyebrow. "I thought I just had breakfast."

"You did, Father. A late one."

The head turned back to look at Teresa.

"You're tiny and good looking. Perhaps you should rethink your calling."

"Oh, I'm not joining the order. The sisters raised me."

"And now they're letting you fly free. How kind of them."

The old man's eyes looked anything but kind. His lips turned up into a sneer rather than a smile. His long pointed nose almost overwhelmed his face.

"Come closer, Teresa. We must get to know each other well."

She walked up to the bed, catching a whiff of tainted bodily fluids. His almost-bald head rested heavily on the pillows. His fingers were deformed, and the nails were either crusted in open wounds or blackened.

"You've been fed, but has someone come to bathe you as yet?" she asked.

"No one has the stomach for that," he replied.

Teresa turned to Luis and gave him a list of the things she would need to make his father more comfortable. She knew she should be asking Gaspar, but she wanted Luis out of the room, for he made her uncomfortable.

He watched her too closely, and his dark eyes always appeared to be thinking, planning, or maybe scheming. He excused himself, and she heard him call for Gaspar once outside the room.

"He hates being told what to do. Did you do that to annoy him or to plain get rid of him?" the old man said.

"To obtain what I need as quickly as possible," she retorted, pulling the heavy cover from his body. Her stomach lurched from the stale odor rising from his flesh. "Perhaps we both could use some fresh air," she said, walking to the window.

"No one opens the window," he said.

"That's what makes you so cranky." She opened the window wide and returned to the bed. He chortled to himself and seemed to give over complete control of his body to her. He lay soiled and covered with sores, his flesh a budding garden of infestation.

Gaspar soon appeared with all she had requested and assisted her only when she called to him. Otherwise he waited near the double doors, ready to abandon her as soon as he could.

As she finished with the dressings, Gaspar asked to be excused, his hand resting against his Adam's apple. With generosity she freed him.

"Thank you," said the patient. "You're far gentler than that horror, Señora Toledo."

"This is not her job. She was trained to cook, not to nurse. You should have had professional help long ago."

"I didn't want it. I wanted to ignore my illness. I

wanted to be able to pass into death with a gentle shove rather than participate in a grueling battle. Dying frightens me."

"Most people fear the end."

"I wonder whether as babes we fear our births as much as we fear our deaths. Both are unknowns, and both require some pain to achieve."

"The Lord will give you the strength you need."

"Which Lord? My old One, or the new One that protects my family and wealth?"

"Are you feeling chilly? I can close the window."

"No one talks of the multitude of gods anymore. To survive in Spain during the fifteenth century, one must believe in Rome's God." He reached out a hand and grabbed her wrist. "I'm afraid, Teresa. I don't know what punishment awaits me."

"A priest can be brought in."

"Is it a priest I need?"

"You have been very generous with the Church, Señor Velez."

"You mean I've bought my place in heaven?"

"Only if you contributed out of love."

He let go of her wrist and nodded.

chapter 10

Teresa spent the evening by Señor Velez's bed, counting out the beads of her rosary with prayers until the doctor, bringing another elixir, relieved her. Closing the double doors behind her, she looked down the long hall. The lamps were kept low, causing shapes to take on frightening poses. She wondered what each door hid. Never had she been inside such a huge house.

As quiet as the convent had been, it had never seemed this hushed. Always there was a rustle of clothing or the murmur of prayer, occasionally even the sound of flagellation. At Christmas and Easter the sisters' voices sang out the eternal praises of the Lord. Inside her head she could hear Sister Lucia's beautiful voice hitting the high notes, assuring all that their praises reached the heavens.

A pale, wavering form caught Teresa's eye. A slender shape dressed in long white shimmery fabric came toward her from the opposite end of the hall. A wild halo of white hair circled thin, sharp features. The alabaster complexion glowed under the light of a candle that the form held in its almost skeletal hand.

Teresa took a step back, wondering whether she should retreat into the senior Velez's bedroom, but she halted, hoping the form would take the stairs down to the ground floor.

The form seemed to be that of an elderly woman, risen from a grave to search for warm blood to give her back her youth. The woman wore an expression of yearning, of sadness, touched with the knowledge of where to find what she wanted. She passed the staircase and finally caught sight of Teresa, her own step faltering, unsure of the risk she took. The eyes squinted, flesh wrinkling, and the lips formed a single word. "Catrin?"

Teresa forced herself into the light of a lamp.

"No. I'm Teresa. I'm Señor Roberto Velez's nurse."

"Catrin isn't allowed on this floor," the woman said.

"I'm not Catrin. I've just arrived from the local convent."

The elderly woman's hand shook, making the candlelight flicker across her face.

"Why wasn't I told about you?"

"I arrived yesterday. Perhaps no one has had a chance to announce that I'm here. Señor Luis Velez asked that I come to care for his father."

"He is dying."

"I'm trying to make him as comfortable as I can."

"Then why do you stand here in the hall?"

"The doctor arrived, and I was about to return to my room."

"Go."

Teresa's body seemed set in stone. Moving toward the elderly woman did not appeal to her. But she knew she couldn't stand in the hall forever. Her feet made tiny motions to move forward.

"Are you an invalid?"

"No." Teresa's loud, startled voice brought the doctor to the bedroom door.

"Who is it?" he asked. Seeing Teresa looking back at him over her shoulder, he scowled. "Señor Velez needs his sleep," the doctor said in a harsh whisper.

"No, Dr. Perez, he needs to absorb as much of this world as he can before he rots in his grave." The older woman heaved these words like a weapon.

The doctor looked past Teresa and saw the white figure. He seemed as surprised by the elderly woman as Teresa had been, and not willing to deal with her, as he immediately stepped back into the bedroom and closed the door.

How could he leave her standing alone in the hall with this apparition? Teresa asked herself.

"He'll bring Roberto to the grave sooner than nature would have. He has with everyone else." The woman opened her gown with one hand to show the white flesh underneath. Gradually she lowered the candle until the light gleamed on a ragged, red scar that cut her abdomen and stomach in half. "He tried to speed my departure, but I fooled him. I survived to torment him. He's not sure whether I am dead or alive." She lowered her voice. "And I'll never tell." A grin spread the woman's lips within the shadow of the candlelight.

Teresa returned to the bedroom door but found it locked. She knocked several times, but the doctor refused to answer.

A slender hand rested on Teresa's shoulder. A hand smelling of the sweetness of flowers and the decay of age.

"Go to bed before the demons return, requiring their revenge of blood." The rancid smell of the elderly woman's breath enveloped Teresa, causing the hall to tilt and blur.

Teresa slipped easily out of the weak grasp and ran for the staircase. She almost slipped on the top step, but she grabbed the banister in time to stunt her fall. She pulled herself back on her feet and dashed down the steps until she ran into Gaspar's chest.

"Is the master asleep?" he asked.

"The doctor . . ." She couldn't get out a complete sentence.

"Is the master all right? Should I call for Señor Luis Velez?" Gaspar suddenly looked panicked.

"No. The doctor is with Señor Roberto Velez. He is giving him something to sleep."

"And where are you going?"

"To my room." She pushed the butler aside and made for the servants' quarters.

Inside her room she found Hilaria lolling on the bed.

"Why don't you sleep with Señor Roberto Velez?" Hilaria asked.

"What are you doing here?"

"I asked a question. Why don't you sleep in one of

the rooms near the old man? What if he should need you during the night?"

"I'm very tired. Please leave my room." Teresa held the door open.

"A nurse should sleep near her patient, not on the other side of the house. It makes no sense."

"You know Señora Toledo assigned me this room."

"Only because the young master complained. She would have put you in the barn had she thought she would not be questioned. Who cares for the old man at night?"

Teresa sighed, giving in to Hilaria's barrage of questions.

"I presume Señor Luis wishes to care for his father at night. During the day he has other tasks to do."

"You don't have much in the way of clothes, do you?"

"I'd rather you not go through my things." Teresa noticed that the bureau drawers were partially opened.

"There's nothing to find anyway, is there?" Hilaria stood, letting one of Teresa's garments slip from her lap to the floor.

"Stay out of my room, Hilaria, or I'll inform Señora Toledo."

As Hilaria left she reminded Teresa she shouldn't be late for breakfast because Señora Toledo wouldn't tolerate it.

chapter 11

LUIS AND JOSE RODE ALONG THE PARCHED ROAD leading to the mansion. The clouds hid what little moon there was to see. Both had been quiet for a long stretch of the road, allowing their horses to take the lead.

"She's pretty." Jose's voice reminded Luis that he had company.

"A new girlfriend? You'll make Carmen jealous."

"Carmen doesn't worry about who I look at or where I go. She cooks too well to bother herself about the way other women look to me."

Luis laughed.

"Food before love, is that your philosophy?"

"At my age, eating takes far less energy than the other. No, I'm talking about this nursemaid, Teresa. She is fragile. There is an awesome beauty to that."

Luis ignored Jose's comment and let silence fall upon their travels again. A mile on, Jose, who had fallen slightly behind Luis, managed to pull up alongside his master.

"Does your father like the girl?"

"What girl?"

"Teresa."

"She's just arrived."

"Your father would have complained five minutes after he met her if she displeased him. He hasn't said anything at all?"

"When I visit Father he doesn't want to speak to me. He stares up at the frescos on the ceiling or looks toward the window. If I ask a question I will get a very direct answer, but that is all." But wait, he thought, the window had stood open that afternoon. *Why?* "Perhaps she has brought new life into that sickroom. It's not as stifling and claustrophobic as it once was."

"And you, Señor, what do you think of the newest member of our household?"

"I haven't had a chance to decide."

"But you chose to bring her home to care for your father."

"Sister Agatha offered no one else. Do you think my choice would have been a young, attractive woman barely out of her childhood?"

"Ah, Señor, she is not that young."

"So Sister Agatha said."

"Teresa may face some problems, though."

Luis looked at Jose for a moment before asking what he meant.

"A slight bit of jealousy, perhaps. Carmen felt superior when caring for your father. Yes, she took it on as extra work, but it enabled her to lord it over the rest of the staff. Carmen tends to set the mood for the household servants. She can encourage good or bad behavior. And I think she has not set a good example in the way she relates to Teresa."

"Is this household gossip you've chosen to share with me?"

"Not gossip. It is what I see with my eyes and hear with my ears. I am not all the time in the barn muttering and soothing the horses."

"That's the safest place for you to be, Jose. Then you can stay out of these petty jealousies that worry you so much."

"Even the animals nip and kick sometimes. I put a little more hay in one stall, and you can bet the whinnying will start. They make their grievances known in far more direct ways than female humans."

"Teresa will have to take care of herself. I'm not the nursemaid, she is." Luis hurried his horse for home, and the horse seemed glad to be heading for its stall.

chapter 12

THE NEXT MORNING AT THE BREAKFAST TABLE, Teresa managed to push in between Jose and Juana. Jose gladly made room for her, while Juana seemed to cringe away from her. There were several household staff members that she had not met the day before. One, a boy of about ten with crudely cut hair and a missing front tooth, would steal food from the plates of others when they weren't looking. Another male, probably in his mid-twenties, kept staring at Teresa until she finally introduced herself. Realizing he had been caught staring, he ignored the introduction and went back to scooping spoonfuls of porridge into his mouth. The third unfamiliar person didn't look like she belonged in the servants' quarters. A woman who could be anywhere between thirty-five and fifty sat stiffly in her chair, holding her utensils with grace, taking small bites unlike her companions. The woman dressed in black had a removable circle of lace around the collar of her dress and wore an expensive ring on her left hand. She politely nodded at Teresa before she spoke.

"Teresa? Am I right?" She didn't wait for Teresa to answer before continuing. "I'm Sylvia. I help Carmen with most of the ordering and shopping, and I cook on the days Carmen has off."

"Which is never," added Hilaria.

Sylvia's face pinched into a sour grimace, but Hilaria never looked up to notice.

"And who are you, young man?" Teresa asked the boy.

Stunned, the boy looked around the table as if he needed assistance in remembering his name.

"Manuel," Carmen answered.

Relieved, the boy went back to his own food.

"And you, Señor?" she asked of the young man who had been staring.

"Fernando. Unlike Sylvia, I try to stay out of the house. Like it better with the barn animals, and I usually sleep with them."

"Smells like them, too," Hilaria commented.

"When I left Señor Roberto Velez last night, I saw an elderly woman in the hall. She looked frail and . . ." Teresa didn't know the right word to use. Finally she said the only one that came to her mind, "ghostly."

No one bothered to look up from their food.

"Can someone tell me who she is?"

"She's the walking dead. Neither alive nor a ghost. Someone forgot to bury her, and now she wanders on the upstairs floor trying to remember how to play dead." Hilaria sniffed and pushed her plate away.

"She is related to the Velez family?"

"Roberto Velez's sister," Hilaria mumbled.

"She didn't seem to like the doctor."

"I heard she died under his knife."

"The woman is obviously not dead. I presume you mean she has stopped living in the world and has cloistered herself away in this house."

"We're not supposed to speak of her," Juana said.

"Why not?"

"It's bad luck to speak of the dead," insisted Hilaria.

"Señora Toledo, maybe you could help me understand what Hilaria is talking about."

"I never met Señor Roberto Velez's sister. I've heard she's here in the house. She never requires anything from me."

"She must dine with the family."

"Only if she eats under the table, because I've never seen her myself." Hilaria propped her elbows on the table and rested her chin on the palm of her hands. "I think the family dreamed her up so we wouldn't wander around on their upstairs floor during the night. The person to speak to is Gaspar; he goes everywhere any time he wants. Even wandered into poor Juana's room one night. Her scream didn't have the fearful echo of yours, but then maybe that's because it was cut off before she could reach a higher pitch. His massive hand left a bruise on Juana's left cheek. It healed before Gaspar had to answer for it. But Juana never complained."

"Keep your odious stories to yourself, Hilaria." Jose

had dropped his spoon into his plate. He would have stood, but Carmen patted his arm.

Juana's cheeks were a bright red. Her brown hair drooped onto her forehead, and a few tears fell to the table. Teresa searched in her clothes for a handkerchief but found none. Perhaps that's best, Teresa thought; she might have embarrassed the girl further by her action.

"Gaspar doesn't eat with us?" Teresa asked.

"He doesn't deign to sit with us, and we never invite him." Hilaria rose out of her chair. "Maybe you ask too many questions, Teresa. Some things we try to forget. We must stay at our positions to survive. After the senior Velez dies, you can return to the arms of the sisters."

"I'm not prying. I'm trying to understand my place here, and I want to get along with all of you."

"You are an outsider, Teresa." Señora Toledo stood to clear the table.

"Weren't you all outsiders at one time?"

"But we minded our own business. Time gave us a common history." Juana turned to Teresa. Her watery eyes looked defiant. Her hands lay on her thighs, gripped into fists.

"I'm sorry, Juana, if I've made you uncomfortable," Teresa whispered.

"Then leave her alone," Carmen ordered.

Everyone in the room scattered away, leaving Carmen, Jose, and Teresa in the kitchen.

"Nothing wrong with asking questions," said Jose. "You had no way of knowing what the answers would be."

"How did Gaspar get away with hurting Juana?"

"Hilaria claims she knows what happened. No one else knows the true story, and Juana hardly ever talks."

"If she went to Señor Velez, I'm sure he'd do something about Gaspar." Teresa said.

"That is her business," Jose warned.

"I'll give you Señor Velez's tray to bring up to him," Carmen interrupted. "He doesn't eat much these days, but we act like we don't notice. So even though the tray is full, don't expect more than a few mouthfuls to be eaten."

"Did you notice Juana's scream the night Gaspar visited her room?"

Carmen placed a tray of food in front of Teresa.

"You little bitch . . ."

"Enough, Carmen." Jose's voice spoke in a low growl. "Teresa, take the food up to Señor Roberto Velez; he needs some sustenance if he is to fight for his life."

Teresa scooped up the tray and stood. Her hands shook, but she managed to make it to the kitchen door without spilling anything. Jose intercepted and opened the door for her.

chapter 13

LUIS WALKED INTO THE KITCHEN TO FIND CARMEN and Jose huddled together by the stove, whispering. He wondered what the latest gossip among the staff was about. Catrin had filled many hours of their time, he knew, but he doubted that after several months she could still inspire such intense discussion. No, most likely Teresa's name was upon their lips. Teresa, the bastard child. Teresa, the woman unfit to be a nun because of her birth.

Luis moved a chair out of his way, making enough noise to force the two servants to turn toward him.

"More love chat?" Luis asked. He noticed that Carmen didn't blush because she had already been flushed by the animation of the conversation.

"That is all I know, Señor Velez," said Jose. His smile hid the dark shadow that had been upon his face.

Carmen poked him in the ribs with her elbow and curtsied to the young master.

"Is there something you need, Señor?" she asked.

"I'm dining at the bishop's house this evening."

"I'll just make a little soup for your father, then."

"Thank you, Carmen. Jose, I'd like to check the horses with you this morning."

Luis and Jose left immediately and began walking to the barn.

"What were you talking about with Carmen?" Luis's curt question sounded hollow.

"I think you know, Señor. You and I spoke of the way Carmen feels about Teresa last night. This morning at breakfast Teresa became too inquisitive."

"How do you mean?"

"She saw your father's sister last night."

"I hadn't thought of that. I'm a fool; I should have told her about Isabella. Why would asking about my father's sister cause a problem?"

"The staff has not met your aunt and thinks of her as a ghost. But Teresa pushed for information about her."

"That's impertinent. My family is none of her business."

"She is caring for your father, Señor. She needs to know who is visiting."

"Isabella is a harpy. She's no kind visitor."

"Harpy or no, she lives in the house and has access to your father."

"Do you think I was wrong in bringing Teresa here?"

"No. You need someone who knows how to care for the sick. Carmen tried, but she doesn't have the patience or stomach for nursing. When her husband was dying, she moved back with her own family. The poor man died with only the sexton to wait by his side."

"What did he die of?"

"He was trampled by a bull."

Luis looked at Jose, who shrugged his shoulders.

"I understand he had been imbibing just before the accident."

The two men walked to the barn where Manuel was cleaning.

"It is none of my business, Jose, but why are you interested in Carmen?"

"She's easy," Jose said, brushing his hand through Manuel's hair.

To Luis this made some sense. He himself didn't want the emotional challenge of catering to the needs of any woman. Frequently he would visit a whorehouse, and he never chose the same woman. Women of easy virtue knew what was expected for the money they earned and used to support themselves and their families. They didn't give details about their lives or ask questions. Most didn't even know who he was. When a woman did recognize him, she managed to ruin the encounter by acting as servant rather than as a lusty mate. Only once did he make the mistake of acting on his appetite close to home, and he would always regret the farce he enacted with the poor girl.

Remembering the indecipherable handwriting he had found mixed in with the report on Catrin, Luis cursed himself. He had meant to look again at that note the night before but had conveniently forgotten. Didn't he want to rescue Catrin from the hands of the Inquisition? Was it easier for him to forget the girl and go back to a life devoid of emotion?

"Señor Velez!" shouted Manuel, pointing up at his father's window.

Luis looked up to see his father standing at the open window, leaning on Teresa.

What the hell did that woman think she was doing? His father was much too ill to be out of bed.

He watched his father wave down at him before he rushed up the steps to the mansion. He flung open the door and pushed Gaspar out of the way in order to take the stairs two at a time. By the time he reached his father's bedroom, Teresa had his father sitting in an old velvet chair, scuffed and threadbare with age.

"Why is he out of bed?"

"Because Hilaria is about to make the bed," Teresa answered.

"Hilaria has never required my father to get out of bed while she changed the linens."

"No, but it will make her job easier, and your father is able to get a little fresh air."

"Please, Son, I am not such an invalid that I cannot walk across the room. Besides, I've been sleeping much better lately with the doctor's help, and a little exercise might help me build up an appetite for the banquet Carmen insists on making me for breakfast." He pointed to his morning tray on the table next to him.

"You haven't touched it, Father."

"But I might. Especially since I will have to work up the energy to return to bed. Although Teresa feels I should spend some time sitting by the window watching . . . what kind of bird did you call it, Teresa?"

"The hell with the birds. What if you caught a chill, Father?"

"Then all this suffering would be over. I'm tired of being trapped in a dying body. Lying in bed will not heal me. It will only prolong a life of past memories. Teresa informs me that new events are happening every day, even inside the walls of this house."

"The doctor did not want you out of bed." Luis came and squatted in front of his father.

"And I didn't want to stay in my bed. I've tried to trick myself into believing that there wasn't anything to live for. Your blessed mother is in her grave. And oh, the patience she had with me."

"She loved you, Father."

"Did I love her enough? Enough to truly make her happy? I gave her a son, then took my seed to other women. I said that I didn't want to hurt her since she had almost lost her life giving birth to you. She never told you about the priest coming to give her the Last Sacrament on the night of your birth, did she?"

"She loved us both very much."

"I used it as an excuse to slake my physical desires wherever I wanted. She cried, and I held her. But there were many times that she cried alone."

"What is all this maudlin gibberish? This must be your fault," Luis said, standing to face Teresa.

"Your father needs to talk, Señor Velez. He needs to share all that is burdening his mind."

"Liar! He is physically ill, not mentally deficient."

"My sister, Isabella, would disagree with you, Son. Have you met my sister, Teresa?"

"Last night I met her in the hallway after I left this room."

"And what did she say to you?" asked Luis.

"She thought I was Catrin."

Luis saw his father blanch. The old man's head fell back against the chair, allowing his hands to fall heavily on the wooden arms.

"Are you all right, Father?" Luis reached out to grab his father's shoulders. "I'll help you get back in bed."

"Get away." The old man used his hands to chase his son away from him.

A rap came to the door.

"I'll get it." Teresa crossed the room and opened the door only a crack at first until she saw who stood in the hallway.

"I've the sheets. Should I make the bed now?" asked Hilaria, with arms full of clean, perfumed bed linens.

Teresa turned to look at the old man, who waved Hilaria in.

Luis reached for some juice, but the old man wouldn't accept it.

"Catrin. Does the Inquisition still have her?" The

old man took in a deep breath.

"Yes, but they haven't tortured her yet. At least as far as the last report indicated. I'm trying to get more information about her crimes. The Inquisitor doesn't believe she is a witch, that much I know. Where did she come from, Father? Who are her parents?"

"How should I know? She came to the door one day seeking employment. She mentioned something about being raised on a farm. A peasant upbringing, no doubt."

Hilaria slowed a bit while making the bed, obviously seeking to gather additional gossip for the next morning's breakfast table. Teresa moved to the bed to quicken the task. Hilaria scowled at Teresa, who couldn't find a graceful way to send her away.

The fluffed-up pillows and the clean sheets enticed the senior Velez back into bed. When Teresa pulled a chair up next to the bed, the old man asked for privacy. He needed solitude to sort out what should now be done. When asked what he meant, he simply closed his eyes and allowed his breathing to succumb into a steady rhythm that might have been construed as sleep, except for the fact that no one believed it.

chapter 14

"Señor Luis Velez."

Upon hearing the formal address, he turned to Teresa.

"May I speak with you?"

"I'm listening."

"Not here in the hall, Señor. Is there a room in which we could be alone?"

"My bedroom."

Teresa's cheeks burned.

"Something a bit more proper, Señor." Her voice sounded prissy even to her ears.

"Pretend I'm ill."

"But you're not. I don't want to play this game. I want to talk to you about your father."

Luis looked at the double doors leading to his father's bedroom before answering.

"We can go down to the library." He allowed her to lead.

As she passed one of the alcoves, she spied Hilaria bunching and rebunching the soiled sheets taken from the old man's bed. Hilaria stared back at her defiantly.

At the foot of the stairs, Luis turned left to open the doors of the library. He dramatically bowed and bade her to enter.

The library had few books. Most of the shelves had account sheets tied up with thin cord. A broad desk with ink stains and two large oil lamps, one on each end of the desk, took up much of the room. The dark wood needed to be polished, and the lamps looked well used. On either side of the desk were two large chairs meant for relaxing instead of working. Across from the desk a striped settee stood, the fabric new but the wood badly used.

He indicated she should sit on the settee, and he drew up one of the chairs. She didn't like this arrangement. She would have preferred sitting at the desk. The chair allowed Luis to sit higher and made it easier for him to peer down his nose at her. His handsome features were ruined by the hostility glistening in his eyes.

"Your father is very unhappy about the way he has lived his life. I think he would like to set many things right, but I'm afraid most actions he has taken cannot be forgiven by those he offended. A few people still survive, and I believe it would make it easier for him if they approached him first."

"Should I post a notice in town? 'Anyone who ever felt offended by Señor Roberto Velez should hie themselves up to the Velez mansion immediately. They will be rewarded with . . .' what?"

"Don't be obtuse, Señor Velez. There are hundreds of secrets poisoning this household. One of them is Catrin."

"You've never even met her. What's so secret about a servant?"

"The Inquisitor thinks her important enough to imprison."

"The staff accused her of witchcraft."

"She is either a heretic or a threat being held over your father's head."

Luis stood.

"Please don't pace, Señor Velez. Pacing only serves to release the tension inside. Deal with the problem instead."

"What has my father told you about Catrin?"

"Nothing, but I saw how he reacted to her name, and you did also."

"I've asked to see Catrin but have been refused. I have been told not to intrude on Church business. You know my father belonged to the Jewish religion at one time."

Teresa nodded.

"My father has taken pains to remain on good terms with the religious establishment. He has even made a pilgrimage to Rome, where he had an audience with the pope. The trip to Rome only made the local religious leaders more suspicious of him. They were afraid that my father reported on the work of the Inquisition. It took a long time to win back their favor, and during that period we all lived in fear of being driven from our land, or worse, burned at the stake. When the Inquisition took Catrin, we feared someone else from this house would be next."

"Was Catrin taken because she was an easy target or because she is important to your family?"

Luis laughed.

"Why does a young woman like you care?"

"Because I believe your father is dying, and I want him to be at peace."

"Thank you. I doubt my father relies on you to bring him that peace."

Teresa ached with the knowledge she had, but worried about saying too much. If she kept quiet, nothing would be resolved.

"Señor Velez, there is talk among some of the staff that your father had a relationship with Catrin. Is this true?"

"Yes, a master and servant relationship." Luis sat back down on the chair with a smug expression on his face.

"Do you love your father?"

"Of course, I do. How dare you question that?"

"Then do something to help him. Were your father and Catrin lovers?"

"No. Catrin and I were."

At first Teresa sat stunned. Luis sat motionless, watching for the next question.

"Did your father know?"

"I never told him, and I can't see Catrin sharing the information with him. You see, the staff acts and speaks on speculation. Because poor Catrin is different from the rest of the rabble in this house, therefore she must be a witch who charmed the master into her bed."

"She could have been lovers to the both of you."

"You're very impertinent. Surely you must want to return to the convent."

"Your father is dying, Señor Velez. Do you want to make amends with him before he dies, or would you rather pitch dirt into the grave of a man who became a stranger to you?"

"Are you here to rob him of his will to live?"

"I can pack my things today if you would ask Jose to return me to the convent."

She watched Luis turn inward with his thoughts. How far back did he travel to find the innocence of his childhood, when he could still believe in his parents? The chapel bell rang, and she could hear the movements of the other servants in the house. Luis didn't appear to hear any of this.

"My mother died a stranger to both my father and me. The last few years she spent in prayer and knitting piles of junk now stored upstairs in the garret. Did you notice them when you were up there?"

"I'm sure they've been put away inside a trunk. I touched nothing during my short stay in the garret."

"We should give them all to you before you return to the convent. I'm sure there are many poor people who could put my mother's obsession to use. No, don't look perturbed, Teresa. I'm not sending you back to the sisters yet. My father and I have distanced ourselves from each other, just as you have said. He is physically ill, but I think he's dying because he has lost the will to live."

"How did your mother die?"

"Gaspar took her to the chapel every day. My father and I didn't have the time and thought this a silly female request. Later she refused food. One day I entered her room to find most of her hair chopped off. She said she had done it herself. Wouldn't answer why. But later, in the chapel, I noticed that the figure of Christ on the large cross had real hair upon its head. I recognized the color. She had even managed to plait rose thorns through her dark brown hair. I thought she must have had help, for how would she have climbed that high with her numb legs?"

"Did Gaspar help?"

"I don't know. I saw no purpose in accusing any of the staff. They only did what my mother required of them."

"Did you ask your mother why she did it?"

"Why should I? I didn't want to hear my mother compare herself to all the other martyrs in history. No doubt that's what she would have done. Finally my father got her to eat small amounts of food by sitting with her through her meals." Luis laughed. "In the end she ruled his life, or at least the hours he kept."

"A sad way to steal away some of his attention, don't you think?"

"I guess for her it was the only way. Eventually she came down with a bad chest cold, her breathing grew more difficult, and she sank into long bouts of sleep, until finally one morning she didn't wake."

"I'm sorry."

"For making me talk about this? You should be. I've spent the last few years ignoring what happened. I haven't visited my mother's grave since she was buried, and she's in the cemetery at the back of the house."

"I'd willingly visit her with you."

"My dear, are you saying that I've been too much of a coward to face the ghosts of my past?"

"Haven't there been times when you wanted to talk with her?"

"She has nothing to say to me now. However, you are right. I should try with my father before he, too, is speechless."

chapter 15

AFTER A PROLONGED SILENCE LUIS EXCUSED HIM-
self, saying that he had to prepare to have dinner at the
bishop's residence. He walked Teresa into the hall.

"I'll check on my father. I'll send for you if he has
need of company."

She waited at the foot of the staircase for close to fifteen minutes before deciding that the senior Velez had
probably fallen into a deep sleep.

Turning, she caught sight of Gaspar measuring her
body with his eyes. His clipped short hair almost stood
on end, and his sullen face looked sunken and cold. He
stared into her eyes directly but remained silent.

"Why are you lurking in the hall?" she asked.

"My job is to see that the household runs smoothly,
and often I just observe to make sure nothing is amiss."

Without responding she turned away from the butler
and found her way through the house and out to the backyard. The cemetery Luis had spoken of was only twenty
yards from the house. Rotting sticks of wood separated

the small patch of earth from the rest of the property.

She pulled gently on the gate, careful not to cause the wood to come apart.

There were at most ten graves and a single mausoleum cut out of stone and marble. The family name had been decoratively etched above the door of the mausoleum. There were no crying angels or crucifixes in the cemetery. Most of the tombstones were dressed simply with the name of the deceased, dates of birth and death, and a short prayer in remembrance of the departed one's life.

She had to be careful as she walked because some of the graves lay sunken, unkempt grass and weeds spraying the dirt. She thought she would find Luis's mother resting in the mausoleum, but only one name appeared on the stone parchment near the door, and it was not that of a female.

As she retraced her steps, she checked each tombstone, sure that someone must have planted a marker in the woman's memory.

"What are you doing among the family plots?" Hilaria stood just beyond the fence with her hands resting on her hips.

"Searching for Señora Velez's grave."

"She's not buried here. They sent her body back to her own family to be buried with her own mother."

"But . . ." Had he lied to her? Had the whole story been fabrication?

"She's buried at least one hundred miles away from here. I understand it was her last request. Guess she'd had enough of Señor Roberto Velez."

"Shhh, he might hear you."

"He never leaves his room. But wait, I forgot you have him toddling around; next he'll be hobbling downstairs getting into the staff's way."

Teresa hadn't been paying close attention to the steps she took, and suddenly the ground gave way under her feet as her entire body sank into the sodden earth. Her skirt, covered with dirt, rose up around her waist, and her elbows rested on the damp soil.

"Help me!" she cried.

"I'll get Jose."

"No, just give me your hand." Too late. Hilaria had already started for the barn at the side of the house.

Teresa tried to pull her body up, but the soil gave way and fell back into the hole, packing her body in more tightly. The dirt under her collapsed further, and her chin barely rose above the level of the ground. The taste of soil parched her mouth and caused her to cough.

"How did this happen, Teresa?"

She looked up to see Jose running toward her.

"Be careful, the ground is dangerously soft," she warned.

"Can't have you joining the Velez ancestors before your time," he said, grabbing her forearms tightly. After several false tries, he pulled her out, and Teresa found herself sitting on solid ground.

She immediately pushed down her skirt and looked at her bare feet.

"My sandals," she said.

"Don't see them. Hate to put my hands into that grave and come up with a useless bone."

"That was my only pair of sandals." She pulled herself up on all fours and crawled over to the open grave. Earthworms wove in and out of the soil. She stretched her hand out, holding it over the tumultuous dirt. Closing her eyes, she jammed her arms deep into the grave, waving her fingers to capture a hint of the missing sandals.

"What's she doing?" asked Hilaria from a distance.

"Looking for her sandals."

Teresa's hand grabbed on to something hard, but when her fingers wrapped around the object, she realized it was too slender to be a sandal. She gagged and shut her mouth tightly, letting go of the object.

Jose grabbed her shoulders and forcefully pulled her away from the grave.

"*Dios*, I have an extra pair of sandals," Hilaria said, coming closer to the cemetery fence.

"It isn't often that Hilaria is generous. Perhaps you should allow her to help you for the good of her soul," Jose said. He helped Teresa to stand.

"What the devil? You're now digging up graves, is that it?" yelled Luis on his way toward the fracas. Gaspar stood smirking in the doorway.

"You lied!" shouted Teresa. "Your mother isn't buried here."

"And how many bodies did you have to dig up before you came to that conclusion?"

"Only one, I think." Hilaria's soft voice irritated Teresa.

"I wanted to help both you and your father. I thought both of you would find peace in your souls if you understood the pain that came from so many misunderstandings and slights."

"Wash up and change, and then do what you're supposed to do. Nurse my father back to health."

As Luis turned away, Jose clasped a hand over Teresa's mouth.

"Do not respond, Teresa. Your words can only cause more wounds. He carries enough pain for one so young. Pain from which he may never be released." He lowered his hand.

"But he lied to me."

"Does he owe you the truth?"

chapter 16

"Why did you go to the cemetery?" asked Hilaria. She had arrived a few minutes earlier with a pair of sandals dangling from her fingers.

"I wanted to see Señora Velez's grave."

"Why?"

"Because I'm stupid." Teresa grabbed the sandals from Hilaria.

"But it doesn't take much brains to realize Señora Velez will have nothing to say to you."

"I wanted to see the words on her tombstone. I hoped to see a tiny bit of passion."

"Passion? I thought you were closer to that when you were standing outside the old man's bedroom earlier today."

Teresa recalled the conversation that took place between herself and Luis.

"He made fun of me."

"You should have agreed."

"What?"

"Finding yourself in Señor Luis's bed might change your status in life."

"He'd never marry someone like me."

"But he might be disposed to give you gifts. The family is very wealthy. Someone in the town I come from slept with a wealthy man, and she ended up taking care of her entire family with the money he provided."

"That is not the way the sisters raised me to live."

"The nuns raised you to beg for food and wipe the asses of the sick. Certainly that doesn't seem like a proper way to live."

"If I'm with a man, it must be someone whom I love and someone who loves me back."

"How old are you? Twenty? A little younger? Your body is desirable. Wait much longer, and no one will consider you a prize. Seems to me you're wasting one of God's gifts to you."

"Have you ever slept with a man?"

"Only local trash. I haven't had my opportunity yet to advance my station. I wouldn't turn down Señor Luis."

"Has he turned you down?"

"Very cruel, Teresa. The nuns would not be proud of you."

Teresa's cheeks burned in shame.

"If that silly barb could make you blush, I fear there is no hope that Señor Luis will ever bed you, either as a mistress or a wife."

"I must go," said Teresa, pushing aside Hilaria in order to leave the room.

"If Señor Luis should knock at your door one night, tell him to send for me, for I will ease the pain in his loins," Hilaria's voice echoed after Teresa.

Blindly Teresa found her way to Señor Roberto Velez's bedroom. She knocked softly, and when bid to do so, she entered.

"I'm sorry to be late, Señor Velez, but I had a slight accident and needed to change my clothes."

"You fell into a grave," the old man calmly said.

"Your son told you."

"No, Luis tells me very little. He fears that bad news could cause me a setback. Gaspar informed me of the circus going on in my backyard."

"He should not have bothered. Your son set the situation right."

"I'm surprised he didn't send you packing. He has no tolerance."

"He thinks I am needed here to care for you. He doesn't want you spending long periods of time alone."

"You mean he doesn't want me wasting his time."

"That is not what I meant. You and your son suspect the worst from everyone around you. He loves you, and if you allowed the words to pass your lips, you'd admit you loved him, too."

"Why poke around in the cemetery, Teresa? Are you a morbid child or simply curious about our family?"

"Your son mentioned that your wife is buried in the cemetery."

"She is not."

"Why would he have lied?"

"He may believe she is buried there."

"But he said he had been at her graveside."

"Had he? He attended the funeral mass in the chapel. He never followed the casket outside. Instead he locked himself in his room with several bottles of port. I may have let him believe she is buried there."

"You mean you told him she was."

"My wife had become very confused toward the end of her life. She worshiped two Gods. One her husband made her follow. The other resided in her heart. The cemetery in back of this house is consecrated. The bishop made sure to bless the ground before the Inquisitor came here. She didn't want to be buried there. I sent her body to be buried with her mother in a Jewish grave."

"The Inquisitor doesn't know?"

"He knows and has forgiven me for a . . . donation. After years of neglect I had to repay her somehow."

"At the risk of your own life." Teresa's words were the last spoken before the old man closed his eyes and pretended sleep.

chapter 17

LUIS CHOSE TO TAKE THE CARRIAGE TO THE BISHOP'S residence. Jose even attempted to dust off his own livery in order to make a better impression on the bishop's staff.

The road was fairly safe, but Luis didn't want his mind wandering in the midst of a long, dark ride home. Teresa had given him much to think about, including whether he should allow her to stay at the Velez mansion. She had overstepped her position, perhaps because of her unworldliness or the fact she had never been trained to work for her betters. The sight of her standing in the cemetery with her filthy dress, bare feet, and specks of dirt freckling her face proved her naïveté. She had had the nerve to yell back at him instead of cowering and curt-sying before him.

When the bishop's villa came into view, Jose slowed the horses and rounded the dirt road leading up to the front door.

Luis exited the carriage before Jose could open the door for him. He had been so enthralled in his own thoughts he almost bowled over his driver. Jose quickly stepped out of the way, aware that his master didn't see him.

The bishop met Luis warmly at the door, offering his blessing and apologizing for the long distance Luis had to travel.

"I don't leave the villa very much. Some of the local people have become churlish since the last *auto da fe*."

"Certainly no one can blame you for the acts of the Inquisition."

The two men entered a sitting room where two glasses of red wine had already been poured. Each man took a chair facing the other.

"Some people don't understand the severity of the threat to the Church, I'm afraid. Heretics pour their venom into the ears of simple men, driving those men to deride their religion and lose faith in the true God."

Luis knew that the bishop spoke of the *conversos*, people like his father who had left the Jewish faith. Many only did so in name. Others were easily seduced back into the ways of their parents, celebrating the old religion in secret services.

Soon the topic changed to the arts and a special need the Church had to rebuild a decrepit cloister that housed some ancient nuns.

The rich food and liberal amounts of wine at the dinner table made Luis glad he had chosen to ride in the carriage. He might even doze off on the ride home after the filling meal. How strange it was, thought Luis, that a religious man could be so well fed while the poor of his parish suffered from hunger.

"There was something you wished to ask me, as I recall," the bishop reminded Luis.

"After such a perfect meal I'm embarrassed to ask anything else of you, Bishop."

"Ask, Luis." The bishop sipped his wine while eyeing the young man seated across from him. His rotund belly served as a resting place for his partially filled glass.

"It is about Catrin." Luis saw the bishop's teeth bite gently into the glass. "She has been jailed by the Inquisition for the past five months, and no official charges have been lodged against her. I know at least one of my servants has testified against her, but the merciful Inquisitor didn't accept the testimony as fact. At least that is what the Inquisitor himself told me."

"He has a difficult task, Luis. Sorting through the truths and lies that spread through our people is demanding."

"I understand that, Bishop. But Catrin is delicate in both mind and body."

"A bit demented, you mean." The bishop's sly smile looked unpleasant.

"She means no one harm. More likely others would take advantage of her."

The bishop rested his glass on the arm of his chair, holding the stem between two of his fingers, and sat straighter.

"Why do you take interest in this servant of yours? From what I hear, she didn't get along with her peers and was rather lazy."

"These are minor faults, Bishop, that hardly require her imprisonment in the Inquisitor's manse."

"What do you want me to do?"

"Intercede. Ask the Inquisitor to allow me a brief visit with Catrin so that I can check on her health."

"Sometimes it is better not to have too much knowledge. The girl barely touched your life. Let her pass into your history."

"I can't. My father and I feel responsible for her. We don't want to abandon her."

"She has abandoned her own soul. You need not take on that burden."

"Please, Bishop, rethink this." Luis stood to leave. "Of course our family's donation will be forthcoming either way."

The two men parted on friendly terms.

chapter 18

TERESA AWOKE TO THE SOUND OF THE DOUBLE doors being opened. Luis entered his father's bedroom slowly, his rich clothes crumpled from the slumber he took in the carriage while returning home.

"Has he been asleep long?"

"I've lost all track of time. He had a light dinner, and I read to him for a while, but when I heard his sharp snore, I put the book aside and fell asleep myself."

Luis smiled down at her.

"Go to your room and sleep the rest of the night. I shall be here if he needs anything."

She arose from her chair and pressed her palm against the old man's forehead to assure herself that he had no fever. The coolness of his skin made her sigh in satisfaction.

She crossed the room, turned to take one last look at father and son, then opened the double doors and left the family to a peaceful night.

"Is he asleep?" The hush whisper came from an

alcove nearby.

"Isabella. That is your name, isn't it?"

The phantom in the darkest corner of the hallway moved its body along the wall. It carried no flame and depended on the dim lamps for light.

"That was the last name I was known by in your world. But I've left it and taken a new name."

"Will you tell me what it is so that I may address you?"

"No. You haven't proven you're worthy of pronouncing my name on your lips."

"And how can I prove that?"

"By taking Roberto's life."

"He is your brother. You wouldn't want me to hurt him, would you?"

"He is Isabella's brother, not mine."

"*Your* brother is sleeping. He can't be disturbed, and his son is sitting sentinel by his bed."

"You don't look like Catrin."

"You know I am not."

"Then why does my nephew talk to you?"

"Because I am his father's caretaker. What do you know of Catrin?"

"I know very little about her. Isabella knew all the secrets."

"Didn't Isabella share the secrets with you?"

"They wouldn't have been secrets if she had shared them with me."

"May I see you safely back to your room?"

"So many doors," Isabella said, looking down the

long hallway. "Do you know which is my room?"

"You could tell me instead of making me guess; then we both would be getting the sleep we need."

"I sleep during the day. I can't sleep at night."

"Late at night do you sometimes sit with your brother and talk about the past?"

"We have no need for words anymore. Words only blurred our reality."

Teresa put out her hand.

"Come, I'll see you back to your room."

A long, bony hand reached out to Teresa. The withered flesh appeared mottled in the dimly lit hallway. The long, unkempt nails scraped Teresa's palm, causing her to wince.

"Is my touch that cold?" the apparition asked.

In answer Teresa gripped the woman's hand tighter.

"Lead the way," Teresa said.

The woman smiled, showing porcelain teeth, for but a moment before turning her head away toward the far end of the hallway. Linked together, they moved gracefully along the wooden floor, the woman moving leisurely as if walking in the country on a summer day. She stopped at the door at the very end of the hall and touched the palm of her free hand to the center of the decoratively carved portal. It swung back slowly, revealing a nursery. Stuffed toys covered with dust circled the room, waiting for an infant to fill the empty cradle in the center of the room.

"This is for you, Catrin," the woman said proudly. "I've chosen everything in this room. It is difficult at night to see the pretty colors, but when the sun shines through the window during the day, the room throbs with the brilliance of its colors. You will sleep soundly in here. Only the birds chirping from their little nest will intrude on your quiet."

Stunned, Teresa saw cobwebs joining the paws of the inanimate animals. The moon's glow spotlighted the cradle with its delicate linen and crocheted coverlet.

"I am not Catrin. You know that. Catrin is an adult now and doesn't reside in this house. She hasn't been here for months."

"Five months," the older woman said. "Five months she has been gone." The woman turned her sad eyes to Teresa. "Do you know when she'll come home?"

"Who is Catrin?"

"She is you and every young girl who walks the halls of this house." The older woman rested her free hand on Teresa's cheek. The cold hand sent a chill through Teresa's spine.

"Where do you sleep? Allow me to take you back to your room."

"I sleep wherever I can fall asleep. Sometimes it's in this room. Often it is next to Roberto's room, where I can hear his breathing and know he is still with me."

"Then let me take you to that room tonight. His presence will comfort you and warm your flesh."

"My flesh is no longer a temptation." The old woman unclasped Teresa's hand and looked at her arms and hands. "I can remember when nothing marred the silky softness of my skin. Look now," she said, moving her arms closer to the moonlight. "The flesh is flabby and discolored. The swollen veins, overburdened with blood, distort the smoothness."

Teresa took hold of the woman's arms, the mottled flesh flaccid with age.

"Come with me." Gently she tugged the woman out of the room, closing the door behind them. Moving back down the hall, Teresa tried to remember whether she had ever seen inside any of the rooms bordering Roberto Velez's bedroom. She hoped by the time they had moved closer to the other doors, the woman would give some hint as to which led to her own room. Instead the woman placed her hand on the handle to her brother's bedroom.

"No," Teresa said, removing the woman's hand from the door. "He's asleep. His son is sitting with him. Let them have some peace tonight." She moved the woman past Señor Roberto's room to the next. The door did not give right away; she had to use additional force to budge it. Inside only a single portrait of Señora Velez hung on the wall; the rest of the room stood empty. Isabella glided past Teresa to enter.

"I remember when she sat for that portrait. The artist was my lover. He told me how much more beautiful I was than her. What do you think?" Isabella stood immediately under the portrait. "Ignore my dress. I had no idea I would be posing." She touched her simple garment of white.

"You are a beautiful woman," answered Teresa.

"But am I more beautiful than his wife?"

"You mean Señor Velez's wife."

"The artist's wife." Isabella looked up at the portrait, backing farther away to attain the proper perspective.

"Did Señor Roberto Velez paint the portrait?"

"He told me secrets about her. She hated the feel of his body against her flesh. She hated the product of their union."

"No, you are confused. Let me take you to your bedroom."

"He loved me very much, you know, before she came into his life. He loved me far more than a brother should." With a stern look, Isabella turned to Teresa. "We didn't sin, though. We couldn't sin because we were blessed by God."

Teresa backed up into the doorway.

"There's a hidden door that leads into my room. Sadly it hasn't been used in a long time. I'm not sure I can still find the secret hinge." Isabella began touching the wall panels.

Teresa retreated from the talking woman, the white of Isabella's dress flashing briefly under the pull of the moon's light. After closing the door, Teresa scurried down the hall for the staircase.

chapter 19

ONCE INSIDE HER OWN ROOM, TERESA immediately packed her few belongings. She couldn't imagine
residing any longer in this house of sin. She was not a
confessor who could bring forgiveness for all the horrors
practiced in this house. Sister Agatha had said she would
take her back. The sister would never expect her to wade
through so many sorrows.

A scream. The laugh of a hyena. She didn't know
which invaded the house, causing the beat of her heart to
increase. She waited for the padding of feet in the hall,
but not a sound fell on the stone of the floor. Opening
the door to her room slightly, she peeked into the hallway.
Every other door remained closed.

The alarm rose once again from the mouth of some
woman. Not nearby, but still in the house. *Why doesn't
someone respond?* She had decided to leave the house and
didn't want to involve herself in further turmoil.

But the high-pitched sound resounded again.

Troubled by the maniacal sound, Teresa rushed to the

bedroom shared by Señora Toledo and Hilaria. Pounding hard, she had to wait far too long for an answer. When Señora Toledo did open the door, she looked angry.

"Go back to bed," Carmen ordered.

"Can't you hear that awful cry?"

"Ignore it and go back to bed. Don't be foolish enough to let them know you hear anything."

"Let who know? You've heard this sound before, haven't you?"

Hilaria pushed Carmen out of the way and grabbed on to Teresa's arms and pulled her into the room.

"You'll get us all in trouble standing out there," Hilaria whispered.

"She needs to go back to bed," Carmen insisted.

A wail replaced the shrill sound.

"Someone's been hurt. We have to help," Teresa said.

"How?" asked Hilaria.

"We have to find where those sounds are coming from."

"Not from this part of the house. It's coming from upstairs on the master's floor."

Teresa turned to make for the door, but Hilaria pulled her back.

"These screams are almost like lullabies to us. They ring in our ears at least once a month. Sometimes more. When Señora Velez was alive, we'd often find her crying. She'd drag herself out of bed and into the chapel to pray, her arms wrapped around the foot of the crucifix. No one ever told her husband. We would gather her up and return her to bed."

"Her husband was unfaithful to her." Teresa did not speak this as a question. She had already been told about the women.

"We think she comes back to mourn her marriage. It is always after midnight when the sounds occur. Always after the witching hour. Señor Roberto Velez buried his wife away from his land, but that doesn't keep her spirit from returning." Hilaria gripped the top of Teresa's arms with fury.

"No. This is a real scream from a flesh-and-blood person, and we must see that this torture stops." Teresa pulled away from Hilaria and walked out of the room.

"Let her go," she heard Carmen say, and the door slammed shut behind her.

For a few moments she stood quietly in the hall, waiting for another scream or wail. Instead a muffled sob came from one of the rooms down the hall. Slowly she approached the sound until she stood in front of the door from which it came.

Juana's room, she thought. The most timid person on the staff. Teresa knocked softly and whispered Juana's name.

"I want to help you," she said. "This is Teresa. If you're afraid, we can sit together for comfort. Open the door, Juana."

She waited until she finally heard a heavy step approach the door. Instinctively she took several steps back, not sure she should remain.

"Juana?"

The door flew open, and Gaspar stood half-naked in the doorway.

"Care to join us, Teresa?" His voice was rough from the activity in which he had been engaged.

Teresa ran back to her room, grabbed the bowl that sat on her water stand, and was ill. The rosary around her neck cut off her breath. She reached inside her blouse and pulled out the crucifix, raising it up high to free her flesh from the black beads, which she then threw to the floor.

chapter 20

In the morning before the others rose, Teresa carried her bundle downstairs. The cold kitchen felt unusually empty. No fire had been started as yet, but she knew Jose always lit the stove for Carmen. He'd be down shortly, she kept saying to herself as the minutes passed and the kitchen grew brighter with the rising of the sun.

"*Dios*, what are you doing up so early? Has Señor Roberto Velez's condition worsened?" Jose asked.

"I don't have any idea how he is doing. I'm here because I want to be taken back to the convent."

"Does Señor Luis know of your plans?"

"I am not one of his servants. I freely came here to care for his father, but I've seen that I can do very little to help. After you start the fire, would you mind taking me back before you've had breakfast? I'm sorry to be asking this of you, but I have no other way to leave."

"At least stay for Carmen's hot breakfast. We both need sustenance before we begin our chores."

"My work is back at the convent, not here."

"The cries last night frightened you?"

"You heard them and didn't check to see whether anyone was hurt?"

"It is Señor Roberto Velez's sister. She has bad nights when sleep is impossible."

"It couldn't have been her. She's too frail to make so much noise."

"From what I hear, you did a good job the other night when Spider surprised you in the garret, and look at you. Those thin arms and slender waist. No, we must fatten you up with breakfast." Jose gathered the wood for the fire.

"I can't walk back to the convent. I could meet a highwayman on the road or even be run down by a racing courier."

"That's true," Jose said completing his chore.

"Please, Jose, you've been kind to me. I ask for only one more favor."

"You would have me take you back to the convent and then return to answer to Señor Luis and his father. Do you think the good nuns would also take me in?"

"You want me to inform Señor Luis before I leave."

"I treasure my job here, even if you find the place obscene."

"Jose, it's still cold down here. What have you been doing?" Carmen entered the kitchen, halting her step when she saw Teresa. "Are you making more trouble? If the breakfast isn't done on time, I'll make sure everyone knows it is your fault," she said staring directly at Teresa.

"I don't think she will care, Carmen. Look on the table."

Teresa's bundle sat boldly in the middle of the wooden table.

"Running away from home?" Carmen asked. "Good riddance!" Carmen whirled into motion. First she tossed the bundle on the floor, and then busied herself with setting the table.

On her way out of the kitchen, Teresa bumped into Hilaria.

"Finished already? Or are you still searching the house for the ghost of Señora Velez?"

"There is no ghost, you fool."

"Ah, then you agree that you heard nothing last night when you intruded on Señora Toledo's and my sleep."

Teresa didn't answer. She walked around Hilaria, heading for the front staircase. She didn't hear a sound coming from the second floor. She grabbed hold of the banister and ascended, wary of what she might find. The empty landing looked serene. She started down the carpeted hall, intending to find Isabella. First she opened the empty room where Señora Velez's portrait still hung over an empty bare wood floor. She remembered that Isabella had said there was a door connecting her room to Señor Roberto's bedroom.

In the hall Teresa paused but a moment to listen at the invalid's door. No sound. Isabella had to be in the next room. She touched the handle of the door when the sound of muffled boots caught her attention. Señor Luis Velez stopped when he saw her.

"My father?"

"I haven't looked in on him yet." Her hand dropped to her side.

He continued toward her.

"That is my aunt's room."

"I thought I'd check on her since she didn't seem well last night."

"She sleeps during the day. There are too many fiends hiding in the shadows of night for her to close her eyes."

"Who are these fiends, Señor?"

"Memories. We all share them."

"I'm returning to the convent today."

"That's impossible. We need you here. Sister Agatha said you would stay for as long as you were needed."

"There are too many horrors burdening all your souls."

"And the longer you live, the more you shall find, wherever you are. Does that mean you intend to stone yourself up inside the convent for life?"

"Life is simple there. We praise God and care for those who need our help."

"Isn't that what you are supposed to be doing here? Or are you a coward, Teresa? Like the rest of us in this house."

"You are blind, Señor, and refuse to see how the lives are being crushed around you."

Luis put his hands in hers and placed them over his eyes.

"Remove the blindfold, Teresa, for I don't know how."

Teresa saw a movement just beyond Luis's shoulder. Hilaria stood with a smirk on her face.

"Teresa, Señora Toledo said if you want breakfast, you should come now because she won't be making any special meals for you." Hilaria winked and retreated back down the stairs.

Luis let go of Teresa's hands.

"Go have breakfast. I'll wake Father and try to build up an appetite in him." He walked past her, and without bothering to knock, he opened his father's door.

chapter 21

AT BREAKFAST TERESA REMAINED SILENT. JOSE never spoke of her request to be taken back to the convent. Juana's hand shook as she passed the bread, her fingers gripping the basket so hard that the straw began to unravel.

Gaspar had to be stopped. Why didn't anyone else stand up for Juana?

"Shall we go into town today, Carmen?" asked Sylvia, wearing a fancier than usual dress.

"We have everything we need."

"How can you say that? We haven't stocked the cupboards since Tuesday."

"That was two days ago, Sylvia."

"But, Carmen, it's a sunny day, and tomorrow may be rainy."

"We need some rain." Carmen began clearing the table.

Sylvia's fingers beat against the table.

"I would like to go into town," Sylvia said.

"You're dressed for it," Jose murmured. "But I'm

afraid Señor Luis will need my help today with the horses, and Fernando is too antisocial to be allowed in town."

Fernando merely groaned.

Sylvia looked at Teresa.

"I used to live in the city. I could shop when I wanted, ride in cabs, and eat at lovely small taverns. Accompanied, of course."

"Accompanied by men with clinking gold coins," Hilaria clarified.

"Hilaria is jealous. She's never seen a gold coin." Sylvia handed her plate off to Carmen. "When Carmen and I go to the market, we always stop and stare at the jewelry. Of course, you'd never find a ring this exquisite," she said, lifting her hand in the air to show her ring finger wearing a dazzling stone.

"Did you steal it?" asked Manuel innocently.

"The boy lacks manners, Carmen," said Sylvia with a frown.

"He's Jose's problem, not mine, Sylvia."

Jose chased Manuel out of the kitchen. The bewildered child grabbed an extra sausage before escaping through the open door.

"I should go upstairs and check on Señor Roberto," Teresa said.

"Go ahead. I'll send Hilaria up with his breakfast as soon as it's ready." Carmen rested both hands on Hilaria's shoulders.

Teresa found her patient alone, sitting up against several pillows.

"I thought you had forgotten me."

"Never. I let your son have some time alone with you."

"He wants me to be nice to you. 'Have patience,' he said. Have I ever been disrespectful to you, Teresa?"

"Not at all." Teresa inwardly smiled, thinking about how dense Luis could be. "You've been one of the most pleasant people in the house."

"My son thinks you're not happy. It isn't very exciting spending your time with a dying old man. Are you bored?"

"No."

"Ah, but I forgot. You were raised in a convent. I suppose they don't throw too many parties. Was it difficult?"

"I enjoyed my time at the convent. The sisters were kind to me."

"And will you return to them?"

"I don't know. Part of me wants to. Choices are simpler when God is your only love."

"And what of mortal men, Teresa? Do you have any interest in them?"

"Besides the priests who said mass for us, I didn't meet many other males. Occasionally I would be called in to nurse a husband or a son for a few days. I would know it was time to leave when the husband or son became frisky."

"You mean when they were well enough to appreciate your beauty. I shouldn't say that, because even a sick man knows you are an attractive woman. But the sick man would never say so for fear of driving you away."

"And when the sick are well?"

"Then it is time to move on their sexual needs before

you disappear. Does that sound crude to you, Teresa?"

"It sounds too simple. Most men have appreciated the care given to them. They do not seek to take additional advantage. I didn't mean to imply that all patients were the same."

"Besides, you were sent to them by the sisters. It would be an insult to press themselves on you. Do you fear men?"

"Only highwaymen and drunkards," she said, opening the window to allow the day's fresh air to circulate throughout the room.

"Wise of you," he said, grinning. "But what of marriage? Do you want children?"

"I haven't had time to think about it."

"Everyone considers children. Women are so mad for children that they risk their lives to have them. Have you ever watched a woman give birth?"

"Only once."

"And did the pain and blood horrify you?"

"The woman was strong and had already birthed three children. She knew exactly what to do."

"I have seen two women I love give birth for the first time. One silently held my hands and did as the midwife instructed. The sweat poured off her brow. Her breaths were gasps. Her fingers made deep indentations on my flesh. I once was a strong man, but the grip of that woman pained my arms for days after the birth."

"Was this your wife?"

"No. Does that shock you?"

"I don't know the circumstances. How can I judge?"

"I'm the father to at least two children, Teresa. Neither knows me intimately, and one doesn't even know her father's face."

"Catrin," Teresa spoke the name softly, allowing the old man to close his eyes and see the babe once more.

"You are clever, Teresa. Luis has no idea." The words were muttered almost inaudibly.

"I shall not tell him. It must come from your lips."

Roberto Velez's eyes opened, and he watched Teresa as she moved about the room, performing her duties.

"There is no reason for him to know."

"He has a sister in trouble with the Inquisition. That would seem to be a reason to tell him."

"And what if she should die at the hands of the Inquisition? The guilt he would feel when he fails to save her would be on his conscience. I'll not burden him with my own sins."

Teresa stopped moving. A chill swept through her body, but not from the open window.

"You confuse your own sin with a separate person, Señor. Catrin is not the sin. She has a right to be saved."

"I had forgotten. My son mentioned that your mother left you at the convent. I apologize for the hurt I may have caused with my words."

"I am sorry that you refuse to recognize your child. You damage the lives of both your children by keeping your secret."

"My son doesn't know that I'm aware he had an affair

with Catrin." The old man paused to watch Teresa turn away from her chores to look at him. "Yes, with his sister."

"They didn't know. You are the one at fault for that."

"Too bad women may not become priests, for you would make a good one. Laying blame, brandishing hell as your weapon."

"I know also how to forgive, Señor. Your pride keeps your secrets buried. Tear yourself away from that pride and ask forgiveness."

Hilaria rapped on the door, bringing the old man's breakfast. Teresa watched Hilaria wink and smile coquettishly at Señor Roberto. The innocent play brought color to the man's pale cheeks. A simple game, she thought, that could make Roberto Velez happy to be still alive. Harmless, yet painful when one considered the impossibility of fruition.

chapter 22

LUIS SAT IN THE LIBRARY PORING OVER THE SINGLE page of the report that had not been written in the hand of his agent. Could Catrin have written this and somehow managed to get it out of the prison? And if she had, what had she been trying to communicate?

He had never seen Catrin write and did not know whether she could. Her giddy childlike behavior had initially lightened the dark sadness of the house. But after his mother died, the girl became estranged from most of the residents of the house. Her interests became dark, the clothes she wore matronly, and her interest in the dark arts increased. She spoke of speaking with the dead and of herbal concoctions that could control the behavior of others.

The staff complained about her moods and said they feared the violence of her temper. A temper which had never been evident before his mother's death. *Why?*

He couldn't depend on the bishop to help to acquire her release from the Inquisition's dungeon. Even the offer to fund the bishop's pet project hadn't changed his mind.

Spider whined by the doors leading to the yard.

Luis stood and walked over to the dog, rubbed its glossy coat, and swung open the door, allowing the dog to run free to seek out the sole occupant of the yard. Luis leaned out the doorway to see where the dog headed.

Teresa jumped when Spider brushed her dress with a fallen branch. She backed away from the dog.

"He only wants to play," Luis said.

The look of fright turned to surprise when she heard his voice.

"He's certainly not a puppy."

"In his mind he is. We've never been able to use him as a guard dog or as a working dog in the field."

Teresa brushed away the soil that the branch left on her dress.

"I apologize for my behavior. I haven't helped you to settle in here. I've forgotten how to be civil."

"Between your father being ill and a servant being taken by the Inquisition, it would be hard to give much thought to other matters."

"You will stay, though?" He lowered his voice to prevent anyone else hearing their conversation. "I'd like you to stay. My father is doing better under your care."

"Yes. I almost ran. But instead I should confront many of the problems in this house. If you will sit down with me a while, we can talk of them."

Luis smiled. "I thought I was the major problem."

"In a sense you are, because you ignore what is happening around you. Did you not hear the screams last night?"

"My aunt can be difficult," he said.

"Difficult? Are you sure she wasn't being tortured, or torturing some innocent herself?"

"She hasn't joined forces with the Inquisition yet. Although that might enter her mind one day. My aunt is . . . Father used the word 'eccentric' to describe her once. I tend to think she is mad. Mad or an incredibly vicious harpy. She finds ways to make my father's life miserable."

"She suggested I do away with him."

"I'm surprised she hasn't done that herself."

"Her mixed feelings about him would prevent her from doing so. She both loves and resents him."

"You didn't use the word 'hate.'"

"It isn't hatred. She feels abandoned by your father."

"Because he is ill?"

"Because he married your mother. Has your aunt never married?"

"No. She had been engaged once, I understand, but refused to show up for her wedding vows."

"She left the poor man stranded at the church?"

"I believe she was fourteen at the time, and rebellious. Her parents gave up on marrying her off and almost found a place for her at a cloister, but she would have none of that, either. My father came to the rescue by promising to care for her. That satisfied my grandparents, and they no longer pushed to have her made independent of them."

"Why does she sleep in the room next to your father?"

"It soothes her to be near him."

"What will happen if he dies?"

"I will place her in the garret and forget about her." He saw Teresa's face darken. "I'm teasing, Teresa. My father made me promise to care for her in the same way he had. She will live out her life in this house with everything she could need."

"Except your father."

"She may visit his grave. He'll be but a few yards from the house. Although I pray that will not happen for a long time."

Spider nuzzled one of Luis's hands.

"He wants some attention. Must take after my Aunt Isabella."

Luis picked up the branch and threw it, sending the dog running to the far end of the yard.

"I wish human beings were so easy to entertain."

"You don't like people, do you?" Teresa moved closer to him.

"Emotions run too high in people." The dog brought back the branch, and Luis repeated the cycle once again.

"Wouldn't it be boring if all you had to do was throw sticks to cement relationships?"

"But safe. Unless, of course, another person gets in the way of your throw."

"I suppose you want me to stand a good distance away from you to give you a better swing."

"No, Teresa, I don't want you far away from me. You give me a chance to see the world in a different context.

Ever since I was a child, there's been a constant aloofness among our family members. Mother complied with her duty by presenting Father with a child. Even better, I was a male child. Father saw to the future by increasing his wealth and training his scion to continue our heritage. The servants performed their tasks well and made infrequent demands on the family. Even Gaspar, the most churlish of the servants, manages to deal with most problems without assistance."

"He is one of your problems."

"Gaspar? He's our guiding light when we have problems."

He saw her forehead furrow.

"Has he given you any problems?" he asked.

"I'm not free to discuss anything about Gaspar right now."

"Anything? Don't be coy, Teresa. Tell me what has Gaspar done?"

"Nothing to me."

"Implying that he has been harassing others on the staff? I wish you would trust me."

Spider jumped up on his owner's leg, the stick protruding off balance out of his mouth.

"I should check on your father. He enjoys my reading to him around this hour." Without asking leave, Teresa hurried back indoors.

chapter 23

Once inside the front door, Teresa started for the staircase but stopped when she saw Juana cleaning in the library. She desperately wanted to talk to the girl about the situation with Gaspar. If only Juana would listen to Teresa's plea. She turned away from the staircase, choosing to confront Juana now.

"May I speak with you a moment?"

"Is there something that Señor Roberto Velez needs?" asked Juana, laying down the cloth she had been using.

I hope not, Teresa thought, realizing that he would be waking from his nap now.

Teresa walked into the room and closer to Juana. She wanted to be able to communicate in a soft voice. Juana's problem with Gaspar wasn't anybody else's problem, and no one wanted to assist the poor girl.

"It's about last night. I'm sorry I ran away. I should have confronted Gaspar."

"I don't know what you're talking about, and I need to keep working. Señora Toledo gave me a heavy load of tasks for today."

Teresa prevented Juana from returning to her polishing by gently resting a hand on the girl's arm.

"Gaspar should not be in your room in the middle of the night, Juana, and I don't think you want him there."

"You'll have me on the street."

"No. You should speak to Señor Luis. I will go with you if it would help."

"What do I need to speak to the young master for? He barely lives in this house. Frequently he is away from home. He remains now only because his father is ill. He'll see it as being my fault. Even at church the sermons speak of the women of temptation who drive men to commit vile sins."

"That is just said to give men an excuse. Señor Luis is wiser than to think that."

"Is he? Why do you think that? It is known that he frequents whorehouses and will pay his full amount to cleanse his soul. He will never bicker about the price as some men do."

"Juana, this is not a whorehouse. Señor Luis understands that this is his home. He can't treat any of you like a prostitute."

"He treated Catrin like one." Juana's eyes defiantly stared back into Teresa's. "To whom was she supposed to go when Señor Luis bedded her? His father? A man who left his invalid wife alone for months at a time, traveling the world on business? And do you think he practiced celibacy?"

"Allow me to speak to Señor Luis for you."

Juana smiled.

"Have you become close enough to Señor Luis that you can intercede? Hilaria spoke of his asking you into his bedroom. And would you have gone if you hadn't anticipated that Hilaria might be nearby? She also caught you both in the hall touching each other."

"This is ridiculous. Hilaria doesn't understand what she heard or saw. She's driven only to besmirch me."

"You may deny what she told me, yet I have seen through this window how you bide your time with him." Juana pointed at a nearby window where the drapes were drawn. She could see Luis tossing the branch for Spider to retrieve.

"There is no romance between myself and Señor Luis."

"I said nothing of romance, Teresa. Señor Luis is incapable of love."

"I wouldn't allow him to touch me."

"Even if your livelihood depended on it?"

"When his father dies, I will return to the convent."

"I can't." Juana pulled away and continued her cleaning.

Teresa turned to see Gaspar standing in the doorway.

"Señor Roberto Velez is in need of your company, Teresa." He backed out of the doorway to let her through. The heat of his body seared her flesh, causing a chill to shake her shoulders.

chapter 24

"Ah, Teresa, I hoped you would come and sit with me. This room grows larger while my body shrivels into a corpse. Even the dead like company. Isn't that why we visit them and take flowers to decorate their final home?"

"I thought the visits were meant to console the living, and the flowers were to assuage our guilt."

"That can't be what the nuns taught you. They wouldn't have been that coarse. Besides, isn't it the Church's duty to sell indulgences for the dead? I never understood how many masses took how many years of purgatory off. The easiest, of course, is prayer. One can sit for hours counting out the rosary. Should one keep a tabulation on paper to pass on to the local priest, or can it be passed directly to the Lord?"

"You don't sound like a man who believes in the Catholic Church, Señor. We both know how dangerous that is."

"I don't care anymore. I've been deserted by both Gods. My muscles wither. My lungs fill too easily with water to allow me full breaths. And I don't know whose flesh covers my body now. The pustules and cuts weary this flesh, which isn't even the same color as the skin of my youth. Come closer, Teresa, and I will tell you a secret."

She sat in the chair near the bed and leaned toward the old man.

"Someone came one night while I slept and switched bodies on me. Yes, the size is almost the same as the one of my youth, but this is a much weaker body. Sometimes at night I imagine my wife sitting by my bed. Her body wrapped in the funeral shroud. Her shrunken legs renewed with both healthy flesh and muscle. She never touches me, because I am much too disgusting for her now. Imagine seeming putrid to a dead woman. She'll ask if I've prayed for her, and I can do nothing but tell her the truth. 'Never,' I say. But why should I pray for her, Teresa, when she did nothing else during her life except pray?"

"You could ask her for forgiveness for the way you treated her in life. Her willingness to do so would bring peace to your soul."

He tried to raise himself higher on the pillows but was too weak to lift himself without Teresa's help. He reached up to touch her cheek. The frailness of his fingers prevented her from pulling away.

"I remember touching soft flesh such as yours with passion, and now I only seek to steal some warmth from your body."

She pulled away, and his hand dropped back down on the blanket.

"I'm afraid, Teresa. One God I have turned my back on, and I have disregarded the other God's laws. Neither will want my soul, and both will wreak punishment upon me."

"There is only one God, Señor Velez."

"And you know who the true God is. There are no doubts in your eyes. You are confident that He made a point of taking you into His bosom. He never sent you on a quest to find Him. Since the time you slid from your mother until now, He has held you within His arms. Why did He choose you, Teresa, and not me? He gave me family and wealth but withheld Himself from me."

"He revealed Himself to you when you converted."

Tears rolled along the old man's cheeks, some dropping to the sides, others flowing into creases in his flesh.

"I go to mass. I say the words that the priests have taught me. I kneel in a narrow box before a man who is no better than me and confess my deepest secrets. On occasion I allow the same priest to place the host on my dry tongue and I answer, 'Amen.' While I die I expect that a priest will pray over my body, giving me the Last Sacrament. However, your God may never reach my heart."

She took his hand.

"Don't ever speak of this with anyone."

"I'm beyond fearing the Inquisitor, Teresa. God is the One who fills my thoughts in my last days on earth." He grasped her hand as tightly as he could. "Reveal your God to me, Teresa. Allow me to see Him through your eyes."

"I wish that I might be able to. If I could sketch a

picture of Him or have the fluency of words to describe His beauty to you, I would. But you must find Him in your own heart."

"Don't let me die yet. Keep me alive until I can sort out this dilemma."

"You've been confessing your sins to the wrong person, Señor Velez."

He looked at her, not understanding her words.

"Don't confess to a stranger, to a priest. Confess your sins to those you've sinned against. Your sister sleeps in the next room. Luis stands in the yard, wondering whether you love him. Give them what they need."

"Do you think Luis will walk away from me?"

"Only Luis will know what he needs to do. At least he will have answers to questions he doesn't even know how to ask."

He let go of her hand.

"Go to the window and see if you can spy him."

She crossed the room and leaned carefully out the window.

"I see him, but he is too far away to call. Shall I go down and get him?"

"Will I lose both my children to the Inquisition, Teresa?"

Teresa faltered over her words. The Inquisitor's punishments were hard to predict. He might fine one man and for the same offense burn another at the stake. Only the Inquisitor had the knowledge of both the accusations and the testimonies. The mobs that filled the streets on the day of the *auto da fe* listened to the announcement of punishments but heard nothing of the evidence. Often the public tormented the prisoners, throwing vegetables or spitting as the prisoners walked by. She couldn't stand to imagine Señor Luis stripped naked and subjected to such abuse.

"You cannot answer me, Teresa? I fear your eyes see into a future we both dread. Look how pale you've become from sitting with a dying old man. Let me rest now."

Teresa nodded her head and pulled the chair near the window to catch the coolness of the late afternoon on her perspiring skin.

chapter 25

"GASPAR," CALLED LUIS.

The butler took but moments to respond.

"How are you getting on with my father's nursemaid?"

"We hardly speak, Señor. I don't have time to dally with staff."

Luis sometimes felt inferior to Gaspar, who carried himself incredibly erect despite his rapidly growing paunch that must have weighed down his body. Gaspar had been with the family for at least thirty-five years and came from a family of servants. He could advise on clothing and dinner etiquette, and he could lie to anyone without flinching when the family had need of this skill.

"Earlier this morning she wanted to leave and return to the convent. She changed her mind after I spoke to her."

"Your aunt woke most of us last night, Señor."

"I thought there might be something more to her uneasiness."

"She did get up and wander around the hall in the servants' area last night. I believe she spoke with Carmen and

Hilaria. Their voices often carry. Hilaria can be unnerving when she rambles on with her stories. She delights in implying that your aunt is not among the living."

"Father and I wonder about that ourselves, Gaspar."

He saw Juana coming out of the library, her head down, her hands full of cleaning materials.

"Juana, may I have a word with you?"

She timidly looked up into Gaspar's face before turning to Luis.

"I should like to put these things away first. If I have your permission?"

"Yes. Why must you tiptoe as if you were in a den of lions, Juana? Go, go, I'll speak to you later."

"Wait, Juana," Gaspar called. "Pardon, Señor, but I can put away Juana's working tools if you wish to speak to her now."

"Actually I hoped you could give me more insight into why Teresa acted so odd this morning."

"Juana spends more time with Teresa than I."

"Oh, here!" Luis scooped the materials out of Juana's arms and let them drop to the floor. "No one is going to steal them, Juana. I had a few questions to ask the both of you. Gaspar has said that Teresa woke Carmen and Hilaria last night after my aunt's dramatic screaming. Did she knock on your door at all, Juana?"

Again she looked first at Gaspar. This bothered Luis. Why should she owe more allegiance to Gaspar than to her own employer?

"Why would she wake me?" she asked.

"I hadn't warned her about my aunt's behavior, and she may have been seeking an explanation."

"She asked me nothing about the yelling, Señor."

"Did she speak to you at all?"

Juana's lips trembled, her fingers knotted into a tight ball.

"Why are you so damn afraid, Juana?"

"Señor, I heard no other voices last night. Carmen is very good about taking charge. I'm sure she saw Teresa back to her bedroom."

"Teresa was right! This house is writhing in secrets." Luis kicked Juana's bundle across the floor and walked out the front door.

chapter 26

"WHAT DID YOU DO TO GASPAR?" ASKED HILARIA.

Teresa had handed off Señor Roberto's dinner tray to Hilaria at the door of his bedroom.

"What?"

Hilaria peeked around the door and gave her seductive smile to the old man before backing away to whisper again to Teresa.

"He's furious. Juana's hysterical. Carmen thinks you make too much trouble. Jose is attempting to defend you, which doesn't help your case with Carmen."

"And Sylvia, Fernando, and Manuel?"

"Their opinions don't matter."

"I'm sure they do to them." Teresa felt sure of that.

"Manuel is a child. An orphan like yourself, except he didn't have the luck to be fawned over by a group of childless nuns."

"Teresa, ask Hilaria to come in if she wishes to join us." Señor Roberto's voice held no sarcasm or irritation.

"She needs to take the tray downstairs, Señor. She

merely wanted to know how you were faring."

"Let her come in and see for herself."

Hilaria gladly pushed the door farther back to allow her and the tray to fit through the doorway.

"I see we have gained some color, Señor Velez." Hilaria's smile appeared instantly on her face.

"Liar. But I could do with listening to lies for a while. The real world wearies me, especially at night."

"Could it be caused by the company you keep?" Hilaria asked. "Not that I mean to insult Teresa, but day and night you two are locked away in this room, with only an occasional visitor to break up the monotony."

"Dance for me. Dance for me the Dance of the Seven Veils, Hilaria. Remind me what wantonness is like." The old man's voice sounded dreamy.

"You embarrass me, Señor. I have neither the courage nor the body for such a dance."

"You're a minx," he said.

Before Hilaria began swiveling her hips, Teresa attempted to sweep Hilaria out the door.

"No, no. Don't make her go, Teresa. I'm tired of serious conversations. I want a jester to brighten the rest of my day. Hilaria is certainly capable of taking on the role."

Hilaria handed the tray to Teresa. With tiny, emphatic steps, she approached the chair by the side of the bed.

"Mmmmm, have we been bathed yet?" she asked, leaning forward to display her breasts.

"Hilaria, stop. He's ill."

"And nearing the gates of heaven," Hilaria said, raising an eyebrow.

"Or hell," he whispered.

Teresa put both her hands on Hilaria's shoulders to guide her out of the room.

"Señor Roberto, since when have you given over authority to a mere woman?" cried Hilaria as she shrugged off Teresa's hands.

"When I first married, my dear Hilaria. When it was announced that we were man and wife." He laughed hard until he fell into a coughing fit.

Teresa immediately poured him some water, and Hilaria lifted the top half of his body off the pillows to make it easier for him to drink. Each woman had rested a knee on the enormous bed.

Gaspar knocked softly on the bedroom door and Teresa invited him in.

"Are you all right, Señor?"

Señor Roberto pushed away the glass.

"I'm in bed with two women, Gaspar. What man can say that on his dying bed?"

"Señora Toledo is looking for Hilaria." Gasper stood neither impressed nor intimidated.

"Tell her she is doing the Dance of the Seven Veils."

"Señora Toledo has a poor sense of humor, Señor."

Roberto Velez didn't want to dismiss his company, but his son entered the room.

The scene melted into slow-motion tragedy, with Hilaria grabbing the tray, Gaspar following her out, and Teresa reclaiming the chair by the sickbed.

"I thought I heard laughter," Luis said.

"From a dying man's room? Son, do not debase the lugubrious air of this room."

"I'm sorry we were making so much noise. Your father had a coughing fit, and we all tried to assist him. As you see, he is fine now."

"Laughing at a dying man. Is that what you're telling me the three of you were doing?"

"Oh, no, Son. Gaspar never laughs. Only the young ladies have the heart and innocence to enjoy humor. Gaspar is way too old and jaded. Sometimes I'm afraid you are, too, Luis."

"I've inherited enough difficulties to rob me of any laughter for the rest of my life."

Luis hurried out of the room.

"That was cruel, Señor. He came worried that something had happened to you," Teresa scolded.

Roberto Velez frowned.

"He is right. I have left him nothing but trials to overcome. His mother raised him in both the Jewish and Catholic faiths. One is his heritage, and the other will keep him alive."

"He loves no God." Teresa had sensed this about Luis from when they first met. He didn't give proper respect to those wearing the robes of the Church.

"I raised him to be a Midas. I taught him how to take without giving. I saw no value to religion unless it served to make me wealthier. Yet I end up here in this bed, waiting for God's judgment."

"He is merciful."

"And righteous. You have forgotten to close the window, Teresa. Would you allow a chill to settle in my chest and rob me of my final breaths?"

After she closed the window, she lowered the lamps and sat quietly by his bed, listening to the straining of his lungs.

chapter 27

"BISHOP, IT IS GOOD TO SEE YOU. I HOPE YOU bring good news."

"I bring a terrible headache that may only be soothed by a bit of port." The bishop sat, raising his feet upon a convenient hassock.

"Gaspar."

The butler entered the room, his nose held high when in the direction of the bishop.

"We'd like some port."

"Yes, Señor." Gaspar left the room without a second look at the bishop.

"Your butler has been with the family for many years, hasn't he?"

"Yes, Bishop. I grew up watching him grow old."

"Don't mention old, or my gout will start up."

"I'm sorry. Is there anything I can do to make you more comfortable?"

"No, no. Sit, Luis. I'm not used to traveling. Even as a young man, I tried to stay close to home, but given my duties I failed most days."

Gaspar entered the room, leaving a glass of port on the small table next to where the men were seated.

"Gaspar, I hear you are hardly ever seen at church." The bishop lifted his glass, holding it short of his lips, waiting for an answer.

"I'll be sure to greet the priest this Sunday. I fear I get lost in the crowd."

"I wish there were such a crowd. Thank you, Gaspar."

The bishop sat in silence until he felt sure the butler had gone.

"I came to give you some information about Catrin."

"How is she?"

"She is in the Inquisitor's dungeon, Luis. How do you expect her to be? Besides, I haven't seen her myself. However, I've been . . ." the bishop paused to think of the best word to use, "notified that the young woman has not been baptized. Were you aware of this?"

"There was no reason for us to ask."

"No reason? Luis, the woman is a pagan, or possibly even a Jew."

"Why come here and tell me this?"

"I should think you would be grateful for the warning. The Inquisitor is disturbed that she was serving in a Catholic home. Also, it proves difficult in obtaining information from her."

"Why?"

"She hasn't said much of importance. She can't be tormented because she is not baptized. This makes for a stagnant affair. Torment does ease the tongue in the telling."

"Hardly, Bishop. Many men would confess to anything to limit the bone-crunching pain of the rack. Even brave men, when they hear their bones popping, will confess to heinous crimes. Wouldn't you, Bishop?"

"Praise God that I'm not the sort to stumble into heretical groupings. No, my faith is firm, Luis. I don't fear the Inquisition."

"I thought everyone did. Isn't that why it exists?"

"Its function is to wipe out heresy. Pope Sixtus IV was wise in giving the regents Isabella and Ferdinand the right to appoint inquisitors. They began a cleansing that had been long overdue."

"It has continued for decades, Bishop. Will it ever end?"

"The devil is always searching for the weak and the depraved."

"Certainly you don't believe Catrin to be either."

"She is not a married woman, and yet she is not a virgin."

Luis couldn't take his eyes off the swollen bishop. His immense body filled the chair, and the cost of the elaborate fabrics he wore could have fed many poor families.

"She may have engaged in her sins in this very house, Luis."

In my very bed. Luis waited for the direct accusation. He wanted to remind the bishop of his own three bastard children who had managed to achieve superior positions within the Church.

"Of course, she may have found her pleasure behind

a tavern with a drunken traveler who stopped for comfort one night. On the other hand, Gaspar does seem the kind to take advantage of a slightly demented girl."

Luis's hands opened and closed into fists, but the bishop carried on.

"It's important that you give some thought to this. I don't see the Inquisitor tiring of Catrin. The taint of your father's old faith brings up many questions in the Grand Inquisitor's mind. By the way, this port is quite good, Luis. Could you spare a few bottles for me to ease the cold nights ahead?"

"I'll have Jose deliver a case in the morning."

"Your kindness will always be rewarded, Luis. Might I spend a few moments with your father?"

"If he is awake, of course."

The two men climbed the stairs. The bishop, old and slow, began huffing halfway up the staircase. Luis slowed his pace to allow the bishop to catch up to him. When Luis knocked softly at his father's door, Teresa opened after a few seconds.

"The bishop is here. Do you think my father is well enough for a visit?"

"Of course." Teresa opened the door wide for the two men.

Luis noticed his father push back the covers and drop his legs over the side of the bed.

"I wanted to greet you myself at the door, Bishop, but Teresa is a cruel woman. She whips me mercilessly when I disobey."

"A few lashes help us all to follow the strict guidance that is necessary for our bodies and our souls, Roberto."

"Come, Teresa, let's allow these two old friends some private time together," Luis said.

"No. The nurse should stay. I would not deprive your father of his handmaid. But you, Luis, I have taken too much of your time already. Your father and I will probably get bogged down in recalling our histories. Go and take care of the business of the house."

Once Luis left the room, the two older men embraced. The bishop offered his support to Roberto, gently helping the invalid back onto the bed.

Allowing the bishop to take the chair closer to Roberto's bedside, Teresa sat near the door in case they should change their minds and ask her to leave.

"I have truly missed your company, Roberto. My dinners no longer have the sting of your wit to enliven them."

"My wit is gradually slipping away, old friend."

"I think it is becoming stale locked up with these morose people. Not that I don't understand the pain Luis is experiencing. I remember when my parents' health began to fail. I busied myself with as much work as I could to avoid the sadness. But he has become obsessed with this servant of yours, Catrin. Now he even wants to visit the poor girl. This can't bode well for his own soul."

"Catrin must be freed, Bishop. What does the Inquisitor want from me?"

"Don't ask that question, Roberto, because you wouldn't like the reply."

"My land? My wealth? Or does he hate me because I am a Jew?"

"A Jew by birth, but a convert to the true religion. However, you are an easy target. Sending your wife to be buried with her Jewish mother was not wise."

"My parting gift to her."

"It may prove to be an expensive gift. I don't think the Inquisitor is quite sure how to use Catrin, but the more questions your son asks, the more intrigued the Inquisitor becomes. Perhaps you could make Luis understand."

"My son feels close to Catrin, Bishop. You and I can vaguely recall the women who moved us to do unspeakable, unwise things."

"Luis and Catrin were lovers?"

"She is a lovely girl, and my son is at a vulnerable age, unlike us."

"You should hide your nurse away, then," the bishop said, nodding in Teresa's direction.

"She comes from a convent."

"Have you taken vows?" the bishop asked Teresa.

"No. I didn't enter the convent willingly."

Roberto laughed.

"Perhaps we should explain what you've said before my friend thinks he is in the presence of a wanton woman."

"It would not be the first time, Roberto, both professionally and for leisure." Both men laughed.

"Teresa's mother birthed her at the convent and left the babe there to be cared for," Roberto said.

"Far better than dragging the child through the streets.

Your mother showed good sense, Teresa, at least at the time of your birth." The bishop nodded in her direction.

Her heart pounded. These men didn't know what her mother's situation had been. Many married women were forced to give up their babes when food was in short supply or when the father had died or abandoned his wife. While at the convent, Teresa didn't think of her mother often. The nuns never spoke with judgment about the circumstances of the birth. But many outside the convent walls were eager to stain her mother with sin. Even these two men, who themselves abused the trust of females.

"My time is drawing to an end, Bishop. There is little for me to ask of you except one favor to save the life and dignity of my son. Please, help free Catrin. Whatever you need to do I will gladly pay for."

The bishop smiled.

"Your son already bribed me, Roberto. A cask of your best port will be sent to my manse tomorrow. Not only that, but Luis is interested in supporting the project to build a new convent for an order of cloisters that I watch over."

"The one to which your youngest child retreated?"

"Yes, the girl will either achieve sainthood or martyrdom, I'm sure. The folly of youth. She spends her time in penance for her father's sins, not knowing I have already paid."

"Have you? A man who allows himself the finer drinks and foods doesn't sound like he's atoned to me."

"There are limits to everything, including atonement."

Teresa watched the two men chuckle. The bishop hugged his old friend and blessed him with the sign of the cross before departing.

chapter 28

"YOU LIED, SEÑOR VELEZ."

"Lied? About what?"

"You told the bishop that Luis and Catrin were lovers, but never mentioned that she is also your daughter."

"That doesn't sound like a lie. Do you want me to admit to being poor Catrin's father? What will that do for her status? Mark her as a Jew? A heretic? No, Teresa, I want to save the lives of both my children."

"Through deceit?"

"You are tiresome, Teresa. I merely keep a secret, just as the nuns are doing for your sake."

"My mother forced them to promise to keep her name secret from me."

"And they could have refused. Instead they chose to keep you unblemished. Come, Teresa, what kind of woman leaves her baby at a convent?"

"She might have been poor."

"I have heard of women doing without food themselves, thus enabling their own children to thrive. I've paid women for their bodies, knowing the money will buy food to fill the bellies of their little ones. Or maybe your mother instead was wealthy and couldn't bear the thought of being linked to the stigma of having a child. Are you sure, Teresa, that you don't already know your mother? She may have worn and actually still wear the Dominican habit. Don't judge me harshly when you've seen so little of life."

Chastised, Teresa sat on the chair next to the bed. The rosary hung heavily around her neck, but she couldn't bring herself to touch it. Since the night she saw Gaspar in Juana's room, the rosary weighed her down. She often fumbled now through her prayers.

"I don't mean to be cruel, Teresa, I only want you to understand that simple answers don't exist in life. There are many roads a single word can lead us down. The wrong word might ruin a loved one's life."

"What if Catrin is released? What if Luis wants to resume his affair with her?"

"Let us pray there is no child from the union."

Teresa's body shivered from the sound of his words. How could a father take his son's life so lightly? she wondered fleeing the room before she made an irreverent response. Within seconds she found herself in Luis's arms.

"What did my father say to you?" he asked, seeing tears washing her cheeks.

"He would see your soul burn in hell," she whispered. The concern in his eyes made her heart bleed.

"What are you talking about?"

"Catrin. She is your sister."

Luis backed away from Teresa. Disbelief, pain, and anger caused his features to turn ugly.

"I'm sorry," she said.

"You know what she was to me."

"That is why I had to tell you. Please, Señor Velez, help your sister get free from the hold of the Inquisition. When she is free, give her shelter. Give her love from your heart. But never return to her bed."

"What did you say to my father?"

"He already knew about your union with Catrin. He didn't want to tell you that she's your sister."

"You decided to tell me yourself."

"You have a right to know. God would—"

"Punish us? We didn't think of God when we lay together. We thought only of our own pleasure. Is that a sin, Teresa? Perhaps we are forever damned." Luis walked past Teresa and into his father's room, closing the door behind him.

"I heard only her soft, sobbing whisper. The words jumbled into the wisp of a sigh that broke my heart. She told you the truth, Luis." The old man squinted to see his son's shape come toward him.

"Her mother?"

"You have no need for that information. I've already erred once this evening. I'm not apt to do it again."

"Did my mother know about Catrin?"

"She surmised and took pity on the girl. They never spoke, but your mother didn't abuse her or demand that

Catrin be let go."

"Why torture my mother in such a way?"

"Catrin had been brought up in the country by one of my friends. I hoped she'd have a life with them. They were not wealthy, but they weren't poor, either. She could have made a suitable marriage."

"Why change your mind?"

"Fate, or God, as I'm sure Teresa would say, forced the change. My friends became bankrupt. Had I known, I would have helped them, but they didn't come to me. Instead, they died in each other's arms."

"Suicide?"

"Luckily a servant in their household came to me, asking for work himself. I couldn't hire him, but I sought out my daughter."

"To bring her into the purview of the Inquisition?"

"Certainly not. I meant to help her, not shunt her off to be burned at the stake."

"Catrin has not been tortured because she has not been baptized."

"Although they were atheists, her guardians were kind. And it's just as well, given the circumstances."

"The Inquisitor thinks she can be of some value to him. Does he suspect you are her father?"

"He doesn't consult with me. In a moment of weakness, I told Teresa. I don't know why. She listened and accepted my pain. It's much easier when people don't pay attention to what is said. Exposure comes with opening one's heart. Unfortunately I was vulnerable to Teresa's patience."

"I will try to speak directly with the Inquisitor."

"Don't, Luis. I've already spoken with the bishop. He and I have lost track of who owes what to whom. He'll fulfill my dying wish."

Luis looked at his father's frail body. His hands could barely hold a bowl when he was thirsty. His parched lips displayed a purplish tinge. His eyelids drooped heavily over fading irises. Sleep no longer replenished his body. Roberto Velez fought against sleep and the oblivion it brought. Luis couldn't bring himself to rage at his father. They had only a short time left together.

"Do you wish me to sit with you a while?"

Roberto Velez reached out his arms to his son. Luis grasped his father's hands, remembering how safe his own hands had felt inside his father's when he was a small boy.

chapter 29

TERESA WALKED TO THE END OF THE HALL. THE nursery door remained shut, the wood of the door hardly touched, the mahogany polished brightly. *Catrin's room*, she thought. *The room in which the babe supposedly would lie. It waits, growing old, dusty, sadder with each passing night.*

She opened the door. Darkness hid the shame, except for a candle nub flickering in a corner of the room, shining onto the whitest hair Teresa had ever seen, glistening hair floating softly around a wizened face. A childless mother sat cradling a porcelain doll, its eyes closed, its mouth a smear of color eternally shut to the exposed breast whose teat stretched forward in anticipation.

Teresa entered the room, the cloth of her dress the only movement in the nursery. Isabella looked up.

"Catrin?"

Teresa knelt next to the woman, folding the white linen back over the breast.

"It's time for her feeding, but she isn't hungry."

"Catrin is a woman now."

Isabella looked down at the doll. Finally seeing what was really in her arms, she let it slip to the floor. Teresa lifted the doll, the taffeta of the dress crinkling in her hands. She set the doll against the wall, shocked when the lids lifted, revealing empty sockets.

"I never wanted her to see me," Isabella explained. "I look old and disheveled."

"We can fix that if you'd like."

"You must be a witch if you can make me young again," Isabella said, raising her right hand to her mouth.

"I can't bring back youth, but I can mend the vagaries of neglect." Teresa pushed back Isabella's hair, sweeping it up atop the woman's head. "We can brush some color into those cheeks and plump the lips with a bit of tint. Would you like that?"

"Will it bring Catrin home?"

"Your brother and nephew have taken on that challenge."

"Like knights?"

"We'll give them each a token. Something you'd like Catrin to have." Isabella reached for the doll. "No. Something of yours."

Isabella thought for a long time.

"My most precious possession is the love God gave me for her. No one can see it or touch it."

"Or steal it," Teresa whispered.

Isabella shook her head. She put her hand inside her linen shift, briefly covering where her heart should be. Bringing her empty hand back out, she offered the contents to

Teresa. "Can you divide my love between father and son?"

Teresa's hands covered Isabella's empty one.

"I've kept most of my love for Catrin inside my heart," Isabella said. "I'll give her the rest when I see her."

Teresa kissed the old woman's hand.

chapter 30

A STORM DROVE FERNANDO INDOORS FOR THE night, to bed down on the flagstone floor of the kitchen. He peeled away the drenched jacket and shirt and tried to cover himself with the spare rags he found in the kitchen. He had come home late, and Jose had locked the barn tightly against thieves. However, the forever forgetful Señora Toledo had only turned a single lock in the kitchen door, leaving it vulnerable to break-in. She'd catch it from Gaspar if he bothered to tell. He'd see how well she treated him in the morning before deciding what to do.

The next day Fernando sat shivering at the breakfast table despite the wool blankets Carmen had piled on him.

"Instead of sleeping on the cold floor, you could have come up to the servants' quarters."

"I would have woken everyone up, Señora Toledo. There was no light or sound coming from inside this house. Here I'd be, clomping around with my filthy boots, waking both you and the masters."

"*Dios*, you could at least have taken your soggy boots off."

"My boots never come off."

"Ooooh!" Manuel pinched his nose.

Señora Toledo swatted the back of the boy's head.

"Teresa wakes us up without giving it any thought," Hilaria said.

Ignoring the cut, Teresa offered the breadbasket to Fernando, but he shook his head.

"You couldn't have gotten much sleep last night. Why don't you go upstairs now and rest?" she said.

"But aren't all the rooms full? I mean, assigned," said Sylvia.

"He can use my room if there's no other," Teresa offered.

"He'll take you up on that if you lie in the bed with him," Hilaria muttered to herself more than speaking to those seated at the table.

"I'm fine. I just need to change my clothes, that's all."

"Tell the truth, Fernando. Those are the only rags you have," Hilaria said.

"Is that true?" asked Teresa.

Embarrassed, Fernando threw off the blankets, rose from the table, and headed for the door, his flesh red from the irritation of the wool, and his shoulders hunched against the chill in the room.

"You'll catch a lung ailment, and I'll have to depend on the runt, Manuel, for assistance. That is not good for me, Fernando!" Jose called the other man back.

"We can have a double wake. The old man and his ever-faithful servant."

"Keep quiet, Hilaria," Jose rounded on her in full voice. He turned back to Fernando to look the ill man up and down. "You and I are not the same size, but I will ask Señor Luis for some old clothes."

"Why should he give me anything?"

"Because he needs your hands and legs to get the work done, fool."

"What . . ." Hilaria stopped before Jose could end her comment.

Teresa went upstairs to wake Roberto. Her mouth dropped open when she spied Isabella standing over his body. The woman wore her hair up the way Teresa had styled it the night before, her face a collection of not-well-chosen pastel colors that she and Teresa had settled on the night before. She wore a dress of deep burgundy, the collar smeared with the colors of her face.

Teresa rushed to grab Isabella away from the bed.

"What are you doing here, Isabella?" Teresa's hands rested gently on the top half of the woman's arms.

"I wanted my brother to wake up and see me like this. Maybe he'll remember me."

Teresa saw that Roberto's chest moved in a slow rise and fall. The doctor must have given him an elixir again last night, she thought, thankful he hadn't awakened to his sister's nightmarish image.

"How long have you been in this room?"

"Since daybreak, but I've been quiet. I've hardly even breathed. I want him to wake up without a start and be happy to see me."

Roberto moaned.

"See, he's waking." Isabella pulled away from Teresa and reached out to touch his face, but her hands moved lower and found his neck.

Teresa tried yanking the woman away by the shoulders but couldn't budge her.

"Isabella!" A sharp voice filled the room from the doorway.

Roberto woke and clasped his hands around his sister's.

"Good morning, Sister." Roberto's dry voice could barely be heard.

Luis moved forward, taking hold of Isabella, his arms wrapped tightly around her body.

"Tell my nephew to step away from me, Roberto. He bothers me when he is too close."

Luis eased his hold but didn't let go.

"He worries too much about me, Isabella." The old man managed to give her a wink.

His sister's nails scraped the flesh of his neck. One fingernail left its trail on his flesh.

"Isn't it time for you to be asleep? Daylight wearies you, Isabella. Your bed is warm and soft with secrets that will carry you into sweet dreams."

"My bed hasn't been warm for a long time, Roberto. Lying on the sheets, I count the days that fall into weeks, that climb into months, and turn into years. When will you return?"

Teresa watched Luis release Isabella, letting his arms fall to his sides. The shock of his aunt's words forced him to step back from her. He looked at the old woman with eyes yearning for a dream, a nightmare to replace what he saw.

"Go to your room and wait for me, Isabella. When I am well, I'll come to you."

Her brother's words demanded obedience. She allowed her palms to skim his cheeks before retiring.

Teresa went to follow Isabella but was called back by Roberto Velez.

"She'll do as I say. You needn't persist in your dogged pursuit. Let her have some peace."

"No wonder the fact that I slept with Catrin did not bother you, Father. To you it is normal. It is no sin, but a treat to be savored even when your wife lies in the bed in the next room."

"Your mother didn't mind. She had grown tired of the body's appetites. She knew about Isabella even before we became engaged. Our marriage worked well because there were no lies."

"Are you saying she didn't mind your straying?" Luis came close to the bed.

"She tolerated it, which is different. I loved your mother. Don't make a face, Luis. I did love your mother, yet I felt safe with my sister. Your mother needed care. My sister didn't. Isabella pampered me."

"She can't anymore, Father."

"Now I have you. And Teresa." Roberto smiled at her, waving his hand for her to come closer. "Tell me, Teresa, who dressed my sister in that hideous outfit? Did you? No. You need not answer. Keep the secret. Once she was a beautiful woman. Confident. Spoiled by her parents. Educated. But she had one fault, Teresa: she loved me too much. Now she and I wallow in the memory of our sins. I'm not sorry. I close my eyes, and our relationship gives me delicious scenes of our debauchery. You think a dying old man shouldn't admit such things, Teresa. I can see reproach in the darkness of your eyes."

"Teresa is not part of the family, Father. She isn't required to listen to the trash you spill into our ears."

She turned to go.

"Teresa, I want you to consider what I said." Roberto raised his voice to ensure being heard. "When you lie on your deathbed, what will give you the greatest amount of pleasure? Will it be the rosary you always wear around your neck? The hymns that keep you from going crazy from the stillness of the convent? Or the touch of a man's hands cradling you in slumber?"

"It will be knowing I haven't hurt anyone as badly as you have," she said, whipping around to face him.

"Leave, Teresa, before you say anything more to my father."

In her flight she didn't bother to close the door.

chapter 31

"DID YOU HAVE TO SPEAK IN THAT FASHION TO Teresa, Father? She's not a barmaid or a whore like your sister." Luis's flushed face became ugly in the hardness that fell on his features.

"*Your aunt* has never been a whore. She loved me above everything else, and I took advantage of that love. Once in a while she thought about straying into other men's beds, but only to drive thoughts of me from her mind."

"And you wallow in that insane belief, don't you?"

Roberto looked closely at his son. The boy's hands fisted into tight balls, his body rigid with contained anger, his chin uplifted proudly, and oh, the eyes raging with the inner turmoil of love and hate.

"Sit, Luis. We cannot talk while you loom over me with such dark thoughts."

His son laughed, but no humor fed the coarse sounds he made. A meek knock on the door forced Luis into silence.

"Yes," he said, his eyes still peering down at his father's

withering body.

"It's Hilaria, Señor. I've brought your father's breakfast."

"Are you hungry, Father, or does the devil not need nourishment?"

Roberto attempted to rise to a seated position, but the weakness in his arms kept him from achieving that goal. He tried three times before looking up at his son.

"Now you would abandon me, Luis? Will you have me crawl from the bed to open the door? Must I soil my sheets rather than you handing me a chamber pot? I pity my poor sister when she is left in your care."

Roughly Luis lifted his father to a seated position and fluffed the pillows against the head of the bed to offer a small amount of comfort to his father.

"Come in, Hilaria," Luis said.

"Ah, my favorite dancer," Roberto said. "You know, Son, she had promised to do the Dance of the Seven Veils for me. Isn't that right, Hilaria?"

The servant sensed something wrong. The room sparked with negative energy. Her wide eyes settled first on Luis, then on his father.

"Perhaps not today, Señor." The tray of food wobbled in her arms.

"When? Do you need a bigger audience? Maybe the next time the bishop visits?"

"Oh, no, Señor! The bishop can never know that I have teased you in such a way."

"Ah, you also are afraid of the Inquisition, aren't you,

Hilaria?" Roberto made no attempt to hide his smirk.

"Everyone is, Señor."

"Put the tray down on the table, Hilaria. I'll see that my father eats."

She nodded in Luis's direction and hurriedly walked to the table to rid herself of the tray.

"Hilaria, did you speak against Catrin?" The old man's eyes narrowed, his lips thin beneath his hawkish nose.

She spun around quickly, knocking the tray to the floor, the food spilling onto the young master's trousers.

The old man saw that she couldn't deny her guilt. She froze, ignoring the loud crash the tray had made.

"You did." Luis started for her.

"Son!"

Both Hilaria and Luis stood stunned by the strength of the old man's voice.

"Let her go. Give her enough wages to travel far from here."

"I wasn't the only one," Hilaria defended herself. "No. The whole household talked of her strange behavior. She frightened us. Are you going to let us all go? No one else will work in this house, infested the way it is with sin and ghosts."

"Wait downstairs, Hilaria, while I speak with my father."

She squatted to pick up the scattered broken china.

"Leave it. Juana can pick it up later."

"She's no better than the rest of us, Señor. Ask Gaspar. He can tell you."

"Suddenly she is full of stories, Son. Are you really going to plead for her?"

"Go down into the kitchen, Hilaria, and wait for me." Luis didn't attempt to help her rise to her feet even when she went slightly off balance before catching herself.

The whole way out, she kept her head down while her hands played with the material of her dress. With unnatural care she softly closed the door behind her.

"Now what, Son? Will you spare your sister's enemy? Your sister's and lover's enemy?"

"I didn't know Catrin was my half sister. You never chose to tell me."

"Instead I placed temptation before you, and you eagerly grabbed on to your fate."

"Little did I know how much like you I am. Had I known, I would have . . ."

"What? Taken yourself off to a monastery like that pathetic Teresa?"

"She's honest, not pathetic."

"She's a woman who is still a child. She knows nothing of men. She'll die a withered hag if some prince doesn't sweep her off her feet. Are you up for the job, Luis?"

"I'll never harm her."

"I didn't ask whether you would bed her. No, will you save her virtue by marrying the bastard?"

"When it is time, she will return to the convent. The nuns will welcome her back. They were unhappy about sending her here in the first place."

"And is that where she belongs?"

"What do you care? She wipes your ass and listens to your meanderings. Teresa means nothing more than that to you."

"I like her. Oh, don't look at me as if I were mad. The purest soul in this house is probably hers. Certainly our own souls are covered with thick layers of sin. And Hilaria would be in close competition with us."

"Hilaria! She must stay, Father. I don't think it would help Catrin if she disappeared. It may even make Catrin appear guiltier. I don't see how an obviously wanton servant such as Hilaria can be much of a threat in front of the Inquisitor. I'll see to it that her activities are limited."

"I don't want anything to happen to Isabella."

"Nothing will happen to her that is any worse than what you have already done to her, Father."

"You've never liked your aunt. I never could understand. Sometimes I thought you might have had knowledge of my relationship with her, but now it is proven that you didn't."

"She always stood in the way of Mother. Whether Isabella wanted a certain food to be served or social gatherings to be arranged seemed more important than what Mother wanted. Isabella was your real wife. My mother merely gave you social status, covering the fact that you preferred incest."

"I loved your mother in a different way. She gave me a son."

"Whom you now despise."

"Oh, no! I can't imagine the pain it must give you to say that. I know how much I love you and how much I have failed you. My sister is an obsession. She's not a choice for me. I must have her. I can't cut myself off from her. Your mother I wanted and had to fight to gain. Her gentleness and intelligence were prizes that made our first few years of marriage perfect. And then she presented me with a son, even though it brought her close to her deathbed. A handsome baby who bawled interminably, but when that babe smiled, my heart melted. I worked hard for that child. I struggled to make sure he would inherit a fortune. I abandoned my daughter to build a strong home for my son."

"And I don't admire you for the choices you made."

Roberto's fingers reached up to touch his lips. He swallowed several times before lowering his hands back onto his bed linen.

"I robbed some time for my own pleasure, Luis. Was that so bad?"

"I'll have Gaspar send Juana up to clean and make sure Señora Toledo understands that Hilaria is no longer permitted in your room."

Roberto saw his son step around the mess on the floor and walk to the door.

How straight a back he has, thought Roberto. *How easily he walks away from matters that offend him. Have I trained him to do so?*

chapter 32

Teresa found Hilaria in the kitchen sobbing into the arms of Señora Toledo. A pot's contents boiled over onto the fire, and several utensils had dropped to the floor. Vegetables had spilled from a cabinet, and some liquid stained the flagstone floor.

"Did something happen here? Are you all right, Hilaria?"

The two enmeshed women stared back at Teresa. Hilaria tried unsuccessfully to hold back her tears while the cook looked down her nose at Teresa as if she were the cause of whatever had disturbed the young maid.

"I came to ask whether a tray had been sent up to Señor Velez." Teresa felt something rub against her dress. When she looked down, she spied Spider quietly sneaking into the kitchen, a place from which he had been dragged many a time.

"Damn you!" shrieked Hilaria as she reached for a glass bowl on the table. With blinding speed she threw the bowl at Spider, who barely escaped out the doorway. The glass shattered and sprinkled harmlessly across the floor.

"I thought you liked the dog," Teresa said. "He will leave if ordered to. There is no reason to hurt him."

"It is not the dog, Teresa." The cook grabbed hold of Hilaria and forced her to sit on a chair, then she turned and faced Teresa. "The tray has already been taken up, but there was an accident and Juana will have to bring a new one up to Señor Roberto Velez."

"Accident? Was anyone hurt? Hilaria, are you . . ."

"She is fine, or she will be. The master is in a bad mood today, and Hilaria caught the brunt of his ire. Otherwise no one was physically hurt."

"I should have warned you."

Both women looked toward Teresa, seeking an explanation.

"He and his son had an argument this morning about a family matter. I'll take up the tray. There's no point putting Juana in harm's way."

"The young master has pointedly requested that Juana take up the tray. I don't believe we should disobey his order," the cook said, the furrows in her brow converging into heavy lines.

"I'll take responsibility, Señora Toledo. Neither you nor Hilaria will be held to blame, I promise."

"You're not the mistress of the house, Teresa. You are no better than any of us servants."

"I meant only to help. I'm sorry if you misunderstood."

"Fine. Go upstairs to your patient and see if he needs anything besides his breakfast. From what Hilaria has said, he may be quite agitated. I'll make a fresh breakfast for him and send Juana up with it when it is ready."

Both the cook and Hilaria stared back at Teresa. No one moved until Teresa nodded her head and turned to the door.

"Oh, also, Teresa..." The cook paused, waiting for her full attention. After she pivoted slightly, the cook continued, "Hilaria will no longer be servicing Señor Roberto."

"I'm sure..."

"Keep quiet, Teresa, and pay attention." The harshness in the cook's voice made both Teresa and Hilaria become alert. "You, Teresa, will have to fulfill most of the needs Señor Roberto has. The sheet changing, the food serving and taking away, the general cleaning of the room, will all be done by you. He has acquired a special fondness for your company, and I see no reason to take up his time with our ministrations. You and he can rot together up in that stinking sickroom."

"Señora Toledo," Hilaria stood and reached out for the cook.

"Don't worry, Hilaria. Teresa knows better than to carry tales to Señor Roberto. She still must eat and sleep with the servants, just as we are forced to tolerate her company. She will wisely take care in the stories she repeats in the master's quarters."

"Whatever happened to Hilaria, I hope you won't hold me accountable, Señora Toledo."

"Alignments changed when you entered the house. Hardly any of us get to see or speak to Señor Roberto.

Even Señor Luis has changed many of his habits. Most nights he used to spend out carousing in whorehouses or with his former schoolmates. Now he spends time either at home or with the bishop."

"That has nothing to do with me. You know that. His father is very ill, and he may even be close to death. What do you expect from a son? And as for the bishop, Señor Luis hopes to influence the release of Catrin."

Hilaria began to sob anew.

A thought sparked inside Teresa's mind as she watched Hilaria pull her own hair and writhe in her self-pity.

"It was you, Hilaria, who spoke against Catrin, wasn't it? Did you see her as a rival for Señor Luis's affections? How foolish you are. To bring the Inquisition's eye to rest on one in a household means that everyone under that roof becomes suspect. Why do you think Torquemada must travel with a guard consisting of 275 men? Too many families have been ruined by his excesses."

"Enough with your speeches, Teresa." All looked to the kitchen entrance where Señor Luis stood. His hands gripped the frame of the doorway. His tense, solid body stood straight and tall, his classic face reflecting an imperious attitude. "Go to my father now. Keep him company, for I can no longer stay in the same room with him."

Hilaria gasped, and the cook looked down at the floor, not wishing to be witness to his remark. Teresa had to stop at the doorway to wait for Señor Luis to drop his arms. He stared into her eyes, wanting something from her, but she couldn't understand what it was. Finally he lowered both his arms and stepped aside. As she walked past him, the heat from his body caused her flesh to flush, and his loud, heavy breaths made her body tremble.

Once past him and farther down the hall, she stopped and steadied herself against a wall. The father and son tore each other apart. The horrible events of the past continued to drive a sharp wedge between the two, and she feared she could do nothing to lessen their mutual pain.

Blinded by her reverie, she did not see Gaspar coming down the hall.

"Are you ill, Teresa?"

"No." She used her palm to push herself back onto her unstable feet. When she wavered, Gaspar grabbed hold of her arm.

"Maybe you've been spending too much time in the sickroom. The next time Jose and Sylvia go into town, you will go with them."

"Yes. Thank you, Gaspar." Amazed at his concern, she wondered whether he had an ulterior motive. No doubt he had heard that she had wanted to go back to the convent. Was he giving her that opportunity in order to be rid of her?

A few days later, Gaspar lived up to his promise.

chapter 33

"TERESA, WHY ARE YOU HERE?"

"Jose took Sylvia into town and dropped me here for a visit, Sister Agatha."

"I'm so glad, but I can't keep you to myself. Let's go find the other sisters."

"No. Not yet." Teresa appreciated being back inside the convent. The familiar old floor tiles, the bland-colored walls, the painted crucifix affixed to the wall in front of her. Sister Agatha led her into the salon where outsiders were taken. Disappointment tamped down her exuberance at having returned. She wanted to be taken deep into the interior where the daily work and prayer were done. She wanted to know that her room still lay unused, waiting for her return.

"Is Señor Roberto Velez much worse?"

"Far worse, Sister." Teresa's voice swelled, filling the room with an echo.

"He is dying?"

Teresa asked if she could sit. Sister Agatha led her to

a bench and sat facing the young woman.

"You said Señor Roberto Velez would be kinder than his son."

"Not kinder, but lighter in mood."

"He's not. Dying has made him an odious fiend."

"Teresa, how can you use such words? He cannot be as bad as that. You are being cruel to someone in great pain."

"His sins rival the devil's."

Sister Agatha raised her palm to cover Teresa's lips.

"Lucifer actively fought against God for power. Señor Roberto is weak. He knows he can never take the place of God. He is more likely to fear God." She moved her palm across to caress Teresa's cheek.

"But only now, when he knows soon he will be judged."

"I have heard that one of his servants is in the Inquisitor's dungeon."

"His daughter."

"That is why she is important to the Inquisitor." Sister Agatha stared past Teresa and allowed her hand to fall back onto her lap.

"His life is blackened by much worse."

"What he has told you, Teresa, keep in your heart. Don't tell anyone else. He speaks in need of lifting the heavy burdens that will crush him otherwise. Act as his confessor, for he may fail to cleanse his soul at the end to a priest."

"I can't offer him forgiveness."

"God is the only One who can. Let the Lord act through you. Offer him comfort without criticism."

"Even if the sins are unspeakable?"

"Especially then. He depends on your mercy. Hold his hand tightly as he steps into the grave. Only let go when you are sure he is in the arms of God."

"I'll go back," Teresa muttered, her head bent in concession.

"You wanted to flee, didn't you?"

"Yes. Was that a sin?"

Sister Agatha chuckled.

"Not everything is a sin, Teresa. This man and his troubles frightened you. Fear keeps us safe and wary of those around us. Rule the fear with your head, Teresa."

"My head feels so full of sordid stories. Never have I known such a sinful household."

"You've never lived in the real world before, Teresa. Since birth you have been isolated behind these convent walls. Visiting homes to care for the ill is not the same as living twenty-four hours a day inside a family visited by illness, deceit, and temptation. Always you returned to the comfort of our chapel and the soft murmurings of prayer."

"I miss . . ."

"Miss what? The escape into the arms of God? Were you truly happy here, Teresa? A few short weeks outside this convent cannot be enough to make up your mind."

"But I wasn't unhappy here."

"We have kept you a child much too long. What about love? The love of a husband and the love of a child? Are you willing to give that up for scrubbing these tile floors and kneeling for hours in the chapel?"

"But you gave up having a family for this."

"Yes. At the time I was a young girl with little potential. I didn't have your beauty. Even so, at night doubts sometimes flood my mind. Did I enter the convent because I loved God or because I was afraid of being rejected by His world?"

"But you do love God?"

"One can love God and still raise a family. A few of the sisters are solid in their choices. Sister Roberta thinks of nothing but fulfilling God's intentions. In the deep of night, when I am returning from a visit to the chapel, I pass Sister Roberta's cell and can hear her flagellating herself. She allows no thoughts to enter her mind but those that add luster to God's name."

"How is Sister Roberta?"

"A bit cross because she has not seen you in such a long time. Let's go and surprise her before you must leave."

The two women stood and embraced.

"I have your rosary with me." Teresa pulled away to withdraw the rosary from inside her blouse. "Many times I've had to pray on these beads. Soon I'll wear them down into slight nubs."

"That is what they are for." Sister Agatha laughed and drew Teresa into the warmth of the inner sanctum of the convent, where Teresa had so much wanted to be.

But after a short while she found herself checking the time, worrying lest she be left behind by Jose. And if she were, how would she be able to return to the Velez household before dark?

Luis had not approved of her visit to the nuns, but Gaspar had emphasized she had had no time off since her arrival. If Teresa fell ill, who would care for Señor Roberto? Seeing a chance to regain her status, Señora Toledo volunteered to fill in for the day. Hilaria could see to the meals, especially since neither the father nor the son had much of an appetite anymore.

Teresa had been tempted to pack her bundle, but realized she wouldn't leave her assignment until Sister Agatha had excused her. However, after spending the entire day away, she found she missed the miserable, sullen mansion. Ridiculous, she thought.

When she heard a knock on the door, she ran to greet Jose before anyone else could.

chapter 34

"I THOUGHT WE WOULD BE RETURNING TO THE mansion without you, Teresa. When we left this morning, you seemed preoccupied, hardly bothering to listen to anything I said."

"I'm sorry, Sylvia. It's the first time in a while since I've seen the sisters, and I've missed them."

"How odd, growing up in a den of women. Did they ever tell you how pretty you were or encourage you to play house with dolls?"

Teresa smiled.

"I had a doll made of cloth, with finely drawn features. I kept wanting to dress her in a habit, but the nuns kept making baby garments for her. She slept in bed with me, and during the day, she decorated the cover." She turned to Sylvia and rested her hand on the woman's arm. "Best of all, I knew I was gorgeous. I was not pretty. I was beautiful. Dramatically so. Can't you tell?" Teresa blushed at the brashness of her words.

"Most definitely. I wondered whether the nuns would

permit you to have ideas like that. Besides, they were all women. How did you know men found you attractive?"

In truth Teresa had never been sure if she appealed to the opposite sex. Most men spoke politely to her, and those who hinted at romps in the hay she guessed would mount most anything that moved.

"I was too busy to give much thought to that, Sylvia."

"Well, now you can. There's Jose, Fernando, and Señor Luis."

"And Manuel."

"He'll break your heart when the dinner bell rings."

The two women laughed.

"Oh, I think we have a welcoming party," said Sylvia, straining to look out her side window.

Señora Toledo, Hilaria, Juana, and Manuel huddled together near the front door. Señora Toledo made a point of waving around a handkerchief, bringing the lace first to her eyes before shaking it at Jose.

"Have we been gone that long, Teresa?" Sylvia began to primp.

"It must be Señor Roberto Velez," Teresa said, anxiously willing the carriage to move faster.

"The doctor is here!" yelled out Carmen. "He's with him now. The poor man took ill suddenly."

How could she say that? wondered Teresa, stepping from the carriage. Señor Roberto Velez had been ill quite some time.

"He coughs constantly, bringing up gobs of greenish bile." Carmen felt it her duty to set the scene in great detail. "He complains that his chest is set in a vise, and he can't bear to take any food or liquid."

Teresa ignored the waiting household and rushed upstairs to see her patient.

Roberto sat up in bed, a tray of soup spread across his dwindling hips.

"The doctor. Where is he?"

"With Fernando. The doctor is doing the best he can for him, but Fernando waited much too long to admit his illness. Now he may be lost. What's the matter, Teresa, didn't you enjoy your trip to the convent?"

"The shock of hearing about Fernando takes my breath away, Señor. I thought you were the one who was sick. I'm speechless."

"He looked so fit. Never complained. This morning Jose had him running around doing errands. Never did he say, 'I must sit for a while.' Instead he fainted, falling off the ladder at the back of the house. Manuel found him. He immediately came to me. Thought he'd find the doctor here. Poor boy thinks the doctor lives here. Sometimes I think the same thing."

"I should check to see whether I can help the doctor."

"Teresa, before you go . . . Did Sister Agatha soothe your doubts? We must seem like the most depraved family in the world to you. She talked you into coming back here, didn't she?"

"I wasn't sure what to do, Señor. I think I understand a little better."

"Please stay, Teresa. Your outraged morality gives

me hope. You may even save the soul of my son."

As Teresa reached the door, Señor Roberto called her back again.

"That girl, Juana, she's not much fun. A bit timid. Moody. Do you think Hilaria is still too upset to return to her old duties?"

"I understand it was you who caused the fuss over Hilaria."

"Catrin is a strange child. And the servants tend to come from superstitious families, with little, if any, education. Hilaria had no idea Catrin was my daughter. Perhaps you could impress Hilaria with my willingness to forgive."

"This is another instance that can't be turned around to suit your whim, Señor Roberto. Hilaria performs new duties where there is less danger of her spying on others."

"Has she taken Manuel's place with the horses?" The high-pitched sarcasm of his voice made Teresa flinch.

"She simply has less contact with the family. I'll be back in a bit for your tray, Señor Roberto." She nodded her head and gently closed the door.

chapter 35

"How is he?" Teresa asked, ducking under Jose's arm, which spanned the doorway into the sickroom.

"He can't even keep water down. He's flush from fever, delirious. He thinks the doctor is some drunken *amigo* from his local tavern."

Teresa moved closer to the sickbed.

"Get out!" the doctor barked rudely, pushing her against the wall.

"I'm here to help. Don't you recognize me? I'm Señor Roberto Velez's caretaker."

"Get out, I said." The doctor's eyes narrowed, and he gripped his lips into a grimace. "I don't know what this man has, and I want no one near him until I do."

"But he simply caught a chill the other night during the storm."

"Maybe. Or he may have picked up something in his travels through the various whorehouses. Get the hell out!"

She backed out of the room, watching Fernando toss in his bed, screaming at the invisible images that flitted through his mind. Because of his strength, his arms and legs had been tied to the bed.

"He didn't have to visit any whorehouses. We all heard you invite him into your bed," Hilaria said. "Remember the other day at breakfast?"

"To rest in my empty bed only." Teresa's eyes flashed at the sight of the servant. "He seemed very ill. It was wrong of us not to make him rest."

"You would have taken care of him well in your bed, I'm sure. Or maybe he'd be dead by now from one of your witch's brews," Hilaria said.

"Then why isn't Señor Roberto dead yet?" asked Manuel. "She's been sitting with him, feeding him, and bathing him. Shouldn't he come down with the same fever?"

"Shut up, Manuel. You shouldn't be here." Jose pushed the young boy back into the hallway.

"Why not? I found him. I should be able to watch what's going on, too. You can't send me away. Not if you allow her to stay." The boy pointed at Teresa. "What if she puts a hex on him? She never liked the way he looked at her."

"He's ill because he slept in his wet clothes on the stone floor." Teresa heard her voice from far away in the midst of the small grouping that watched and shivered while Fernando convulsed. The frame of the bed trembled. The doctor slipped something into the man's mouth to prevent Fernando from biting his tongue before the smell of urine and feces overcame the stale air in the room.

The other women hurried away, but Teresa stayed to

watch Fernando stiffen gradually into a corpse by nightfall.

She volunteered to wash the body and find a clean shroud in which to wrap him.

His muscles lay slack, his flesh paling into deathly gray, and his eyes stared into the demons of his fever. No one else wanted to touch the body. Teresa would enter the room alone.

"Teresa."

She turned to see Luis standing in the doorway.

"My father needs you."

"But who will care for Fernando?"

"I've sent for a woman who does these things. Manuel should return soon with Maria and a priest to give the final rights. Fernando is beyond caring who washes and buries him."

The doctor agreed with Luis, adding that he did not wish for her to carry any illness to the master of the house.

"And what of you?" she asked.

"I am more able to understand illness than you."

"I've been trained to assist . . ."

"Teresa, do what you are told." Luis's sharp voice made her jump. "Living at the convent must have at least taught you how to be obedient."

"The nuns taught me to have mercy for others. Both the living and the dead."

Teresa nearly walked into Gaspar, who led a petite woman dressed in black with a black lace shawl covering her gray-black hair. Heavy lids almost hid the irises of her eyes, and the lines branching out from the corners of her eyes reflected the amount of weeping this woman must have done. She held her weathered hands in a prayerful pose, the cuffs of her sleeves fallen back to reveal a psoriatic rash on her forearms.

"I'm surprised you returned, Teresa." Gaspar paused momentarily. "I gave you the option to leave before you caused even more trouble for yourself and the members of this house. Stupid woman." He continued on, and the petite woman looked at her with curiosity.

chapter 36

No one remembered whether or not Fernando had family. Manuel suggested that Fernando's closest friends were the animals he slept with in the barn. They tolerated the man who saw to their needs, allowing him to share their beds. For this observation Señora Toledo slapped Manuel on the back of the head.

Maria immediately took charge of the body. No one had bothered to untie Fernando's arms and ankles. The lips on his gaping mouth lay back, allowing his oversized teeth and his blackened tongue to hang out. His wrinkled shirt, bunched up in the back and ripped open at the front, obviously did not belong to him. The rich material could not be afforded by a servant, and the shoulders appeared a bit too large.

"Will you need any help, Maria?"

She turned to see Señor Luis standing a few feet behind her.

"The bindings are extremely tight. Perhaps you could give me a hand with them."

"Of course." As he worked the cloth free from Fernando's flesh, he inquired about the priest. "Manuel was told to bring both you and Father Sanchez back."

"We stopped at his home and told his housekeeper we had need of him. She didn't know when he would be back, but said she would inform him immediately upon his return. But sometimes simple prayers from those who loved the deceased mean more to God, I believe. Has he family?"

"None that we know of. He was not very open with anyone here. If we had paid more attention to him, he might be alive now."

"Father Sanchez may not come."

"Why do you say that?" He undid the last of the bonds.

"The Inquisitor is asking questions about this house. One of your servants is in his prison, isn't that so?"

"She doesn't belong there."

"I don't mean to judge, but often priests fear being branded as heretics, especially when they visit the house of a *converso*. I have managed to service all, including *conversos*, without any repercussions. But someday I may also have to answer to the Grand Inquisitor Torquemada."

"I'm sorry, Maria. If you think you may be in trouble for coming here, leave now. The woman caring for my father volunteered to prepare Fernando's body."

"Is she the one I saw in the hall when I first came in?"

"I suppose. She had been the last to stay with the body. I ordered her upstairs to see to my father."

"Where does she come from?"

"The convent."

"She looks very familiar. She resembles a dying woman whom I cared for several years ago. This young woman, she didn't wear a habit."

"She isn't a nun. Her mother left her at the convent when she was a babe."

Maria hesitated in removing the clothes from Fernando's body.

"Is something wrong? Do you wish to leave? As I said . . ."

"No!" She faced Señor Luis, her face laden with fear. "The nuns sent her here, to the house of a *converso*?"

Luis had been leaning against the mattress but now moved onto both his feet and stood erect.

"We are not demons!"

"No, you are just as human as any Christian. I didn't mean to offend. But the young woman should never have been sent here. It is not safe."

"The nuns don't share your objection. As a matter of fact, I wanted someone else. Someone more mature to care for my father."

"You don't understand. If the Inquisitor found out who she was, that she lived under the roof of a *converso* family, and a family so in question . . ."

"What do you know of Teresa?"

"Teresa? Yes, she asked that they call her that. She wanted a Christian name. A name that would not give away her daughter's parentage. Susanna will never find peace if her daughter is at risk."

"You know Teresa's mother?"

Maria paced the floor, her doubts visible in the lines forming on her face. With her bony fingers clasped together, she began to sway back and forth.

"Maria, what troubles you so? Is it Teresa? What do you know of her? Please tell me. My father lies weak in his bed, unable to defend himself, and she is the one who spends most of the hours of the day with him. Can I trust her?"

"Lord, there is no reason to believe she would do anyone harm. Neither would her mother. God rest her soul."

"Her mother died? When?"

Swiftly Maria made her decision. She approached Señor Luis with hands folded in sufferance.

"Señor Luis, you and your father are *conversos*. You know the penalty for being a heretic. And you know the importance of being extra careful if you once prayed within the Jewish faith. I am about to share a secret with you because Teresa needs protection." Maria hesitated, not quite sure if she was doing the right thing. Finally Luis saw determination fill her weary eyes. "She is the daughter of Susanna Diego."

Luis searched Maria's face, wanting to be sure she spoke the truth.

"The skull on *La Calle de la Muerte.*"

"Yes. She did not mean to betray her family. The man she loved proved false. She was left with nothing but a babe within her womb. A babe whom she could not care for."

Luis retreated several steps before responding.

"How foolish of the nuns to send her here."

"Perhaps they think so many years have passed that no one would connect Teresa to Susanna Diego. I'm sure they would not have purposefully put Teresa in danger. They've cared for her all these years. What is she now, twenty?"

"She appears younger."

"Teresa has not had to deal with some of the world's brutalities. She has had a roof over her head and food in her belly. And presumably no man to torture her soul."

"She now has my father."

"I didn't mean to sound so crass. I only remember the agony her poor mother suffered. My own husband is a treasure. Our love has bloomed through five children, two deaths, and old age. I pray every day to God in thankfulness for our lives together."

"Teresa does not know the identity of her mother."

"And she never should. Think what sadness it would bring, knowing that her mother's skull rests above the lintel of her old family home."

"It's barbaric."

"On her deathbed Susanna requested the shameful act."

"I'll do what I can to prevent Teresa from learning the truth. And as for the Inquisitor, he will never hear the story from me. I will do everything I can to protect Teresa, whether she stays with us or returns to the convent."

"Thank you, Señor Luis. I've spent all these years

with this secret. Sharing it has lightened my burden."

"Continue with Fernando's preparations. If you need anything further, ask Gaspar."

Maria nodded and quickly returned to her burden.

They buried Fernando in the cemetery at the back of the house in the evening with the sun descending. Jose dug the hole, piling the dirt neatly to the side. There was no box, only a shroud that enveloped Fernando's muscular body.

"Shouldn't we say some prayers?" Manuel dared to ask.

The group looked at each other. No priest had shown, and they had wanted the body underground before a new day broke.

"We really should say a rosary or ask God to accept this poor soul," Carmen said.

"She comes from the convent," Juana said, looking at Teresa.

"Do you still remember your prayers, or has Satan robbed you of the words?" Hilaria taunted Teresa with her words and eyes.

"Hilaria, Fernando never used Teresa's bed to rest. I got dry clothes from Señor Luis and put Fernando immediately to work. If anyone must take the blame, it's me. I should have given him my bed in which to sleep that day," said Jose.

Sylvia made the sign of the cross, reciting the Lord's Prayer slowly and with deep reverence. Teresa thought the sound of Sylvia's voice too staged. Sylvia acted the role of priest, but did she feel it in her heart?

chapter 37

"I SAW ALL OF YOU BURY SOMEONE TODAY."

Teresa shook herself awake in the chair next to the sickbed. Roberto Velez slept, his breathing more labored than she had remembered. His mouth hung open, emphasizing his sunken cheeks.

"Who did you bury?"

Teresa looked up into Isabella's light eyes.

"I peeked out the nursery window when I heard the sounds of a shovel. The body was wrapped so well that I couldn't guess who it was."

"Fernando. He spent most of his time in the barn. You may not have met him."

"I had a lover once by the name Fernando. Roberto didn't approve of him. He told me Fernando didn't love me. Did you get to ask him if he loved me before he died?"

"This was not the same man."

"How do you know?"

"Because this Fernando was only in his twenties."

"That's about how old my Fernando was."

"But that was many years ago, I'm sure."

"I don't know how to pile my hair high the way you did it. Strands keep escaping, flying about my head, teasing me." Isabella's hand swirled in the air, circling her head.

"I'll fix it for you again tomorrow. Right now I'm much too tired."

"Do you think Fernando would have been a faithful lover?"

"I never met him."

"But you buried him."

"You're confusing me, Isabella. Are you talking about your old lover or about the servant who died?"

"Aren't they the same?"

"Definitely not. I doubt you would have been attracted to the man buried in the cemetery. He was rough, not at all a gentleman."

"He was to me. Maybe he didn't like you."

"He didn't like any of us. I'm afraid he lived his life in misery because he didn't know how else to live."

"He sang."

"I doubt this Fernando did."

"Did Roberto call for his death?"

"No. I told you, the man we buried was not your Fernando."

"He wants you to lie to me. Roberto is jealous of every man I talk to. Once he lay in wait outside my door, sure he would catch a young man leaving in the middle of the night. Instead, just after midnight my personal maid took leave of my room. Roberto captured her in his arms in the dark and threatened horrible cruelties. Finally he felt her breasts and realized his error. The woman fled this house. That's when I no longer had anyone to see to my hair and my color."

"But he had a wife."

"She slept lightly. She listened to us in bed, her ear against the door with the flats of her hands pressing against the wooden portal that separated us. Roberto never noticed. Only I sensed her presence. She haunts me at night now, laughing at me, grinning. The white teeth long, straight."

"Is that why you sleep during the day?"

"The dead can't roam the earth under the sun. It burns their flesh, dries them into ash. That's why she visits at night. She wears the dress in which she married Roberto. The long train rustles across the floor. That is how I hear her coming."

"I'm so sorry, Isabella."

"About Fernando? He wasn't a good lover anyway. Are you sure he is dead? What if he climbs out of the grave?"

"This is a completely different man we buried. The doctor pronounced him dead at three today."

"Did he call my name on his deathbed?"

Teresa stood.

"I think your brother should sleep through the night. Your nephew sent me to bed a while ago, but I thought I would stay a few minutes just in case. I dozed, and now it must be terribly late. I should go to bed." Teresa looked at Isabella.

"You want me to leave. No one trusts me around Roberto. They think I will seduce him into his death. He's withering in that bed, Catrin."

Teresa shivered at the sound of the daughter's name.

"You'll not have your father for long." Isabella shook her head in pity.

Without saying another word, Isabella guided herself out of the room. By the time Teresa stood in the hall, she saw Isabella's figure disappear into the nursery.

chapter 38

SCREAMS FILLED THE MORNING SKY. OVER AND over Teresa heard the high-pitched sound coming from outside the house. Throwing a shawl over her dressing gown, she hurried out of the room and down the stairs to the back door. Gaspar barred her way.

"What is it, Gaspar? What's happening?"

"It's not for you to see. Jose is calming Carmen."

"Did something happen to her?"

Hilaria and Juana now pressed against Teresa's back.

"You can't leave us here not understanding what is happening. Tell us. How do you expect us to carry on with our day?"

"It is Fernando. His grave has been opened."

Hilaria and Juana backed away from Teresa.

"Why would you do that, Teresa?" Hilaria asked.

"Stop! Don't take your hate out in such an evil way. Why must you always imply I have something to do with things that can't be understood? You even have Juana looking at me like I'm growing horns."

Hilaria reached out to pull back Teresa's hair to search for those horns before Teresa could swat her away.

They were interrupted when Jose moved the tearful Carmen back through the door of the house. Teresa briefly caught sight of the open grave, Fernando's body half-in and half-out of the earth. The shroud had been torn apart. A strip of the white linen surged upward, caught in a strong breeze.

Juana whimpered on her way to the back stairs.

"An animal would have carried parts of him off," Hilaria said, staring at the body. "He seems to be in one piece. You think he wasn't dead? Perhaps that old woman who bathed him didn't realize he still breathed. Didn't you help her, Teresa? Did you sense he still lived?"

"If I had, I wouldn't have allowed the burial to proceed. Besides, the doctor examined the body before Maria took charge."

"He could have died from exhaustion scratching his way out. I've heard stories about such cases."

"It doesn't matter. Now he is dead, and Jose will put him back in the ground before breakfast," Gaspar said. "Have you checked on your patient, Teresa? Carmen's loud screams may have traveled to the rooms at the front of the house."

By the time Teresa reached Roberto Velez's room, his son stood by the bed, plumping the pillows. Luis's wrinkled clothes indicated he had been in a rush. His shirt lay open on his chest; a pale scar marred the skin on his shoulder.

"What's happened? Has Carmen gone mad?" Luis asked.

"Fernando's grave has been opened."

"By whom? What for?"

"No one has any idea."

"Jose may not have dug deep enough. He can be lazy," the older man said. "Some animal may have smelled the meat."

"His body is whole."

"Perhaps Carmen's screeches frightened the animal away before it could start its meal." Señor Roberto took pleasure ridiculing the sad scene.

Teresa didn't like the calm way the older man dealt with the situation. Certainly no other graves had ever been dug up by the local animals. Why now? Jose did nothing carelessly.

"I'll help Jose. Fernando won't be climbing out again."

Teresa watched Luis leave. His tired walk indicated he had not slept most of the night.

"My son is handsome, isn't he?"

Teresa looked back at Roberto Velez.

"He's been with many women. Almost as many as I. None of the women are equal to him."

"Maybe he's not looking for a wife."

"While I'm alive he would never marry below himself. I wouldn't approve."

"He may stay a bachelor all his life."

"I don't want that to happen."

"Most parents don't," she said, fixing a blanket that

touched the floor.

"I felt my heart beat fast when the screams started. A dream didn't want to let go of me. At first I thought they were the screams at my grave grieving for me. Am I too full of myself, Teresa?"

"We all want to be mourned."

"There's no one left to scream for me."

"There's your sister."

"She's insane. Her ravings are for delusions springing from her own mind. Reality doesn't bother her."

"Why did you limit her life so much, Señor? She told me that you denied her the possibility of marriage."

"I denied her lovers, Teresa, and never bothered to arrange a marriage for her. You think it's because I'm selfish. No. My sister's mind was never strong. She fell prey to many devious men."

"Like yourself."

He smiled, his tongue sliding across the edges of his teeth.

"I admit I did many wrong things. And my sister is one of my victims. Can you believe, though, that in my warped mind I wanted to protect her? It's even entered my mind to take her life."

Teresa held her breath for a moment.

"Others will take advantage of her. My son thinks she is more harpy than mad. He has no patience for her rambling and skulking. Sometimes he even locks my door at night to keep her out."

"But there is a secret door."

"She told you."

"Your wife would be in this bed while you lay with your sister."

"Often my sister needed comfort at night after the bad dreams from which she has always suffered."

"I think you have been her bad dream, Señor."

"You may be right." Roberto's head fell back against the pillows, his eyes closed, his breathing ragged. A burst of tears forced themselves from beneath his eyelids and rolled down his face, sinking into his sunken cheeks.

Teresa kneeled beside the bed and took one of his cold hands. All strength had left the muscles, making it difficult for him to clasp onto her hand.

He turned his head to her and opened his dark eyes. He smiled while his eyes remained sad.

"If only I could beg for mercy. I'm scared, but proud. I don't regret my sins. Does that mean your God will burn me forever in His hell?"

"He is your God also, Señor Velez." She bit her bottom lip, fearing this journey into heresy.

"I don't have a God, Teresa. When one abandons the God of his birth, it is almost impossible to take on a new deity. At first the alternative God meant very little to me. As long as I could retain my wealth and power here on earth, why should I worry about the next world? I had my son receive the proper sacraments. My wife took to bed in a statement of disapproval. Adamant that no one would drive me from my home, I donated to the most public religious charities. Most of the money I'm sure went into the bishop's personal coffers. I sighted no change in the streets. The poor begged. Children ran around in rags with bloated stomachs, and women continued to weep at child-sized graves. Some women should be barren, Teresa. They shouldn't have to long for children who can't be saved. My sister would have been better off barren."

"No, Señor Velez, she would never agree. She simply chose the wrong man to father her babe."

He clasped her hand tighter, his smile broadening into a malevolent grin.

"You serve God well with your recriminations, Teresa. Have you no pity for a dying old man?" When she went to speak, he waved his free hand at her. "No, don't answer. I don't want to know. I'd rather believe that you will find some tears to shed over my grave. Let's talk of my son. What will happen to him?"

"What of your daughter, Señor Velez?"

"She was lost to me at birth. Only once did I see her, and she was covered with blood and dripped with her mother's juices. I had her immediately taken away. The midwife bathed the child and delivered it to the family I had chosen. But never once did I visit the girl. Nor did I ask about her health or whether she needed anything. The family happily cared for her, relieving me of any responsibility."

"Would you do it again?"

"Definitely. Why would I force my wife to raise a bastard? A bastard coming from the belly of my sister. I'm not such a cruel man."

Amazed, Teresa forced herself to hold back her words.

"I look at your face and see the horror you feel at my pronouncements. But you must know more of life before you judge me. I loved my wife, even if you can't understand that love. And my son is my flesh. I couldn't have people making fun of him or belittling him for having a bastard sister."

"What of your own sister, Señor? How did you deal with her feelings?"

"I didn't. She always put me first, and I relished being on her pedestal. Yes, I put her on a pedestal, too. Made her believe she was my goddess."

"You don't even believe in God. She never would have thought you'd consider her a goddess." Teresa wanted to pull her hand away from the old man, but fought the instinct.

"Now that I'm dying, I'd truly like to believe in a God. Someone who would forgive my sins and never ask me for explanations." He gripped her hand with all the strength he had left. "Why wouldn't He forgive me, Teresa? I exist because He wanted me here. Everything I've ever done He could foresee. Why put me on this earth if He didn't approve?"

"You have free will, Señor. Don't blame God for the wrongs you have committed." She tried to pull away, but he refused to release her hand.

"What free will do I have? The freedom to live comfortably? The freedom to see my family's bellies full? Or should I have chosen to worship the God to which I was born and starve?"

"The Church you now belong to is the true religion of God."

"Then why did He cast me into what He considered the evil synagogue? As a babe why wasn't I baptized?"

"God gave you challenges, Señor, as He has done with the rest of us."

"Ah, and does that make me a better person?"

"We must all pay for the original sin of Adam and Eve."

"The nuns have taught you well. An answer for every question, even if the answers make no sense."

"Please let go of my hand, Señor Roberto."

He released her, and she tried to rub the redness away from the flesh of her hand.

"I'm sorry, Teresa, I didn't mean to harm you." He smiled. "I didn't mean to harm anyone. I merely am trying to survive."

chapter 39

LUIS SAT IN THE LIBRARY, REVIEWING THE UN-readable page given him by his spy. He hadn't been able to speak to the man since he had received the package of papers. The handwriting looked weak, scribbled in a childlike hand.

A soft knock and Luis immediately rose from his chair to open the door. He didn't want anyone else in the house to see what he was looking at.

Hilaria stood stiffly in the hall. She must have taken several steps back after knocking, since her arms would not have been long enough to reach the door from where she stood. She worried her bottom lip, and her hands crushed the fabric of her dress in her fists.

"Thank you, Señor." She made to turn away when he called her back.

"What are you thanking me for, Hilaria?"

"For not dismissing me. I don't know where I'd go if . . ." Her eyes filled with tears, and she couldn't complete the sentence.

He consciously prevented himself from ranting at her. What good would it do to embarrass her? Most probably she had learned her lesson while in his father's bedroom.

"I could ask you why you did it." He watched her look down at the floor, her hair falling in front of her face like a veil. She mumbled something. "What did you say?"

She looked at him but didn't bother to sweep back the hair that still partially covered her face.

"It was wicked of me. Only . . ." she thought about her words for a few moments, "Catrin was different. And none of us were sure why she was taken on. She didn't have many skills. Sylvia seemed to be the only person who could speak to her. Sylvia even took the time to teach her to write."

"Sylvia?"

"Yes. I don't know what she expected Catrin to do with that talent. Maybe Sylvia was just bored."

"I didn't know Sylvia could write."

"Long ago, when she was married, she helped her husband in his business. When he abandoned her, leaving her with nothing but debts, she begged your father for help."

"Send Sylvia to me."

Hilaria became flustered.

"I didn't mean to say anything against Sylvia, Señor. I'm sure she tried to help Catrin."

"No one is in trouble. I'm sure the Inquisitor didn't imprison Catrin because she could make a few strokes with a pen. I'd just like to speak to Sylvia for a few minutes."

Hilaria curtsied and flew down the hall in search of Sylvia. Luis returned to his desk, leaving the door to the library open behind him. Ten minutes later, he heard the sound of laughter in the hallway, and Sylvia appeared in the doorway, smiling widely.

"Heavens, Señor, Hilaria is upset. She thinks she is sending me off to the Inquisition as she did Catrin, but I can't think of a single reason why that would be true."

Sylvia entered the library without being invited and sat in the chair directly across from Luis.

"You wanted to know something about Catrin, I believe," she went on. "At least Hilaria made it sound that way. I loved Catrin. She had a wonderful grace and had more brains than the rest of the staff put together."

"Is that why you taught her to write?" Luis watched Sylvia straighten her dress and make a few primping motions around her hair.

"One of the reasons."

"And the others?"

"Boredom. A maternal urge. Your father."

"My father asked you to teach her to write?"

"He worried a good deal about the girl. I think he would have liked to have seen her trained as something, but what? She had no desire to join the convent. Raised as an atheist, you know. She knew nothing of the Bible stories or of the sacraments. That's really what I should have been teaching her. Religion would have kept her alive."

"She is still living."

"At the Inquisitor's prison. Hardly a life. There have been many stories about what happens inside the prison, Señor, and I'm sure she and many others pray for death each day. I wish my husband had been that unfortunate."

Luis studied the woman. He had never paid much attention to her before, but now he could see that she had obviously not always been a servant. She styled her hair in the manner of the day, her dress obviously cost more than it should have given her position, and her jewelry, though spare, still appeared to be extremely expensive. She always wore a self-satisfied expression upon her face, but her eyes searched constantly for knowledge. Not the kind of gossipy knowledge that the servants engaged in. No, she wanted to educate herself, better herself if she could. She sat across from him as an equal and not as a servile domestic.

"I take it you have no family, Sylvia."

"Why do you say that?"

"Because if you had family, you wouldn't be working here."

"Wrong. I have in-laws, but we haven't spoken in years. My marriage was barren. My husband took more interest in his work than in me. My parents didn't have much luck themselves with children. Thirteen births and I'm the only one who survived. The others were either still births or died as toddlers. I didn't know you had such interest in me."

Luis ignored her comment and asked how well she knew his father.

"We were not lovers, if that is the true meaning of your question. Your father and I met through my husband's business, and since he always appeared to be a generous man, I thought he would take pity on a . . . wronged wife."

Luis nodded and glanced down at the sheet of paper on the desk. Should he question her about the handwriting? Could Catrin have been attempting to communicate? He quickly lifted the paper off the desk and handed it to Sylvia before he changed his mind.

Surprised, she hesitantly took the paper in her fingers.

"You'd like me to read this?"

"Yes. I'm having difficulty understanding the handwriting. Perhaps you would have more success than I in comprehending the poor script."

"You think it is from Catrin?"

"Nothing escapes the Inquisitor's dungeon," he stated.

"Money can do wondrous things. Magical happenings can spring from gold coins." Sylvia smiled and looked down at the writing. "Yes, she wasn't very good, and I'm sure several months as a guest of the Inquisition isn't going to improve her ability to put pen to paper. This is her writing."

"What does it say?"

Sylvia sighed and squinted intensely at the paper.

"She appears to be asking you for forgiveness."

Luis felt ill.

"Does she say anything else? Any indication of how she is doing?"

"From the shakiness of the handwriting, I'd say she wasn't doing well. Perhaps this smudge is a watermark. A tear, perhaps."

Did he imagine it, or did the look on Sylvia's face when she raised her head appear accusatory?

"I had hoped she would be able to give me information that would aid in her release."

"You and I are aware that heretics know nothing of the charges, nor of who made them." Sylvia cocked her head. "I didn't know that servants could find champions in the wealthy men who employed them. It certainly makes me feel good to know that you care about us so much. Or is it Catrin in particular? I did think it strange when your father asked me to instruct the girl."

"Thank you, Sylvia, for your help. You may go."

"But I haven't helped. All I did is flesh out a few words that simply signaled her contriteness. Doesn't help her or you or your father. I wish I could do more, but it is quite dangerous to involve ourselves in the heretics' plight, isn't it? Especially when one's ancestors were Jews."

"I don't need you to warn me, Sylvia. You may return to your chores." His glance lingered on her face, but she never turned away. An enigmatic smile turned up her lips. "Is there something else?"

"One reason why your father hired me was because we've been longtime friends. Let me reiterate, we were not lovers. I was much too proper to cheat on my husband, even if your father would not have had any qualms. However, I do know who Catrin is. Many men forget their bastard children, and it is rather noble that your father finally managed to take responsibility for her. But this is one child who can never give him any joy. She is much too scarred emotionally, and the Inquisitor surely suspects a deeper relationship between her and your family. I'm telling you this since I never see your father now that he's locked himself away in that malodorous bedroom. Please share my opinion with him when next you see him."

Sylvia stood, took a step forward, and placed the paper back in the center of the desk where Luis could re-read the shaky handwriting.

chapter 40

LATER THAT DAY LUIS STOOD ON *LA CALLE DE la Muerte*, surrounded by grubby children dressed in assorted rags. Several held out their dirt-stained hands seeking coins. Others grabbed hold of his clothes, preventing him from passing on. A toddler stood a small distance away, waiting for his older siblings to return for him. The coins Luis carried were not enough for the number of hands grappling for his attention, but finally he made it past the children into the darkness of the street.

Many of the doors held crucifixes, most handmade and held together merely by string. There was no religious statuary or any sign of a church. He remembered that most of the families here had been of the Jewish faith before the Inquisition decimated their numbers.

"Luis Velez!" someone shouted.

Luis turned to spy an elderly man with a stubble of gray hair on his head and chin.

"You don't recognize me. I look a bit more weathered than when you last saw me." The man nodded to himself, his eyes fading into the past.

"I'm sorry, Señor. Have we met before?"

"It must be six. Oh, no, more than that. Perhaps as many as eight years ago. I've lost track of time. You and your father supped at my home."

"I've never been on this street before, Señor."

"No. I'm new to this street myself. I had a problem with the Church. Some question about whether I lit fires on Saturdays. Whether I bathed on Fridays in order to dress up on Saturdays."

"The Inquisitor accused you of being a practicing Jew?"

"Not the Inquisitor himself. One of my neighbors reported me to him. The same neighbor who now is housed in my wonderful home."

"I'm sorry."

"I had to pay a high fine, practically every *maravedi* I owned, but look at me, I'm still whole, not ashes like some. Though I did come away with a bit of a limp. The rack is an unpleasant business." The elderly man sighed. "I now live with my daughter-in-law and grandchildren. My son has disappeared."

"The Inquisition took him?"

"No. My son fled when the Inquisition took me prisoner. The Inquisition burned him in effigy, assuming he must be guilty of heresy if he ran. He never returned, but it is just as well. His life is better than ours, I hope."

"Jose Pérez."

"Yes, you do remember me."

"If there is anything my father and I can do for you . . ."

"Hush! Keep yourselves safe. I would invite you into our home, but I think it best you not be seen spending too much time with me. My sin is that I couldn't help but call out to you when I saw how splendid you still look. You shouldn't be seen on this street, Luis, or questions about your religious affiliations might spark some gossip."

"I'm here looking for the skull of Susanna Diego."

"Let the dead rest in peace." The elderly man had turned surly, his shoulders raised up covering his short neck.

Luis reached for his purse, then realized this might only distance the man further from him. Besides, he had very little left.

"Recently I spoke to a woman. Her name is Maria, and she told me the sad story of Susanna Diego. I only wished to see whether she told the truth."

"Maria. She dressed the headless corpse before burial. There was talk of burning Susanna Diego's body, but this Maria offered a plot for the burial. You see, Susanna couldn't be buried in consecrated soil."

"Hadn't she already paid her debt?"

"She didn't ask for forgiveness at the end. She died in sin, refusing the Eucharist, even though a priest stood next to her bed until the end."

"Where is the skull now?"

The elderly man moved closer to Luis and seemed to smell the air around the younger male. His nostrils flared, the tip of his nose twitched, and his eyes captured the richness of Luis's clothing.

"You come to view our pain, Luis? To steal what little

respect we retain in this hovel?" The man nodded toward the houses. "We would be delighted to eat the scraps from your table. They would be far more nutritious for our children than the miserable bits of garbage we are forced to feed them. Have you a wife and children, Luis?"

"None. I've not been blessed as yet."

"Blessed. Is it a blessing to watch one's children starve and shiver with the cold? As handsome and as loving as my grandchildren are, there are nights I wish they hadn't been born to my cowardly son. Sometimes they cry, not able to understand why their bellies must grumble and ache. My daughter-in-law, Abril, tries hard to keep us all comfortable, but I see her tears when she turns away from the children. Please, don't come here to gloat, Luis."

"I assure you that is not the reason I am here. I can see to it that the nuns will bring you food with my donation and—"

"You cannot. Even the nuns and priests are careful whom they visit. Have you not heard of the few poor priests who have been burned at the stake for showing too much mercy?"

"My father has been ill, and the convent has sent a woman to care for him. We could make the donation through her. It could be done quietly."

"Is your father seriously ill?"

"We are hoping he may regain his health." Luis paused, thinking about how his father's illness grew worse by the day. "He may not survive into the summer." His breath halted after his final words. His mouth became dry, and a slight tremble made his lips quiver.

"I am sorry, Luis. I've been busy complaining about my life without considering what could be befalling yours. I will pray for him."

"Thank you, Jose, but, please, in what direction will I find the remains of Susanna Diego?"

The old man pointed straight in front of him.

"Another block. The house is now deserted. An occasional street urchin will break in to spend the night. But no one touches the skull. In our fear we barely acknowledge it, for it serves only to remind us of the tortures we face from the Inquisition. Our lives are limited, Luis. We are watched constantly. A neighbor could see a way to lighten his own burden by inflicting harm on someone else."

"Where do you live?" asked Luis.

"No, better for both of us that you do not know."

"But I wish to help."

"Then do not whisper my name to a soul." The elderly man headed in the opposite direction from where he had directed Luis, his pronounced limp twisting his body into an awkward gait.

Luis continued down the street, passersby ignoring him, keeping their gaze steadily on the ground before them. The houses became shabbier, and a few cobblestones were missing, leaving gaping holes that caused a cart to teeter dangerously. But he noticed few carts, and most were old and barely held together.

Finally he came upon the door for which he had been looking. The door stood barren; no crucifix decorated its surface. At one time the wood had been painted; now a few streaks of color only served to mar and cheapen the door. Over the lintel stood the skull of Susanna Diego. Whitened and spotted with dirt, the hooded eyeholes looked beyond the earthly life into a desired peace it would never find.

This was Teresa's mother. He wanted to touch the bone, remove it from its ledge and present it to Teresa for the deserved burial after this protracted punishment.

He felt eyes upon his back, watching, wondering, willing him to remove the insult from their midst. Who would recognize him and report him to the Inquisitor? He thought no one would know him on this street, but just a few minutes ago he had stood talking to a man he hardly recognized. To silence the onlookers, he made the sign of the cross and carried on down the street.

chapter 41

LATE AT NIGHT TERESA EXPLORED THE UPSTAIRS family hallway, seeking to find Isabella. Were her eyes playing a trick on her, or were the shadows deeper than they had ever been before? Perhaps fewer candles had been lit, or were the walls and furnishings protecting Isabella, hiding the elderly woman from a stranger in the house? She thought of checking the rooms on either side of Señor Roberto Velez's bedroom, but stopped when she recalled the silent nursery. She dreaded that room, the somberness so antithetical to the concept of a babe's room. Everything was too perfect and yet covered with the dust from ages of disuse.

Her sandaled feet softly crushed the almost thread-bare carpeting. Neither Velez bothered with keeping up appearances. Money existed for renewing the furnishings, but neither man had thought it necessary. The old man waited to die, but what of his son? Didn't he wish to raise a family here and continue the work his father had so assiduously built for Luis? Both men had become

obsessed with the Inquisition, ruling out any other interests. But, she reminded herself, they had good reason,
with Catrin locked away in prison.

Teresa rested her hands on the mahogany door to the
nursery. Her fingers trembled a bit, but she had to find out
whether Isabella had been the one to dig up poor Fernando's grave. Should she knock or whisper to warn Isabella
of her presence? The woman couldn't escape nor could
she bar the door, for Teresa had noticed there was no lock.
Did the woman desire some semblance of privacy?

"Isabella," she called placing her ear close to the door.
"Isabella, it is Teresa. I'd like to speak to you. May I
come in?" She waited, feeling foolish now, knowing that
Isabella might be ashamed of what she had done and not
be willing to face Teresa.

Ignoring civility, Teresa pushed open the door. The
night's clouds passed swiftly before the moon, causing its
light to flicker across the floor and the bassinet in the
center of the nursery. As soon as she stepped inside the
room, her body trembled from the frosty chill that always
pervaded the nursery.

"Isabella, are you here?"

The door slowly shut behind her, and she turned to
see a black bundle looking almost like discarded rags. A
white hand reached out from the material, seeking to
touch the hem of Teresa's skirt.

"Here, let me help you up." Teresa leaned forward toward the figure, but the hand immediately withdrew, and
the bundle scurried to the darkest corner of the room.

"I won't hurt you. I wanted to talk to you about Fernando."

"He wasn't Fernando," the elderly woman's voice held disappointment.

"He's not your Fernando, Isabella. I told you that. He was a servant here, working mainly with the animals."

"He frightened me. So cold he was and so silent."

"He's dead, Isabella. He can never harm anyone." Teresa tried to gauge exactly where Isabella sat, but found herself confused by the many shadows of the toys cluttering the floor. "Will you sit with me a while and talk?"

"Catrin, I've missed you so much. I've been lonely. He doesn't visit me anymore. I don't think he ever will again."

"I'm Teresa. Remember? I'm taking care of your brother while he is sick. I can't play the role of Catrin for you."

"You see these robes." Isabella stood, stretching her arms out to the sides. "They're mourning robes. I have so much to cry over. I've done so many bad things."

"If you're talking about Fernando, it's all right. Jose and Señor Luis have righted what you did."

"Brother. He is your brother. You need not be formal with him."

Moving forward, Teresa reached out and took Isabella into her arms. The woman's brittle, delicate bones collapsed into the caress.

"Forgive me, Catrin. I had no part in sending you away. He did it. But he paid, and he will continue to pay until his eyes are closed for him."

Teresa wondered how such a frail woman could have opened Fernando's grave. Could she have had help?

"Did someone go with you to the graveyard, Isabella?"

"I told you, he isn't Fernando. He's cold and lifeless, his hands rough with calluses and ground-in dirt. The shabby shroud he wears is fit only for peons, not for a lover and musician."

"But did someone help you to reach the dead body?"

The elderly woman shook her head.

"What did you use then to clear away the soil?"

Isabella pulled back and brought forth her hands. Teresa took them and inched Isabella into the moonlight. Compressed dirt wedged under Isabella's fingernails. A few of the nails were broken or fractured, and the open wounds were unwashed. In the darkness the flesh shone white, but up close Teresa could see they were terribly reddened.

"We must wash your hands."

Isabella pulled her hands back. "But you're not Catrin." Isabella's watery blue eyes glistened. "She looks like me, you know, not at all like her father. If he hadn't been there for her birth, he might not have believed she belonged to him. Should I have poisoned her, too, before I birthed her? He did speak of it. Only I cried so much he caved in and didn't force me to seek help. But I knew what to do on my own. My parents gifted me with a tutor and a witch. Many spells needed but a few ingredients that could be found growing on or mixed in with our soil." Isabella smiled at Teresa, proud and confident. "I could have rid Roberto's world of Catrin, but I wouldn't. Instead I rid him of the sow slumbering in his bed."

"His wife?"

"She had her babe before me. A pinkish, squalling brat caterwauling for cuddles and breast milk, which I tried to sour. But the sow didn't have enough milk. Instead they brought in a wet nurse. When I gave birth, my breasts hung heavy with milk. Catrin would have flourished."

Teresa made the sign of the cross and instinctively reached for the feel of the crucifix beneath the fabric of her blouse.

"Your faith can't protect you from what's inside this house." Isabella began walking around the standing Teresa. "I once had faith in a God different from yours, but He was taken from me. Ripped from my heart to preserve Roberto's wealth. My brother traveled all the way to Rome to pledge his allegiance. His family waited, wondering whether a knock would come to the door, demanding we march ourselves to the Inquisitor's prison. All the way to Rome he went while we sat exposed to the papal Church's wrath. And when he came home, we feasted, but not in the old way. No, nothing of our old traditions could be retained. We could not even kill our meats in the same way. There could be no blessing of the poultry, no separating of veins from meat. The bishop sent us pork, hare, rabbits, and eels. And they were served to us with the bishop sitting at the place of honor at the dinner table." Isabella had made a full circle but did not halt. Her words flowed much too quickly to cause her to stop and think. "Roberto's sow cried night after night until he could no longer stand to hear her blubbering wails and left on the pretense of business. I came to her and held her. In the middle of the night, I whispered in her ear, but all my words were false. She thought I felt the same as she, but no God is more important than Roberto to me."

"Hush!" Teresa covered her own lips, not daring to reach out for Isabella.

"Soon each night I brought the sow an herbal to help her sleep. At first she thought it too bitter and protested, but I soothed her with my hands, with lips pressed against her cheek, and she drank willingly. Oh, how her ugly face squinted in distaste." Isabella laughed and whirled her body around Teresa in a breathtaking spin until she dropped to the floor, her laughter subsiding into a gentle smile. "When he returned, he found her ill. Unable to be a wife to him. Soon she couldn't walk, could hardly manage to sit up in bed, but she stopped her crying. Too concerned she was with her health to harangue my brother with her words and tears."

"Did your brother suspect you had poisoned his wife?"

"He was blinded by love for me. He thought she feared another pregnancy and believed his son had drained the sow of all her energy. He blamed Luis the most. For a short while he couldn't stand to look at the child, but soon the little boy won back his father. The sow had become much too involved in her own illness to be a mother, and the little boy wandered in and out of her room almost unnoticed."

"Did you give her the final dose of poison that killed her?"

"I gave her very little. It would be too easy for her to die. I wanted her to hear my footsteps freely passing through the house, to realize that Roberto slept in my bed instead of hers. Sometimes he would fall asleep next to me and I would rise from the bed to visit the sow. I would bring her a warm cup of herbal. She would ask me where Roberto was." Isabella quickly rose to her feet and stared directly into Teresa's eyes. "She knew. But I would lie and say he must have fallen asleep in the library while poring over some document. The stupid sow drank deeply from the cup I brought her, finishing every drop."

"You will pay in hell."

"I don't care, for I had a few hours, days, months, years of pleasure with Roberto. I kept him from loving another woman."

A scream shattered the emotion of Isabella's words, forcing the two women to turn toward the door. Several more screams followed.

Teresa attempted to reach out for the door when Isabella grabbed her wrist.

"Bring Catrin to me." Isabella spoke in a whisper, but one that seethed of frustration. "Bring her to me as soon as you can. I have so much knowledge to give her."

"She might be better off without your mean-spirited wisdom." Teresa yanked her hand free and opened the door.

chapter 42

IN THE HALLWAY THE SCREAMS ECHOED AS IN A canyon. Teresa rushed to Señor Roberto's room, pushing the door inward with all the strength she had.

Alone in bed the elderly man's head tossed back and forth on the pillow, his mind evidently held inside a nightmare. There was nothing she could do for him. Upon turning, she caught sight of Isabella slinking silently into the room.

"Get out, Isabella, before I call Señor Luis. You know he doesn't want you here without a chaperone."

"You cheat me. You would have me believe you to be Catrin, and then you listen to me as a friend, but quickly you turn on me."

"I never said I was Catrin. I've always denied that to you. Yes, I wanted to be a friend, but now after hearing what you've done . . ."

"The sow would have been rid of me if she could have."

"Isabella," Roberto's raspy voice hung heavy in the room. "Whose wailing do I hear, Isabella?"

Both women went to the bed. Roberto reached out a hand to his sister.

"They can't burn her, Isabella. Not now. She's done nothing wrong. Our child is innocent. Stop the burning." His hand rested on the lower part of Isabella's right arm, his nails scratching the black fabric, causing the wounds upon his fingers to open, spilling trails of blood on the sleeve.

"No, Señor Velez, it is not your daughter. It must be one of the servants. There must have been an accident."

His unfocused eyes scanned Teresa's face, not recognizing who she was. Isabella rested her left hand upon his cheek and gently turned his face to hers.

"Our daughter rests in the cradle. I've just lullabied her to sleep. A stranger cries out in pain. A foreigner to whom we gave shelter, that's all."

"A stranger. But the flames seemed so real. The heat. I could feel the warmth of the fire and the smell of seared flesh." He barely raised his head from the pillow.

"Only a dream, my brother. You've protected us from them. You've promised to praise their false God."

Roberto nodded his head and closed his eyes.

"My sleep is troubled with all that I have done."

"But we love you for saving us all."

He opened his eyes and looked at his sister.

"Have I saved anyone? Look at you, Isabella. Your skin is creased with lines. Your lips," he reached up to touch her mouth, "are dried and cracked. They never smile anymore for me."

Isabella forced a smile and kissed his fingertips, allowing her tongue to lick drops of blood from his skin.

"Let me check on the household," Teresa said, pulling away from the bed. Neither brother nor sister looked at her. She could not be sure they had even heard her. Isabella fell to her knees beside the bed, clinging to Roberto's hand, while her brother slipped back into his drug-induced slumber.

Once outside the room Teresa rushed down the staircase. The screaming had stopped, but she heard the bustle of bodies moving briskly through the servants' quarters. First she entered the kitchen, finding Manuel putting big pots of water over the fire. He wore an oversized shirt that looked as if it had originally belonged to Jose. The water spilled onto the fire, causing sizzling puffs of steam to erupt.

"What's happened, Manuel?"

Surprised by her voice, he almost dropped one of the pots. His large eyes searched out the owner of the voice.

"It's Juana. She's bleeding heavily, not like ladies normally do, says Señora Toledo. She ordered me to boil up some water."

Teresa ran up the staircase to the servants' quarters, her sandals slapping firmly against the stone steps. The door to Juana's room stood open.

"Where the hell have you been?" Señora Toledo yelled as Teresa entered the room. "I couldn't find you and had to send for Manuel for assistance. He's much too young to be dealing with such matters."

"I needed to check on Señor Velez."

"In the middle of the night? You've never done that before."

"She didn't say whether it was Señor Roberto or Señor Luis," Hilaria interjected, unfolding some clean linens.

"I needn't answer to you," said Teresa, moving into the room for a closer look at Juana. "What happened to her?"

"She'll be all right," Señora Toledo said. "She lost her child, which is what she wanted."

"What did she do?" Teresa asked, looking down at the blood-soaked bed on which Juana lay.

"Pennyroyal," Hilaria answered.

"She got it from you, no doubt." Señora Toledo's angry voice quivered, reflecting the nervousness of her shaky hands.

"The doctor should be called." Teresa rested her palm on Juana's forehead.

"We keep things private around here. Go down and help Manuel with the water."

"This is Gaspar's fault. Where is he?" Teresa demanded.

"There's nothing he can do now. He'd only make matters worse. Hopefully he'll keep the young master from poking around."

"We all heard the screams. I don't know why Señor Luis Velez didn't."

"The screams belonged to Juana and this idiot, Hilaria. She gives the herbs to Juana and then doesn't know what to expect. She found Juana writhing in pain and covered in blood."

"This is a sin on both your souls." Teresa turned her back on Juana and looked directly at Hilaria.

"And what do you think would have become of her babe?" Hilaria pushed aside the cook to stand in front of Teresa. "What would have happened to Juana? Do you think she'd be a useful servant with her belly protruding out in front of her? Do you think the Inquisitors would ignore the sight of her? This house is being watched closely by the Church. The bishop visits, not to befriend the masters, but to spy."

"But Señor Roberto and the bishop are old friends."

"The bishop is an agent of the Church. No lay person is his friend."

"Stop bickering, you two, and do something to help. Teresa, I've already told you to help Manuel with the hot water, and Hilaria, we need more clean linens."

"This is all we have."

"Take some from the masters' cupboards, then. And hurry."

On the way down to the kitchen, Teresa ran into Manuel trying to climb the stairs with a boiling pot of water. He had wrapped several rags around the handle, but the steam rising from the pot burned his hands.

"Let me help you."

Inside Juana's room, Manuel's eyes went wide. He stood still, stunned by the sight of the bleeding woman.

"You've seen worse in the barn," Señora Toledo snapped.

"Is she having a baby?" he asked.

"No. It's a woman's problem. Go back down to the kitchen."

Juana's body curved into a fetal shape; her crying came in ragged bursts.

"It's over, Juana. By the morning the pain will have subsided. Try not to make so much noise. You don't want everyone knowing your business." Señora Toledo stepped back away from the bed and tripped over Manuel. "What are you still doing here?"

"I've never seen such messy woman's problems before. Jose said that . . ."

"What is Jose telling you? He should keep quiet and not put wicked ideas in your head."

"He says it's not wicked, just a punishment God put on women because of Eve."

"Get out!"

Manuel rushed past Teresa. She felt sorry for the confused boy, but didn't think it her place to explain what had happened.

Most of the night the women stayed by Juana's bed until she finally fell asleep. Hilaria curled up next to Juana in the bed, her arm flung over the slight girl's body.

Teresa smelled the sweat coming off Señora Toledo's body, her clothes soaked, her brow spotted with drops of perspiration.

"I could prepare the breakfast in the morning if you want to sleep in."

"No. Sylvia took one look at the blood, screamed, and ran back to her room. Let her get up early and see to the morning meal. You've helped well enough tonight."

Relieved, Teresa was moving to her room when she suddenly recalled how she had left Señor Roberto alone with his sister. Should she check to see that they were all right? The heaviness of her arms and legs made walking difficult. The thought of climbing a flight of stairs to get to the master bedroom didn't appeal to her. Instead she returned to her own room and dropped, fully dressed, into bed.

chapter 43

TERESA AWOKE TO A KNOCK ON HER BEDROOM door. How long had she been asleep? Her hair lay across her face, not fitted into the tight braid she usually made before bed. Her body fought her effort to rise, but the knock persisted.

"Who is it?" she called, thinking that Señora Toledo might have changed her mind about breakfast.

"It's Manuel."

She forced herself out of bed and walked barefoot across the room. When she opened the door, she realized she must have looked a sight, because Manuel made a sour face.

"Do you suffer from the woman's problem, too?" he asked.

"No. We stayed up very late."

"Oh. Señor Luis Velez wishes to speak with you in the library."

"It will take me a few minutes to get ready."

"He said for you to come now, and he didn't look happy."

"Manuel, do I look presentable?"

"I'll tell him you need some time, but don't take too long."

"Thank you, Manuel. And, by the way, I don't believe anyone thanked you for your help last night."

"I fell asleep in the kitchen."

"I'm so sorry. No one remembered to tell you to go to bed. You were a great help, though. We wouldn't have been able to do your task and take care of Juana at the same time. Thank you."

Manuel smiled, and she thought she saw a quick wink tick his left eye before he left.

It took Teresa well over fifteen minutes to arrive at the library. The door stood open, and Señor Luis sat at the desk, looking off into the distance, his body sprawled across the chair and his booted feet leisurely resting atop the desk.

She knocked, and he instantly lowered his feet to the floor, rising from the chair.

"You wished to speak with me?"

"Yes. I'm glad you took as long as you did. I was much angrier when I spoke to Manuel. I may have frightened the boy."

"He's sturdier than you think."

Luis nodded and invited her into the room, directing her to the settee.

"I came home late last night and immediately checked on my father. What time did you last see him?"

"It was quite late. The doctor must have given him

an elixir because he woke briefly and appeared rather confused."

"Yes. He was alone?"

"No. I left him with his sister."

She watched Luis's eyes narrow.

"He seemed comforted by her presence. I saw no reason to drive her away. He had awakened from a bad dream. A dream about Catrin."

Luis walked around the desk. He was about to sit next to her, but thought better of it and took the chair across from her.

"What kind of a dream was it?"

Teresa looked down at her hands resting upon her skirt and remained silent.

"Did he tell you?"

"Juana became ill in the middle of the night and there was some screaming." She decided to meet his eyes directly. "He woke and called out for Isabella. He thought the screams belonged to Catrin. He begged your sister to save Catrin from the stake."

Luis buried his face in his hands for several moments before looking back at her.

"And you went searching for Isabella?"

"I didn't have to. She had followed me into the room and immediately flew to her brother's bedside."

"I found Isabella in my father's bed last night. He has grown so frail that he fits snugly in her arms. I became angry, afraid that she had taken his life, but as I drew closer, I could see the rise and fall of his chest."

"She loves her brother."

"And has spoken of wanting him dead. You must remember that, Teresa."

"Yet she seems to bring him peace."

"One day it may be in the form of taking his life. Hence this morning I wanted to berate you. I had assumed you had left them together."

"Did you leave them together, yourself, when you saw them?"

He hesitated.

"I must admit I couldn't bear to separate them. For once he seemed to sleep soundly."

Teresa nodded her approval.

"This morning, when I looked in on my father, they still lay together. Isabella had her eyes open, but I don't think she heard me come into the room. She kept staring blankly ahead of her as if into the past. When I called her name, she cackled like the witch she is and told me to go away. She claimed to have taken back her brother. The woman is mad. I dragged her from the bed and woke my father. She cried out as if I were beating her." He paused.

"What did your father say or do?"

"He tried to get out of bed but was dizzy and fell to the floor."

"Was he hurt?" Teresa bundled her skirt together, preparing to rise to her feet.

"No. He is all right. Angry, but not hurt. I put him back into bed. When I turned around, Isabella had disappeared."

"Why must you try so hard to keep them apart?"

"She wants him dead."

"And he is wasting away. Your father will not survive this illness. He grows weaker each day. Even his thinking is clouded by the elixirs the doctor gives him. Let them have this short time together."

Luis rose to his feet.

"You're here to care for my father, not to predict when he will die. My sister is a threat to him."

"But no longer a threat to your mother."

Luis fell to his knees before Teresā.

"What do you know of my mother's death?"

Flustered for a moment, Teresa held her breath. No good could come from telling him the truth.

"I did not live here then. How could I know anything about your mother's death? I know only what you and your father have told me, that your sister and your mother were rivals for your father's affection."

Luis moved backward to sit on the floor. She saw relief in his eyes. He didn't want the truth. There had been so much torment in his childhood; she refused to feed it any further.

"You said Juana took ill last night. Not like Fernando, I hope."

"No. I haven't seen her yet this morning, but I assume she is resting much easier." Gaspar had to be stopped. If she didn't tell, then Juana would again find herself pregnant and seeking witches to feed her a magical brew to expel her child. "Gaspar was the cause of her illness."

"How is that?"

Teresa swallowed several times before she could finally speak the words.

"Gaspar has been forcing his affections on Juana." She looked at him to see whether she needed to explain any further, but Luis's perplexed expression forced her to go on. "He has been visiting her late at night. From what I've heard, he's not been invited. And last night she lost the child she had been carrying."

"Juana was pregnant?"

"She took something to rid herself of the child."

"And why are you telling me this?"

"Because Gaspar must be stopped."

"If they wish to carry on a . . ."

"You haven't listened to me. He has forced himself on her. She is very young, and he is much older. She dare not say anything because she fears losing her position here."

"You mean she thinks she has to sleep with Gaspar in order to retain her position."

"No, no. She doesn't want to have . . . relations with him, but she's afraid of complaining."

"Teresa, you've set my mind in a whirl with your gossip."

"It is not gossip. I knocked on her door one night, and Gaspar came to the door. He even . . . even asked me to join them."

Luis moved closer to her.

"Did he hurt you?"

"I ran away like a coward instead of helping Juana."

"There's nothing you could have physically done except to tell me. I'll see to Gaspar. I'll warn him that if this situation continues, I'll have to let him go. You shouldn't feel guilty." He took hold of her hands.

She noticed how large and warm his hands felt. When she looked into his dark eyes, he gripped her hands tighter, and she felt her body lean forward toward his.

"Teresa," he whispered.

She wanted to touch his face, memorize his handsome features, allow him to do the same with her, until she remembered Catrin and all the late nights he spent away from the manse. She sat up straight and unwound her fingers from his.

"Your father must wonder where I am. He hasn't eaten as yet. If you need me no further . . ." She looked around, trying to find a space in which to stand without having to brush against Luis's body.

"What about me, Teresa? What do I mean to you?" He still spoke in a whisper. A whisper that frightened Teresa.

"I don't know what you mean, Señor. You are not the patient. As far as I can tell, you are quite healthy." She felt a blush rush up through her cheeks.

He chuckled and stood, offering his hand to help her up. She accepted with reluctance but didn't want to appear unnerved by him.

"Thank you," she said. "And thank you for helping Juana." When she finished speaking, she realized that they still held each other's hands. Immediately she pulled away, moving quickly to exit the room, only to be tripped by Spider. Luis grabbed her waist, and she wavered a moment, feeling faint, before her feet finally steadied beneath her.

Teresa remained conscious of each stair she climbed, knowing Luis followed her departure with his eyes.

chapter 44

WHAT THE HELL WAS HE DOING? TERESA HAD spent her entire life being reared by nuns in a convent. He caught her often blessing herself and grasping for the rosary she persisted in wearing. On top of everything, she was the bastard child of Susanna Diego. He certainly didn't want to get weighted down with a relationship like the one he had with Catrin. Look at the evil he had brought upon her, and, unlike Teresa, Catrin had not been a virgin. She had been the one to instigate the sex play.

Luis slammed the double doors behind him.

Teresa would expect marriage and children. The last things Luis ever wanted to have. No, he had to spend less time in her presence. He had been right in not wanting to accept her as his father's nursemaid. Had he felt the attraction the first time he met her? Yes, quite possibly. He remembered the wet blouse settling against her breasts, her dark hair moist with the rain, her face shining, and her eyes glistening with their jewel green color.

Spider slapped a paw against Luis's leg to get his attention.

"What's wrong with me, boy?" He patted the dog and sat on the settee, the exact spot where Teresa had been. Still warm with her heat, it made his desire grow. He'd slake his desire at one of the whorehouses where crucifixes and virgins never entered.

But first he'd deal with Gaspar. Did he have the right to lecture his butler about the vagaries of having sex within the household? However, if Teresa was correct, Gaspar had not found himself a willing partner. That Luis would never tolerate. He thought back for a moment and recalled how Juana seemed unable to speak freely in front of Gaspar. Now he knew why.

A knock interrupted his thoughts. He bade the person to enter.

Gaspar stood in the doorway. Both of his hands rested upon the open doors. His haughty air, which Luis had previously found so amusing, now irritated him.

"The bishop has just arrived. He is in the salon."

Luis hadn't expected to see the bishop so soon. Could it be that he had managed to obtain permission for Luis to visit Catrin? Or had word already spread about Juana's pregnancy?

Luis sent Gaspar away with a wave of his hand and headed for the salon. When he opened the door, he found the bishop holding an ornate silver candlestick. The bishop might have been getting old, but his hearing still remained acute, for he immediately turned to smile at Luis.

"Your father has such excellent taste, Luis. Or was it your mother who chose this gem?"

"Neither, it was a gift from one of Father's business associates."

"Lovely," the bishop said, placing the candlestick back on the mantel.

"Did you come to take an inventory of our possessions, Bishop?"

The bishop gave Luis a sharp look.

"I cannot imagine what you mean by that." The bishop limped across a small Asian rug to seat himself in the chair closest to the fire. "I try so hard to assist your family, and yet I have the feeling you do not fully trust me. But then maybe it's the Church you don't trust. Think of me as the Lord's representative. You certainly trust in God?" He cocked his head to the side and waited for an answer.

Luis crossed the room and bowed to kiss the bishop's ring.

"My aunt has soured my mood. I'm sorry if I offended you."

"How is she doing? I haven't seen her in years. She never receives Communion, but she might not realize the importance of the sacrament. I assume her mental capacity has not improved."

"Worse. She wishes to live in the past."

"Ah, sometimes I do, too. Life was easier for clerics and laypersons before Torquemada became the Grand Inquisitor. But I've brought good news. You may visit Catrin."

"When?"

The bishop patted his chest.

"I'm a bit parched from the ride."

"I'm sorry, Bishop. I'll have Gaspar bring some sherry."

"Port, please. That lovely one I had the last time I was here."

Luis called for the port, and Gaspar brought two glasses with the bottle on the tray.

"Gaspar, my son, I hope you'll be able to make Sunday mass." The bishop enjoyed scolding the butler. "Besides, a member of your family will also be saying mass."

"I have no one in the priesthood, Bishop."

"Yes, you do. A distant cousin, Pedro. He remembers you very well. Seems you used to playfully beat him up when you both were children."

"He claimed then to be related to me, and I frequently disputed it."

"Quite brutally, from what he says. He'd like to meet you again and make amends with you. He's now a Dominican with the Inquisition." The bishop sipped his port.

"Is there anything else, Señor Velez?" asked Gaspar, turning away from the cleric.

"I don't like being ignored, Gaspar." The bishop lowered his voice.

"I will make an effort to greet Pedro."

"*Father* Pedro, and merely greeting him won't do. I want to see you on your knees in a pew. Is that understood?"

"Yes, Bishop." Gaspar bowed, and Luis eagerly dismissed him.

"He is a weak link for you, Luis. He's not liked by

many people. Oh, I know your father always thought Gaspar did his job well, but his attitude and temper sow bad seeds."

"My father wouldn't hear of dismissing him."

"And you?"

"I'm not the head of the household."

"Why don't I make a visit to the 'head of the house-hold'?" The bishop grabbed hold of the arms of the chair and pushed himself up.

"And Catrin. When can I see her?"

"Day after tomorrow. I'll meet you at the Inquisitor's residence. I know something of the maze he has constructed in that dungeon of his."

"You've seen Catrin?"

"I pray with the poor souls held there whenever I can."

The bishop walked past Luis, eventually calling for his assistance in climbing the stairs. The bishop talked of the town and how well the building of his monastery was going. At the door to the sickroom, the bishop removed his hand from Luis's forearm.

"I want to look whole for your father. No sense in reminding him of how old we're both getting."

Luis lightly knocked, and Teresa pulled open the door, bowing to the bishop as he walked past her into the room. Luis pulled the door shut leaving Teresa, the bishop, and his father alone.

chapter 45

THE NEXT MORNING TERESA WAS SURPRISED TO find the kitchen silent, until she noticed that Gaspar had joined them for breakfast. Juana concentrated on her food and never looked up. When Teresa bade them good morning, only Gaspar responded.

"Teresa, how well you look this morning. Certainly better than this morose lot." He looked around the table, his eyes settling on Juana.

"I'm surprised you've joined us for breakfast," Teresa said.

"Señor Luis insisted that I try to get along better with the staff. And I never thought there was any problem. Did you, Juana?"

She shook her head but didn't meet his eyes.

"I have to hire someone to take Fernando's place," Jose said, distracting Gaspar from the girl.

"I know nothing of barns, Jose, nor of the kinds of people who work in them." Gaspar pulled out the chair next to him. "Sit, Teresa. I long for conversation."

Cautiously she sat down. As soon as she did, she felt Gaspar's leg rub against hers.

"Oops, sorry. I'm too big for this table, I suppose," he said.

Juana rose when she heard Manuel stand. She hoped she could scurry out of the kitchen along with the boy.

"Have you asked for permission to leave the table, Juana?" Gaspar asked.

"She doesn't need to," Señora Toledo said.

"I forgot. This is the cook's territory, isn't it?"

"I'm the one who spoke to Señor Luis, Gaspar." Teresa didn't turn her head in his direction. She waited for his rage to strike out at her, but he surprised her with his calm expression.

"Juana has no guts. She's like a frightened deer in the wood. Pliant and stupid. Scurry away, Juana, and perform your household duties."

Juana took advantage of the release and almost ran out of the kitchen.

"She'll not thank you for what you've done, Teresa," he said.

"I didn't expect her to. I only wanted to stop you."

"Gaspar, there is no way to change what has happened. Don't make it worse." Jose's soft voice did nothing to soften Gaspar's ire.

"I've worked here longer than you, Jose. Longer than any of you." He looked around the table. "No one has ever questioned what I do."

"That's because everyone's scared of you," Manuel

said, a slice of bread in his hand and his eyes opened as wide as they could get.

Gaspar turned to Teresa.

"You either aren't frightened of me or you're very stupid."

"She'll be leaving as soon as Señor Roberto dies," Manuel persisted.

"And how long will that take?" Gaspar's words in her ears and his hot breath, soured by milk, blowing across her face made Teresa want to cringe.

Instead she looked directly at him.

"Don't you dare touch anyone else in this household or I'll demand you be let go."

"Firm in your position, are you?" Gaspar reached out a hand to touch her hair, but she pulled away. "Have you spread your legs for the young master the same as Catrin did? The old man would have bedded you long ago if he had had the strength."

"Enough, Gaspar. You insult all of us with your talk." Jose pulled back his chair and stood. Señora Toledo attempted to pull Jose back down, but failed.

"When the Inquisitor rams a hot poker up into your womb, Teresa, I hope you see my face as you scream." Gaspar stood and left the kitchen.

"Fool," Señora Toledo said.

Teresa was unsure whether the word was directed at her or Jose, for they both had been fools.

"Don't ever allow yourself to be alone with Gaspar, Teresa." Jose started to walk over to her, but the cook held him back. "What you did was commendable, but . . ." He halted, leaving silence lingering for too long in the room.

"I'm not hungry. Breakfast should almost be ready for Señor Roberto, shouldn't it?" Teresa looked at the cook.

"I'll send Hilaria up with the meal. You can take it from her at the door so he doesn't have to see her."

chapter 46

"You are pale today, Teresa. Perhaps you've been spending too much time with me."

She heard Señor Roberto's voice from miles away. She had opened the window and lingered, looking out at the road leading to the manse. She recalled the first day of her arrival, the excitement of something new that tingled through her body. How she had watched Luis pace, not understanding the yearning he ignited inside her. Why did Sister Agatha insist upon sending her? Sister Agatha would call it God's will, but Teresa wondered. Could the devil have had some hand in the decision?

"Do you intend to ignore me for the rest of the day?"

She turned to Señor Roberto.

"You wouldn't allow me to ignore you. You'd whine and bellow like the pest you are." She had fallen into teasing her patient. It helped them both to forget how ill he was.

He tried to bellow, but only succeeded in having a coughing fit. She rushed to him and smiled, thinking how right she had been. After a few sips of water, his chest calmed and his head rested heavily on the pillow. She noticed several specks of blood peppering his garment.

"You shouldn't excite yourself like that."

"Why not? Will it speed my death? How many more minutes do I gain by lying as still as you want me to?"

"You only make yourself miserable, and there must be some pain."

"But I experienced heaven this morning. I woke up in Isabella's arms. Of course, my son ruined it."

"He fears that Isabella may mean you harm."

"What dreadful thing can she do to me now? No, it's my son who must take care. He will be visiting Catrin soon."

"The Inquisitor will permit this?"

"Yes. Why do you think that is?"

"How should I know?"

"You've grown up in the bosom of the Church. Do you not understand its workings?"

"I understand the love the Church has for its people. The Inquisition I don't understand at all."

"Should I tell him not to go?"

"He wouldn't listen to you. Also, you both want Catrin freed."

"Did you know that the Inquisition charges us for her prison cell and the rotted food they feed her? I'm sure most of the *maravedíes* go toward buying food for the Inquisitor's dinner table. Luis will probably find a scrawny child sleeping on contaminated hay."

"The bishop didn't mention Catrin yesterday when

he visited you." She remembered being present for the visit.

"No, Luis told me last night. I think my son is in great danger. The bishop has always protected me, but when I die, he will be free of any debt he owes me."

"But your son still pays homage to the Church, and the bishop doesn't dislike your son, I'm sure."

"He is as indifferent to my children as he is to his own. He has given one or two of his progeny religious positions, but not of the level where they will flourish." With great effort Señor Roberto lifted his right hand and stretched it out to Teresa. She took it in her own, feeling each spindly bone wrapped in drooping flesh. The discolorations had worsened, and the open sores had multiplied. "My son has no one, Teresa. I've taught him to be independent, free of any bonds. I thought it would make him strong. Now I am sorry. He should be married with small children instead of carousing the whorehouses and lying with his own sister. How like me he is. Do you like my son any better than you did before?"

"I never disliked him."

"But you fidgeted around him. Wanted him to keep away from you. Does his handsome appearance frighten you?"

"The way he lives does."

"He's unhappy, and I am the cause. Even my sister aches inside because of the sins I've committed with her."

"Why didn't you stop? Especially after you married."

"It was too easy to continue. I didn't have someone

to curb my appetites. To curse me when I scorned and abused others. Something you're very good at, by the way. If I were not dying, I'd send you away, fearing my son might learn to love you. Now I pray that you both will love each other. This manse will be taken by the Church when I die."

"Do you mean to leave it to the Church?"

"Oh, no. I'm not so generous. No, the Church will rob my son of his inheritance. Help him, Teresa. Don't let the Church rob him of his life."

A cold chill swept the room. Teresa placed the old man's hand on his blanket and rushed across the room to close the window.

"We can't lock them out, Teresa."

"I'll do what I can for him," Teresa said, staring out the window between the shutters' slats, watching the birds crowding on the front lawn. She spied Hilaria spreading bread crumbs while Manuel laughed and chased the birds. Hilaria obviously scolded him, since the boy crossed his arms and pouted, kicking a small rock in the direction of the birds.

"Do you love him?"

Suddenly she turned around to find her patient on his side, leaning almost over the mattress.

"What are you doing? You'll fall."

He lay back and complained that she hadn't been responding to his questions.

"I didn't hear you. And it is just as well, since all this silly talk is totally unnecessary. Your son will be fine.

He'll bring Catrin home and learn to tolerate Isabella. Eventually he'll meet a woman of his station and marry. This house will be filled with children."

"I'm not a toddler to be told fairy tales, Teresa."

"And I can't be who you want me to be. My life is with the sisters at the convent. They need my assistance in bartering with the outside world. When one of them is ill, I nurse her back to health. That is why God chose to birth me in the convent."

"If I had the strength, I would reach up and rip that damn rosary from around your neck."

Protectively Teresa's hands touched the beads of the rosary.

"It was given to me by Sister Agatha. She wisely understood that I would need it during my stay here."

"What are we, Teresa, demons clutching at your flesh? Tempting you into living in the world? Is that why you wear the rosary?"

"My world is different from yours, Señor Velez. I don't wish to hoard wealth or satisfy my base desires. My mother offered me up to God's service."

"Your mother was a whore, Teresa. Don't turn so red as if you would explode. Your mother did the best she could for you. She made sure you had a roof over your head and milk in your belly. She didn't intend to plan out your life for you."

Without knocking, Luis opened the door. His smile slowly dissipated as he took in the scene before him.

"I'm sorry. Did I interrupt?"

"No. I need to take leave for a while, if you don't mind sitting with your father." A pang touched Teresa's heart. Could the old man be right about the danger in which his son would eventually find himself? Luis agreed to stay, allowing Teresa to scurry out of the room.

chapter 47

GASPAR WAS MISSING FROM THE DINNER TABLE
that night, to everyone's relief. But still silence pervaded
the evening meal, Juana sniffling as if she held back tears.
Teresa wondered whether Gaspar had been hard on the
girl that day, but didn't dare ask since she assumed Juana
would burst into tears and flee the room. Had she been
wrong in informing Luis of Gaspar's brutal actions? No,
for as long as she resided in the house now, she doubted
that the butler would take advantage of Juana sexually.
What would happen, however, after Roberto Velez died
and she left to return to the convent? Luis's father pre-
dicted disaster for the household.

Looking around the table, she met no faces except for
Jose's, which smiled back at her. The rest of the staff kept
to their own thoughts, afraid to exchange even the slightest of pleasantries. Even Manuel knew better than to
speak. He gobbled his food as quickly as he could before
rushing out of the kitchen, claiming he had not finished
the day's chores as yet.

Teresa wanted to speak to Juana alone to apologize and explain why she had spoken to Señor Luis. Perhaps she'd try knocking on the young maid's bedroom door that night. On the other hand, she didn't want to frighten the girl and have her think it might be Gaspar. She heard Juana excuse herself and stand. Immediately Teresa stood to follow.

"Where are you going?" Señora Toledo turned to Teresa and asked.

"I'm finished with the meal and . . ."

"Your plate has barely been touched, and you had no breakfast this morning. Finish what you have on the plate."

"She'd rather hound Juana," Hilaria said.

"I wanted to apologize. If I can help her . . ."

"Juana will have to leave the house," Señora Toledo said.

"Why? She isn't at fault for what happened."

"Gaspar has been here far longer than she has. The Velez family will insist upon his staying."

"Why does either of them have to leave?" Even as Teresa heard her own words, she knew that Señora Toledo spoke the truth. Gaspar and Juana could no longer work together in peace. This was what Juana had most feared.

"You have no idea how a house like this works. Nuns forgive, but scullery help is never forgiven. I shall be looking for a new girl and trying to place Juana. She understands this without being told."

"I pray she finds a happier household than this one," Teresa said, throwing down her napkin and walking out of the kitchen.

She climbed the stairs to take a last look at her patient before turning in herself. Better lit than she had ever seen it before, the landing looked almost cheerful, fresh flowers filling the vases at the top of the stairs. This surprised her. Ordinarily the vases sat empty, and neither Velez ever noticed. She stopped to capture the scent from the yellow and white roses. The roses that hadn't opened as yet had a pinkish hue to their buds.

She turned away from the flowers and immediately saw Isabella's black form huddled in front of Señor Roberto's bedroom. Softly she walked over to Isabella, thinking that the elderly woman was asleep. Isabella's face peeked out from the folds of her garment to stare at Teresa.

"What are you doing here? You'll catch a chill sitting on the floor."

"He won't let me go in."

"Your nephew?"

"The doctor. He said I should go away because I smell of death and will only bring my brother to his grave sooner."

Teresa had to knock on the door several times before the doctor finally poked his face out into the hall.

"I told you . . ." he began until he recognized Teresa. "Señor Roberto won't need your services for the rest of the night. The draft I've given him should make him sleep."

"Please, allow his sister to at least say good night to her brother," Teresa said, waving her hand at Isabella.

"I've slept with him many times before. There is no

reason why I can't continue to do so," Isabella said with a childlike pout.

Before the doctor could answer, a voice boomed out from across the hall.

"Admit her to the bedroom, Doctor." Luis stood in an open doorway.

"We've agreed, Señor Luis, that she will only bring harm to your brother."

"I've changed my mind, Doctor. My aunt should have the freedom to come and go as she pleases."

Isabella rose to her feet and flew into Luis's arms, kissing his cheeks as he attempted to pull back his head. Gently Teresa took Isabella by the shoulders, guiding her across the hall, past the doctor, and into the sickroom. Already groggy, Señor Roberto barely recognized his sister, but when he did, a weak smile lightened his face.

"She's a witch." Teresa heard the doctor's voice seething with anger.

Isabella looked at the tumbler beside the bed. She lifted it in her hands and smelled what remained of the contents.

"Bah, rotten, vile ministrations you give my brother to take away his knowledge. This only clouds his thoughts. It doesn't relieve the pain."

"It puts him to sleep," the doctor said.

Isabella leaned back onto Teresa and began to whisper, "He ripped the babe from my womb with his blade. He didn't expect me to live. Wanted me to die and the babe, too, but my brother stood nearby and watched his every move. The doctor gave me the same draft to drink. and I felt that blade cutting into my flesh and his hands lifting Catrin out of my womb."

"I would have killed him had you died," Señor Roberto said.

The doctor collected his medical bag and quickly departed.

Isabella knelt on the bed and embraced her brother.

Teresa wondered whether the elderly man knew that his sister had been slowly poisoning his wife. Could he have been complicit, either allowing it to happen or actively assisting? She looked at Luis standing in the doorway, his eyes half-closed, his lips barely touching, making him look worn, tired, old. How had he managed to survive so long with the secret assignations and the corrupted emotions of those so dear to him? His father should have feared for his son's future long before the shadow of death fell on this room.

As she walked past Luis, he whispered to her, "You are right about them. They give each other comfort. My aunt shan't have that after my father is gone."

She stopped next to him. "Do you think you could forgive in memory of your father? He wouldn't want her punished for what he himself had set in motion."

Luis turned to her, his eyes softening as he explored her features. She placed her hands on her fiery cheeks to hide her discomfiture, but by the broadness of his smile, she knew he had already caught the glow on her cheeks.

chapter 48

LUIS HAD TROUBLE SLEEPING. HIS THOUGHTS WERE filled with the activities of the day and apprehension concerning what he would find when he visited the Inquisitor's prison the next day.

Teresa had been exceptionally gentle with Isabella and wisely faced down the wretched doctor who blindly fumbled through his armamentarium of medicines. Nothing he had done had improved his father's condition. The doctor kept talking of an imminent restoration of his father's health, but Luis now understood it would never happen. His father lay on his deathbed, begging to be released from this earth, yet fearing the consequences he would suffer in the next life. And Isabella? How would she react when her brother ceased breathing? Teresa pleaded for mercy for his aunt in the name of his father. He had originally planned to lock away his aunt in the garret, in the small room that Catrin had chosen for herself. How appropriate that the mother should follow the daughter into exile. He believed his aunt justly deserved that punishment, but had never thought Catrin belonged locked away in the garret.

Soft-spoken, amiable Catrin, her slender fingers so agile in the art of lovemaking. Luis squeezed his eyes shut against the vision. He and Catrin shared the same family blood, the same dishonest and depraved relatives; only Catrin had fared much worse than he. His father had planned on leaving her in the arms of some peasant farmers, to be married off to a young brutish colt for breeding. Yet Isabella felt love for his father amid the disappointment she had experienced when forced to give up her only child.

Luis pounded the feather pillows into shape and dragged the blanket up over his body. He looked over at the window and noticed the full moon so close he wanted to rip it from the sky and send the entire earth into darkness.

He doubted Catrin had seen the moon in months. By now her eyes would not bear the sight of even the moon, never mind the sun, after the months of darkness inside her cell. Would her skin be as blemish-free as he remembered it? If he looked closely, would he see some of his own features on her face?

He got out of bed and dressed before he realized he had no idea where he planned to go. Everyone else in the manse would be asleep by now. Isabella might be bedded down with her brother. But it wasn't Isabella he wanted to see or talk to. No, he wanted merely to be near Teresa. She wouldn't have to say or do anything to give him the strength he needed for the next day's activities.

The moon sprayed his room with enough light for him to find a candle. When he lit the wick, the candle flickered, almost blowing itself out, but he covered the wick with his hand and the flame finally took. Opening his door, he listened for other footsteps. He didn't want to encounter his aunt, but unlike previous nights, there was no sign of her.

He made his way carefully to the servants' part of the manse, the narrow stairs and halls uncomfortable for his large frame. Señora Toledo had mentioned to him that Teresa would be occupying the room across from Jose's. As a child Luis had spent many hours hidden away inside Jose's room when he couldn't bear his mother's sulkiness. Luis heaved a huge sigh, knowing this was not the proper thing to be doing. Maybe he should rap on the coachman's door instead. They could have several drinks together, falling asleep in one of their shared drunken stupors. The idea disgusted him. Besides, he needed the sharpness of his intellect for the next day, when he would go head-to-head with the Inquisitor.

Luis laid his hand on the badly marred door that separated him from Teresa. He set an ear against the portal to listen for any sound indicating she, too, lay awake. But there was nothing, not even the sound of her breath.

"Teresa," he whispered. Speaking the name filled him with the urge to rip the door off its hinges to reach her. His hand lowered to grasp the handle. The servants were not allowed locks, their privacy considered a trivial matter. But Teresa was neither a servant nor a domestic slave. She came borrowed from the convent, the nuns sparing her only because of the money his father had donated to the Church. He could not trespass on Teresa's privacy; whether she be of the Church or hired help, she had his full respect.

Luis turned away but noticed one of the other doors in the hall stood ajar.

"Hello?" he whispered softly.

The door quickly closed.

Unsure to whom the room belonged, Luis decided to ignore the Peeping Tom. Thank God, he thought, he hadn't taken the liberty of invading Teresa's room, or else the breakfast talk the next morning would have been quite lively.

How stupid he had been. Luis shook his head and returned to his room, where he slept for merely an hour or two.

chapter 49

Hired guards stood in front of the Inquisitor's residence. The Inquisitor himself always demanded soldiers from the state whenever he traveled. Too many families had lost loved ones for Torquemada to chance the roads alone with his clerics. A number of stories traveled about, describing Torquemada's odd behaviors, the strangest being his eating habits. It was said that the Inquisitor never ate a meal without a unicorn's horn next to his plate to defend himself against possible poisons. A strange superstition for a cleric of the Church, Luis thought.

A woman dragged at the sleeve of his shirt, begging for coins, her dirt-stained hands and face pleading for alms. When she opened her mouth, he saw no teeth, and her breath contaminated the air with the smell of stagnant waste.

"I have babes at home," she said, her lips chapped with peeling flesh.

Noticing how well Luis was dressed, the guards approached the woman to chase her away. She cringed as the shadow of one of the guards blocked the light of the sun.

"She's all right," Luis said. "I have a spare coin for her." He immediately placed the *maravedi* into her palm, but the coin slipped and fell onto the dusty road. The guard kicked the coin, and the woman scrambled across the ground pursuing it.

Luis wanted to complain to the guard, but before he could, he heard the voice of the bishop calling to him.

"We shouldn't keep Torquemada waiting. He can quickly change his mind if he feels slighted." The bishop waved for Luis to follow, his rotund body swaying with each step.

At the door a guard bowed to the bishop before inquiring about Luis.

"He has an appointment with the Inquisitor and is my guest." The guard stepped back and allowed the bishop to ring the bell.

A hunchback answered the door. He wore the black-and-white rough woolen cowl of the Dominicans. His deformed bare feet caused an unsteadiness to his gait. But his hands were exquisite. The blemish-free white flesh and long slender fingers looked feminine. Obviously the man did not engage in hard labor. He spoke Spanish with an accent Luis could not place.

The two men followed the hunchback across a shiny marble floor into a room filled with books. A flag lay spread across a long table. Luis looked closely at the centerpiece of the flag.

"You must surely recognize that, Señor Velez." The Grand Inquisitor Torquemada came from the shadows of the library. "That is the flag of the Inquisition, a green cross of knotted wood with the olive branch signifying forgiveness and reconciliation. Do you know what the sword on the flag stands for?"

"Eternal justice."

"Correct, Señor Velez. Eternal justice. I'm afraid the words are begining to wear off. The flag has been used numerous times, unfortunately. *'Exurge Domine et Judica causam tuam.'*"

"'Rise up, Master, and pursue your cause!' Psalm 73:27," Luis translated.

"I'm certainly impressed," said Torquemada, looking more disappointed than impressed. "Your Jewish father made sure you studied your religious lessons well."

"My father is Catholic, as you well know, Inquisitor."

"So the bishop here has told me. Frequently he reminds me of your father's generosity, but then the bishop has been the recipient of quite a bit of it." Torquemada stretched out an arm and placed it on the bishop's shoulders, revealing the hair shirt he wore under his Dominican habit. "The Church and the bishop are truly thankful to your family."

"My father believes it his duty to assist the Church in feeding the poor and caring for the sick."

"Yes, I have heard that you have a caretaker nursing your own father right now. The nuns were kind enough to give her to you. An orphan, I believe she is."

Luis did not want to discuss Teresa with Torquemada. He wished to keep her away from the Inquisitor's eyes.

"I appreciate this visit you have allowed. Our family is very fond of Catrin, and we fear that one of her enemies may have given false testimony against her."

"Everyone claims the evidence to be false. The Church must be careful in evaluating the truth or falsehood. Your Catrin is charged with being a witch."

"Even the Church considers witches to be simply a pagan superstition," Luis responded.

"Ah, Señor Velez, in 1494 the *Repertorium Inquisitorum* recognized the existence of witches. It is well known that witches have had carnal intercourse with the devil in the form of a goat. They suck the blood of children to give themselves strength and dabble in powders to control and kill their victims."

"I don't think Luis meant to imply that witches didn't exist." The bishop interposed himself between Luis and the Inquisitor. "Perhaps he finds it difficult to accept that witchcraft may have been practiced inside his own home. Catrin may have used her powers on members of the household to control her environment and to cloud the family's rationality."

Rational. Luis felt quite rational, but he did have some questions about the rationality of the Church.

"I had hoped that by now, Señor Velez, you would have perceived major changes in your household. Some have talked of a heavy darkness pervading the mood of your house. Could it be that Catrin was not the only one communing with the devil?"

"My home is sad, Inquisitor. My father is very ill and has been for some time. Laughter and cheer is something we long for, but are unable to attain with death so near."

"Ah, yes, I am sorry. Does your father worsen? Is there no sign of health returning to him?"

"No. I have tried to retain hope, but all that is left for me now is prayer."

"Prayer is the best comfort you can afford yourself." Torquemada took Luis's hand in both of his. "I will pray for your family and ask the Lord to do His will, but to give all in the household the strength to bear His pleasure."

"Thank you, Inquisitor. You are certainly kind to remember my household, given all the important decisions you yourself must make."

Torquemada nodded and released Luis's hand.

"My scribe, Hugo, will accompany us on your visit to Catrin," Torquemada said.

Luis immediately looked to the bishop, who turned away.

The hunchback limped forward carrying a sheaf of paper, a quill, and a small jar of ink. His face remained somber; barely a snippet of tonsure surrounded his head. Hugo's pale blue eyes shone like a thin layer of ice reflecting the sun on a bright winter's day. His blunt features made him appear ugly, for so readily they seemed to blend into each other.

"Why do we need a scribe, Inquisitor?" Luis asked.

"In case something is said that is worth writing down.

Would you please lead, Bishop, for you certainly know the way. Oh, and would you mind lighting the lantern on the table and carrying it with you?"

The bishop did as requested, then walked out into the hall, followed by the scribe and Torquemada. Luis slowed his pace in order to remain the last in the line. As the bishop approached a heavy door, he whipped out a linen handkerchief, which he held to his nose as he opened the door with a great heave. The refuse of human waste poured forth from the cellar, but Torquemada and the scribe didn't wince.

From behind the linen handkerchief the bishop asked Luis whether he wanted to proceed.

"Of course, Bishop." He held his head high and thought he caught a slight smirk pass across the Inquisitor's face.

The staircase was extreme in its slant, causing the men to turn slightly sideways in order not to miss a step. No banister aided in the descent, and the farther down they went, the stronger the odor became. A milky scum traveled down the side wall, dripping onto most of the steps, making them dangerously slippery. The hunchback's bare feet slapped against the stone while Luis's boots brought about a loud clicking echo.

At the foot of the stairs, two large men sat at a table, one bare chested, the other wearing an old shirt peppered with stains that could have been blood. The pope had stated that the Inquisitors could draw no blood from the prisoners, but Luis doubted Torquemada worried about a visit from the papal clerics.

The bare-chested man stood, his height and build astoundingly large, making him a frightening creature to have hovering over anyone. His belt clinked with the sound of keys.

"We are here to visit Catrin, my son." Torquemada kept his hands folded in front of him.

The man grunted and bowed before leading the foursome down a hall lined with bars. Within each cage at least one poor soul huddled, their faces buried within their own arms, attempting to lock the world out. Luis knew each feared being the next one to be questioned. Many suffered dysentery and sat with overflowing buckets.

"This is a pigsty," Luis mumbled.

Only the bishop acknowledged him by warning against comment with his eyes.

They came to an area of wooden doors. Each door had a small square cut out to pass food and waste. The bare-chested man removed the keys from his waist, flipping through them one by one until he located the correct key. As the lock turned, Luis thought he heard someone from within cry out in fright. The hinges creaked, and the bare-chested man had to stoop low in order to enter the small room.

"Thank you, my son. You may remain outside while we speak to Catrin." The Inquisitor's voice left no room for refusal. The bare-chested man exited and stood to the side to allow the others into the room. "Close the door," the Inquisitor said once everyone had entered.

The door squeaked closed, and the bishop raised the lantern high in the air in order to see the contents of the windowless room. Hay lay piled high in one corner of the room. Luis recognized the flowery scarf he had given to Catrin resting atop the hay, the ends of the material frayed and the colors muted by dirt.

"Come, Catrin, you have a visitor. Someone, I'm sure, you've missed." The Inquisitor moved the bishop's arm, causing the light to fall on a distant corner.

Catrin's bent knees poked out from under her skirt, the bulge of the knees exaggerated in the thinness of her form.

"Haven't you been feeding her?" Luis asked, attempting to move forward, but he was held back by the arm of the bishop.

"In an act of penance, each heretic must be limited in the amount of food they ingest. This is not the site of a banquet, Señor Velez."

With the sound of his name, Catrin looked up at the men, her eyes squinting to accustom themselves to the flame of the lantern. She held up a hand to block the brightness, studying each figure carefully. When she recognized Luis, she rose to her feet and extended her arms.

In a hushed whisper, the bishop warned Luis against answering her plea, but Luis cast the bishop's arm aside and crossed the room to embrace his sister and lover. His arms enfolded what felt like a sack of bones that smelled of sweat, fear, and urine.

"Let them," said Torquemada, putting out a hand to

keep the bishop from separating the two reunited people. "It's been a long time since they've been able to touch. They seem so starved for each other. Wouldn't you agree?"

"Señor Luis Velez has a great deal of compassion for those who work for him."

"Does he greet everyone like this?"

"He understands that Catrin has been under a strain the past few months."

Torquemada stood, searching the floor.

"A stool, Hugo."

The hunchback immediately made the request of the man guarding the door.

"How are you, Catrin?" Luis whispered in her ear. Her greasy hair clung to the side of his face. Her fingers tried hard to grip his clothes, but were too weak. "Catrin, my father has made many mistakes." He halted his speech, knowing that the clerics listened to every word. He heard the stool hit the stone floor.

"Ah, thank you, my son." Torquemada sat, slowly arranging his Dominican garb carefully around himself.

Luis turned to the Inquisitor and asked what exactly the charges were against Catrin.

"Witchcraft."

"But what has she done to deserve such allegations?"

"That is secret, Señor Velez. We must protect those who inform us of heretical actions."

"But surely you can give me some sort of detail. My father and I have already deduced that one of our staff has testified against Catrin."

"There may be more than one person involved in this."

"At least tell me what Hilaria said."

"Ask her yourself if you must, but do be careful, Señor Velez, that you don't implicate anyone else in this matter."

"Are you threatening my family?"

"How could I do that? No, only your own words and actions can do that."

The scribe adjusted his sheaf of paper and knelt down on the floor the better to write. The bottle of ink stood near his writing hand.

"I had hoped to have time alone with Catrin."

"Alone. Is there something you need to keep hidden from the Holy Mother Church?" Torquemada brought his hands together in an act of prayer.

"No one at the Velez manse has secrets from the Church. I myself have dined at their table and had my fill of roasts of pork and usually on the night before our Sabbath." The bishop lowered the lantern to appraise the look on the Inquisitor's face. "I'm sure you could speak to the girl sent by the convent to care for Luis's father. She doesn't seem at all uncomfortable within the walls of the Velez home."

"What is her name again?" The Inquisitor raised a hand to prepare Hugo to copy the information.

"She has only recently arrived, Inquisitor. Certainly there can't be anything for her to add to this matter. Catrin and she have never met." Luis tried to intercede.

"Teresa is her name. She wears her rosary about her neck," said the bishop.

"For protection, no doubt," Torquemada said.

"No harm has come to her, I assure you. If she were unhappy, she would have spoken to me about it on one of my visits." The bishop stood erect; only the lantern wavered slightly in his hand. "Luis's father cannot have much time left. He has lost much weight and is currently bedridden. Those within the manse attempt to be quiet, for they do not want to disturb the poor man."

"The poor man is readying himself for the next world, no doubt." Torquemada looked up into the bishop's eyes, obviously searching for lies.

"He and I pray together whenever I visit."

"Is that often?"

"I have many duties, as you know, and cannot spare as much time as I would prefer."

Catrin buried her face in Luis's chest, and he rested a hand on the back of her head.

"Catrin, is there anything that you need? Father and I have been worried about you. When you come home, life will be different."

"In what way will her life be different, Señor Velez?" The Inquisitor leaned forward to better hear the answer.

"I meant that she would not have to live in a hovel like this."

"Ah, you mean she can return to the glorious life of a servant."

"Our servants are well cared for, Inquisitor. I assure you this cell in no way resembles the way our staff live."

"But they do seem a bit discontented. You have said

yourself that one of your servants spoke against Catrin. Why would the servant do that?"

"Have you asked Hilaria?"

"Shh, we do not speak the names of witnesses here in front of the accused." The Inquisitor stood.

"Why not? Shouldn't Catrin have the opportunity to defend herself?"

"What if Catrin should find a way to cast a spell on the witness? Oh, no, Señor Velez, we protect those who defend the Church."

"This is nonsense." Luis pulled Catrin away from his chest in order to look into her face. "Tell him, Catrin. Tell him you have no supernatural powers, for if you did, you certainly wouldn't have allowed the Church to lock you up in this sewer."

Catrin's eyes filled with tears, and her lips trembled, forming words she did not speak.

"Speak, Catrin. I am here with you. Tell them you've been falsely accused."

Catrin attempted to free her arms from Luis's grasp, shaking her head wildly.

"Catrin, speak at least to me."

Grunts issued from her mouth as she opened her mouth wide for Luis to see that her tongue had been cut out.

"My God, what have you done to her?" Luis let her go and moved in the direction of the Inquisitor, but the bishop intervened. Suddenly he heard the scratch of pen against paper and looked down to see the hunchback writing down the actions he observed. "And what the hell is the scribe for, if she can't speak?"

"Keep calm, Luis," the bishop whispered. "Else neither Catrin nor you will ever leave this place."

"First, Señor Velez, when Catrin entered this cell, she ranted on, blaspheming the Lord with her foul tongue. She was given adequate warning and did not heed it. One of our guards was forced to remove the weapon she wielded against the Church."

Luis looked back at Catrin, but she had already scurried to the far wall and hid among the dark shadows. He heard her muted crying and saw the flash of her foot as she squashed her body into a tighter ball.

"Secondly, as to Hugo's presence. I never said that he would take down what Catrin said. No, Señor Velez, we were more interested in what you had to say."

"This is a trap then!" Luis shouted.

"Quiet, Luis, remember your father is ill in bed and cannot take another setback. You would not want him to die because of a careless word you said." The bishop kept his voice low, turning his head occasionally to view the hunchback who continued to write furiously.

"How can you call this a trap, Señor Velez, when it was you who requested this visit? And, I think, it is time to depart and allow Catrin some time to consider what has happened here today."

"Please, Bishop." Luis raised the bishop's arm higher to throw more light into the cell. He found Catrin shaken and tiny, her arms wrapped around herself, her legs drawn up into her chest. He squatted to speak with her. "I will tell Father that I've seen you. If we must pay for your release, we will, no matter what the cost."

Her head gently leaned against his chest, her eyes closed, imagining a better time. She rested a hand where she heard the beat of his heart and kissed the exact spot with her parched lips.

"I wish I could take you with me now."

Her lips crinkled into a smile, and her eyes opened to memorize his face. She reached her body up, allowing her lips to touch his softly. He heard the hunchback's impudent gasp and the further scribble of the man's damnable pen.

"Let's go, Luis. Your father will be worried if you don't return soon." The bishop rested a hand on Luis's shoulder; as he did, Catrin shrank back away from Luis.

"The bishop is right. Hugo, have the guard remove the stool."

"Can you not leave it? The floor is cold, and she wears so little. Let her at least have the stool." Luis didn't bother to look over his shoulder at the Inquisitor. He heard the awkward movements of the hunchback as he slid the stool to the door and called for the guard. "Is there nothing I can give you, Catrin, to give you hope?"

She tilted her head to the side and reached a hand out to touch his hair. Luis tore a clump of hair from his scalp and placed it into her small palm. Immediately she closed her fingers about the strands and brought them to her lips to kiss. Her smile quivered until she finally bowed her head and he took leave.

chapter 50

Twilight hovered over Luis as he turned his horse into the barn. Jose quickly took the reins, and Luis dismounted, his body heavy. His feet hit the ground with a loud thud.

"Catrin, she is still . . ." Jose stopped upon seeing the look on Luis's face.

"Catrin will never be herself again. We will never hear our names on her lips."

"She is not dead."

"No. The Inquisitor wishes to continue our tortures." Luis walked to the barn doors and stopped. "Have you seen Teresa?"

"She is probably with your father. The doctor refused to visit today. He claimed to be much too busy with other patients."

Luis smiled to himself wickedly. From where he stood, his father's bedroom window was clearly visible, but the shutters were closed, and he could view no movement inside the room. He would have to tell his father about what he had seen. He would not keep anything secret from the old man. His father should know the pain his actions had caused for others. And Teresa, the saint, would be present. He would like to hear her defense of the Church.

Inside the house Gaspar asked when dinner should be served, but Luis ignored the question and climbed the stairs with a slow gait. Gaspar knew him well enough to leave the question unanswered.

"You are back, Luis." His father lay propped against several pillows, his arms resting on bundled blankets. "Teresa, you may go."

"No. I want her to stay, Father."

"But this matter doesn't concern her. She needn't—"

"You've managed to include her in our personal lives. Why not continue to do so?"

"Because, Luis, she is not family."

Teresa rose from her chair.

"Sit, Teresa. I want you to know what my father's selfishness has set in motion."

She looked at his father, who didn't bother to turn his head to her. She sat and stared down at her hands folded in her lap.

"Father must have told you that I visited Catrin today." He watched Teresa nod her head. "Did he mention what he expected me to find?"

She looked at the old man.

"Leave her be, Luis. Why do you want to embarrass the girl with your morose stories?"

"Morose stories? Is this just a story to you, Father? Or are we talking about your own flesh and blood? My sister."

"Your spy said they hadn't tortured her." Roberto's eyes filled with concern.

"They merely are starving her and letting her sit in her own waste. The hay she uses for a bed is infested with lice and fleas. Her cell is so dark that a simple lantern is too bright now for her eyes."

"But she is whole, Luis."

"No. They've cut out her tongue."

Immediately Teresa's hand went up to her mouth. Luis regretted making her stay. What had he been trying to prove? Why make her suffer, too? Just because she had been raised in a convent, Teresa had nothing to do with what the Inquisition did.

"I must apologize, Teresa, for my son's cruelty. What he has seen today has warped his reason, I'm sure. Is that not true, Luis?"

"Yes, you are right. You may go, Teresa. You needn't bear any more of this burden."

Teresa rose and looked at both men.

"I am sorry for the ordeal you both suffer. If there is any way for me to help you, do not hesitate to ask."

"Can those nuns entreat Torquemada to give us back our Catrin?" Roberto Velez's hand waved in the air. "No, Teresa, I already know the answer. Our darling Catrin will burn at the stake as a warning to our friends and neighbors."

"That's ridiculous, Father. She hasn't done anything wrong."

"It's been, what . . . ? Three months since the last *auto da fe*. It is almost time for another display of the Church's power. Torquemada has no mercy, Luis. I pray that I am dead, for I never want to hear the crowd's jeers directed at my Catrin."

"I won't let them burn her at the stake."

"How will you stop them, Luis? You can only make trouble for yourself. Be glad you were able to see her one last time."

"You give up only because you're a dying old man." Luis's eyes flashed fire. "The bishop will help us. He saw Catrin. He knows how badly she's being treated."

"The bishop is Torquemada's accomplice. He will not put his own life on the line, and neither should you." Roberto's voice sounded weary.

"She can't even speak to defend herself."

"And that's exactly the way Torquemada wants it. She will kiss the hem of his robes and be gifted with strangulation before the fire ever reaches her, if she is wise."

Luis threw a look of disgust at his father, and with long strides left the room with Teresa close behind. In the hall she called to him. He stopped but didn't face her. Instead she walked around him to confront him.

"I will speak to the sisters. Perhaps they will be able to give me some advice on this matter. If not, I will help you myself as much as I can."

He scooped her face into his hands and kissed her

lips. Her hands flattened against his chest, but she didn't push him away. When he backed away from her, he glimpsed the confusion and passion in her face.

"Teresa, I want you to promise to avoid any connection to Catrin. Don't even speak of this to the nuns. I would go mad should the Inquisition get you in their clutches. Do you understand?"

Teresa stood dumb, unable to react to what she had just heard. Luis didn't force an answer from her. He turned away to enter his own room.

chapter 51

TERESA STAGGERED OVER TO A LONG TABLE where several vases sat filled with flowers. The roses had been replaced by a panoply of colorful wildflowers, and their scent made her swoon. The sweetness filled her senses with visions of the outdoors, with the blue heavens stretched above her head offering their protection. She remembered hills she had climbed as a child, Sister Roberta's hand firmly clutching a bouquet that Teresa had collected as a surprise for Sister Agatha. "These are quite enough," Sister Roberta had insisted, but Teresa wanted to stay on the hills for as long as she could, the stuffiness of the convent a faraway memory in the outdoors.

"He saw her, didn't he?"

Teresa took hold of the edge of the table, stiffening her back. Isabella's wrinkled hand touched hers.

"Is she coming back to us soon? Did he say?"

"I'm so sorry, Isabella." Teresa's voice cracked.

"What are you sorry for? Isn't Catrin coming home? This is her home now, you know."

"She wants to come home, I'm sure."

"Then why doesn't she?"

Teresa swallowed her words. What could she tell Isabella about her child?

"Your knuckles are so white. Why must you grip the table so tightly?" Isabella clawed at Teresa's hands. "Look at me. Tell me what my nephew said."

"Oh, Isabella, you and your brother are paying dearly for the sins you both committed."

"What sins? We loved. Was that a sin? Come, look at everything we've done for our daughter." Isabella pulled on Teresa's forearms, trying to move her down the hall to the nursery.

"That room will remain forever empty." Tears blurred Teresa's vision. "Poor Catrin will pay the greatest price for all the years of incest you shared with your brother." Teresa felt her heart hardening. She didn't want to turn her back on Isabella or the old man, but she found it difficult to control the rising anger in her. "Did you think of anyone else when you bedded down with your brother? His wife did nothing to you. She married a man chosen for her by her family. All she wanted was to be loved and to have her children."

"A sow! She smelled. He couldn't lie with a sow. Sometimes I could smell my brother on her. I pitied him even when he came to my bed smelling of her stench."

"They were husband and wife. Blessed by the Church."

"Breeding. He needed heirs. She was meant for breeding, and she couldn't even do that well."

"Not with you poisoning her."

Isabella contorted her face into a mask of horror, her features melting into demonic ugliness. Her arms reached out, but Teresa quickly moved away.

"The sow's child kisses your lips tenderly, and you stand stunned, unable to respond. You're no woman. Your breasts are sacred. If he should touch them, you'd scream, not from pleasure, but from fear. Only that odious rosary you wear will ever feel the rise and fall of your passion. What is it like kneeling before an invisible groom? Isn't that what the nuns call God? Aren't they married to chastity for life?

"I know what man-woman love is. The touch of flesh against flesh. The sweetness of his breath mingling with my own. The thrill of having him in my grasp, attentive to my every move, to the curves and heat of my body."

"And what did he do, Isabella, when you presented him with a child?" Teresa's own heart stung with the sound of her words. Why did she stoop to the old woman's level?

"My baby. He'll bring my baby back. The room . . ." Isabella turned to look down the hall at the nursery door. "She'll sleep there."

"Not in that cradle."

Isabella nodded her head. Her hands had fallen to her sides, and her face went limp with pain. "She'll sleep in that room. I'll have Roberto replace every stick of furniture. She'll have the best of clothes. Men will court her, vying for a smile from her lips, for their names upon her tongue."

Suddenly Teresa became physically ill, the gorge in her throat rising into her mouth. She swallowed back the ill-tasting mass, thinking how she would have to always keep the truth from Isabella.

"She'll come home, won't she?" Isabella asked, her face now heralding her innocence.

Teresa stood looking at the old woman. No words came to her lips, no comfort for a mother without a babe.

Isabella turned to the flowers and selected the most colorful, the freshest for a bouquet.

"What are you doing, Isabella?"

"I must begin the alterations. First, there must be flowers." She looked at Teresa. "I don't know her favorites. Should I amass every flower known and line the house with them? You must find out for me what she prefers. I know you can. Luis will do anything for you. I saw the way he kissed you. Much too gently, perhaps, but he will become braver if you do."

How can the woman change so rapidly? Teresa wondered. *One minute she is threatening me, and the next she is befriending me.* With the bouquet complete, Isabella breathed in deeply to catch the multitude of scents.

"Have you ever gotten flowers?" Isabella asked coyly, looking over her shoulder.

"No." Teresa had made many bouquets for the sick, for the nuns' birthdays, but not a single flower had ever existed just for her pleasure.

"Why not?"

"No one has ever wanted to give me flowers. Perhaps

I don't look like a flower person."

"What is a flower person? I suppose corpses are flower people, but they can't enjoy them."

"I think it makes those left behind feel better. It's a family's last gift to a loved one."

"What good is a gift after one is dead? I want to give Catrin everything I can while she is alive. I want her to love me while I can feel the warmth of that love. Waiting for someone to die to give them a gift is silly."

"It's the last gift, Isabella. We give our time, our love, and our material possessions during life, but when someone close to us dies, we need to offer them a departing gift."

"Who is the 'we' you are talking about?"

"The nuns I lived with. The families I helped when they needed me. All of us do for each other."

"So much prattle. I care only about Roberto and Catrin." Isabella spun around to face Teresa. "Catrin must come home before her father dies. She mustn't miss being at his deathbed. I suppose you plan on being there, too. That's all right. I give my permission."

"What are you going to do with those flowers, Isabella?"

Isabella looked down at the bouquet she held in her arms as if surprised to find it there.

"I'll bring them in to Roberto and tell him all about my plans. He'll make a fuss, but I know how to tease him into agreeing. I've done that many times before, you know."

"He may be tired."

"He's never tired when he sees me. I brighten his room, and so will these," Isabella said, looking down at the flowers. She danced over toward the old man's bedroom door, fussing constantly with her dress and hair until she reached the door. She entered without knocking, kicking the door shut with one foot, a young girl still in her ancient body.

Teresa didn't have the energy to stop the older woman. Señor Roberto would have to bear his sister's fantasy world for a few minutes. He'd probably nod off during her prolonged speech about an impossible future.

She heard the squeak of a door being ever so slowly opened. Isabella's long white fingers clutched the wooden bedroom door, her face appearing drawn, her body tense, the opposite of her stance just moments previously when she had entered the room.

"He is very quiet," Isabella said. "His hands are warm, but he won't talk to me. I'm not sure he hears a word I say. He stares up at the ceiling, and when I put my face over his, he sees something beyond me."

Teresa moved quickly, gently pushing the old woman out of the way. At Roberto's bed she stopped short. His pillow had fallen to the side, leaving his head in an awkward position. His fingers lay intertwined upon his chest, the palms limply falling to the side. Upon examination she confirmed the obvious. Señor Roberto was dead.

She sketched the shape of the cross on his forehead before making the sign of the cross on herself.

chapter 52

THE SUN FILLED THE FAMILY GRAVEYARD WITH bright light. Many had attended the funeral mass, but only a few friends stood at the site of Señor Roberto Velez's burial. Some shaded their faces with their hands to watch the slow procession carry the coffin. Others closed their eyes to the sunlight and to the last sight of the casket. Most of the friends present were elderly and remembered Señor Roberto Velez's youth as well as their own. The servants stood in back of the small crowd, looking chastised rather than sorrowful. All probably wondered how this event would affect their employment. Manuel kept fidgeting, scratching his head, rubbing his nose, hopping on one foot and then the other, until Jose gave him a powerful nudge, sending the boy off balance and into the procession. Quickly he righted himself and got back into line with the other servants. Teresa drew the boy close to her, slipping him into the center of the group where he wouldn't be noticed.

The bishop, dressed in formal vestments, preceded the

coffin carried by Luis and carefully chosen friends. Isabella
followed the coffin, weeping into a black lace handkerchief;
occasionally she would command the pallbearers to take
care with her brother's body even though there seemed to
be no danger that the six men would drop the frail body
within the wooden coffin. Fresh flowers covered the lid of
the coffin, all wild and chosen by Isabella.

The crowd stepped aside to allow the procession to
lay the coffin at the edge of the gravesite. Several flowers
slipped to the ground, but Isabella swiftly restored them
to the lid of the casket, shaping the flowers into a specific
order known only to her. When she stepped back, she
almost fell into the grave, except that Luis had remained
alert to her every move and directed her to solid ground.

One altar boy carried an aspergillum to spray the
holy water around the coffin. The other altar boy waved
the censer, spreading incense throughout the small
crowd. The bishop opened his missal and began the
words to the rite.

Originally when the bishop had been called to Señor
Roberto Velez's deathbed, he was disappointed because
the dead man had not been able to make a last confession.
The bishop verbalized his doubts about whether the
dead man could receive a proper Christian burial. After
all, Señor Roberto Velez had converted to the Catholic
Church from Judaism. Had his conversion been true, or
had he still retained allegiance to the religion into which
he had been born? Teresa had sensed the threat in the
bishop's words and knew that he feared acting in a way

not approved of by the Inquisitor. Luis had reminded the bishop of the years of friendship his father and the bishop had shared, and embarrassed somewhat by the memories, the bishop agreed to give the dead man the sacrament of Extreme Unction, but he warned against having a high mass. Instead, the mass had been simple. There had been no hymns or even the distribution of Communion.

Now the bishop moved through the ceremony confidently, or at least that seemed to be his demeanor. Teresa gave the responses quickly while the others lagged behind. She knew that most of the friends present were also *conversos*, and perhaps they hadn't learned the ceremonies the way children brought up inside a religion would. Every word she knew by heart, for the nuns often attended funerals for the poor or homeless who died on the streets of the city.

She heard the cook blow her nose and turned to see whether the woman had real tears on her cheeks. The woman's face and nose were red, but that could have been due to a cold, thought Teresa. Immediately she said an Act of Contrition, knowing that her thought had been unkind.

Isabella leaned against her nephew, his arm firmly set around her body, not only holding her up but keeping her from making an unseemly scene. A scene that was inevitable.

Ropes were placed under the coffin to lower it into the grave. The bishop stood aside, and Luis had to release his aunt to help the men with his father's casket. In but a brief moment, Isabella had thrown her body across the coffin and wailed in a high pitch, causing many to cover their ears.

"My brother!" she screamed. "My lover! The father of my child!"

For some reason Isabella had decided it was time to reveal all.

Isabella looked up into Luis's face and spoke in a tortured voice. "He'll never see our baby again. I wanted Catrin to see her father one last time. Why isn't she here? Why haven't you brought her home?"

Luis attempted to raise her up to her feet, but she flailed about. Many of the flowers had stuck to her black satin dress, squashed into petals. Teresa assisted Luis, capturing the woman's arms in her own, holding them close to her chest.

"Please, Isabella, don't do this to your nephew," Teresa whispered into the old woman's ear.

"He's the sow's babe, not mine." Isabella's words came out in a hiss, sounding like a serpent. "The sow will win even now, long after her death. My child lies imprisoned while her son inherits the land."

Teresa tried to hush the woman by pulling her closer. Suddenly the bishop knelt next to them, leaning into their bodies, a crucifix raised up in his hand.

"Isabella," he said softly. "Kiss the crucifix in memory of your brother. For his salvation."

Is he mad? thought Teresa.

Isabella twisted around and spat on the crucifix. The bishop stood with the crucifix still outstretched, the spit glimmering under the sun.

Teresa checked the faces looking in their direction. All remained quiet. A few turned their heads away in shock. Others grew pale, knowing what this action would precipitate.

She noticed Luis's hands clench into fists and feared for a brief moment he would act on his anger. Instead he leaned over and picked his aunt up to carry her into the house.

"Shall we begin or wait for Luis?" asked one of the men still holding the rope. The people in the crowd turned to look at each other, and the bishop finally lowered the crucifix. His face was pale. He looked ill.

Had the Inquisitor ordered him to make a show of a member of the household? she wondered. *Perhaps the bishop had no choice.* It would be alarming if that were true, for it would be but days before the Inquisition's guards showed at the Velez door.

chapter 53

AT MIDNIGHT TERESA FOUND ISABELLA ENSCONCED in the nursery. The elderly woman diapered the large doll that usually sat on a high shelf. The porcelain doll looked delicate, the face painted in pale shades, its eyes wide and brown with a small round mouth that begged for a bottle. Isabella looked up and hushed Teresa.

"She just stopped crying. She misses her father terribly. I don't know whether she'll ever be able to smile again. All her tears are here in this handkerchief." Isabella held up the black lace handkerchief she herself had used at the grave side. "I'll keep it here close to my heart." She placed the handkerchief down the bosom of her dress.

Teresa knelt down beside Isabella and watched quietly, not wanting to break the elderly woman's concentration.

"Tomorrow I'll take her out into the sun. It will be her first time, but she desperately wants to see where her father lies. Will they put a cross over his grave, Teresa?"

"That is up to you and your nephew."

"No, it's not. The Church will make its demands, and Luis will follow their orders. This family hasn't thought for itself in a long time. We follow rules we don't understand. Roberto always said we didn't have a choice. He asked us if we wanted to live in this big house or wanted to find ourselves crowded together in a coach headed for a land we had never seen before. That frightened me, Teresa. Seeing a foreign country. What would we eat? How would we communicate with shopkeepers and physicians? His sow cried. I stopped crying when Catrin began to grow inside my belly." Her hand rested against her body, rubbing the black satin in small round circles. "My womb grew and grew until Roberto told me not to go out in public. This Church of yours would call it a sin. Is having a child a sin?"

"No, Isabella, it is not a sin."

"Then why did Roberto worry? I told him a baby brought joy, but he shook his head. He let me decorate this room. Every object, I chose. I would have none of Luis's hand-me-downs." Isabella picked up the doll with one hand and smoothed the cradle's sheets with the other before laying the doll carefully on the infant-sized pillow.

Teresa saw tears touch the porcelain face of the doll. She wrapped her arms around the elderly woman.

"Giving birth to her caused me the worst pain I've ever had, but I'd do it again and again for the babe that lay briefly in my arms. Will he rise from the dead?"

"Who?" Teresa whispered, her lips almost touching the woman's white hair.

"My brother. Your Christ rose from the dead, and He brought Lazarus back from the dead. Won't He give Roberto back to me?"

"At the end of the world, we'll all rise again."

"I can't wait that long."

Teresa smiled. "Your brother will come to you when you die. He'll bring you before God for judgment."

With fright in her eyes, Isabella looked into Teresa's face.

"But the Lord is all-merciful, Isabella. He will forgive you."

"What if He doesn't? Will He punish me by forcing me to live forever without Roberto? I couldn't bear that."

"You'll see your brother again, Isabella, and he'll look healthier and stronger than when you last saw him."

"Will he be young again?"

"Possibly."

"And what about me? I want Roberto to still want me. Your God will make me young again, too?"

"You'll be beautiful, and all the fears and troubles you've had will be gone."

"And Catrin. Where will she be?"

Teresa's body stiffened, a terrible chill speeding through her body. Would Catrin still be imprisoned inside the Inquisitor's dungeon? Or would Luis somehow manage to have her freed into his care? The performance put on by the bishop at the funeral did not bode well for the Velez household.

Isabella shook Teresa's sleeve.

"What do you see, girl? Will my daughter join her father and mother in your God's heaven?"

"Why do you call Him 'my God'? He belongs to everyone, no matter what words are used in His praise. The ritual isn't important. It's the intent of the person's prayers."

"Are you saying the God I knew as a child is the same God who tortures people today?"

"Man mistreats man, not God, Isabella. God is merciful." Teresa swept the palm of her right hand across Isabella's cheek, catching the droplets of tears before they fell.

"Your God . . ."

"Our God, Isabella."

"Our God does not approve of what the holy men of your religion do?"

Teresa's eyes searched the dark room. She knew what heresy was. Often she had skirted the fine line when she delivered food and clothing to those left behind by the people the Church called heretics. But the nuns had not believed that God would want so many to suffer, especially the children, still innocent and hopeful of salvation.

"Perhaps the Inquisition is a special trial that God is using to test the faith in all of us."

"What has Catrin done that she must be tested?"

"I can't speak for God, Isabella. We can pray together that Catrin will find peace."

"Death will bring her peace," Isabella said.

"I didn't mean she should die. Let us pray she'll be released and come back home."

"Her father is gone."

"She still has a mother who loves her very much. Remember how you gave me some of that love to share with Roberto and Luis?" Isabella nodded. "You kept some in your heart for when Catrin returned. Isn't it there still?"

Isabella smiled. Her tongue licked her lips shyly while she nodded her head.

"Keep it safe, Isabella. Don't let anyone take it away from you."

"I couldn't continue to survive without that love," Isabella said.

chapter 54

EARLY THE NEXT MORNING BEFORE BREAKFAST, Luis called for Teresa. He waited in the library as he usually chose to do. Instead of pacing he sat in a chair by the window, staring out at the overcast day. It had not yet rained, but the building storm clouds promised a deluge.

"Señor Velez, you wanted to speak with me?" Teresa stood at the door, waiting to be invited into the room.

"Come, sit down on the settee."

She walked slowly, the house's bereavement still lingering in the air.

"I'm watching the swelling clouds and wondering whether the heavens are preparing to cry for my father. Is that puerile of me?"

"Not at all, but there would be nothing wrong in your feeling childlike right now. You've had a major loss, Señor Velez."

"I'm an orphan now, like Manuel. Only my father has seen to my needs with this house and the *maravedíes* he left me. I need not sweep barns housing horses belonging to someone else. Sometimes when I watch Manuel, I better appreciate my lot. He's a young boy with not much of a future."

"Jose was such a boy at one time, I believe. He doesn't appear unhappy to me."

"And you look at me, Teresa, and see a disgruntled fool." Teresa opened her mouth to speak, but he stopped her with a raise of his hand. "No, no, you needn't deny it. I waste my nights attempting to forget what the days are like. I no longer have a father to blame for my misery. I shall have to take responsibility for my own moods now. I can hardly blame my aunt for what happens in this house. She hides by day, and at night she'll no longer linger in the hall, hoping to see my father."

"I spoke with her last night. She wants to remain in the nursery for a while."

"Yes, I know. My aunt has big plans for that room, and she'll not abide my standing in the way. She is the reason I asked to speak with you."

"I'm sorry if I encouraged her fantasies, Señor Velez."

"Her dreams keep her alive, Teresa. I don't mind redoing the nursery. We hardly need one in this house. No, I've noticed you have a special rapport with her. Something I don't have. I'd like you to stay until she has come to terms with our family's loss."

"But after your father died, I presumed I would return to the sisters."

"Would another month or two upset whatever plans you've made?"

"Señor Velez, I normally take care of the ill."

"And isn't my aunt *ill* in her own way? Perhaps not physically infirm the way my father was, but she certainly is not lucid at times. Aunt Isabella and I tend to go for the jugular whenever we are together. You make a good referee."

"You showed great patience at the burial."

"That prick of a priest." Luis halted and thought a moment before he began again. "I apologize for my language, Teresa."

"The bishop was unkind, Señor Velez, but I fear it may have something to do with the Grand Inquisitor."

"Ah, yes, Torquemada. I believe you are correct. We must be wary from now on. Catrin may have only been the first step."

He knows, Teresa thought, relieved to understand he shared the same suspicions. His eyes drifted away from her to cast a glance over the room. Dressed in black, his bronze skin seemed tamer, his black hair wilder. He stretched his long legs out in front of him and turned his face once more to Teresa. His heavy lids barely stayed open, and the pain in his eyes had yet to be relieved by tears.

"I will stay, Señor Velez. I will stay for Isabella's sake," she said, knowing that was not the reason for her remaining.

"My aunt and I appreciate your assistance, Teresa."

"I said no such thing!"

Teresa and Luis caught sight of Isabella standing in the doorway.

"It's cold down here," the elderly woman complained.

"Isabella, what are you doing downstairs?" Luis stood.

"I forgot what the rest of the house looked like, and I wanted to get some ideas for Catrin's room. The nursery won't do, you know that."

"Yes, Isabella, you've explained the changes needed."

The elderly woman walked into the room and cocked her head in Teresa's direction.

"What is she helping us with, Luis?"

"Redecorating."

"Not the nursery. Only I will decide what to put into that room."

"Wouldn't you like her to give you some ideas? After all, you haven't been out of the house in ages. You need someone to advise you on the newest styles."

The elderly woman raised her head proudly. The loose fit of the black satin gown she wore emphasized her slenderness. The bottom of the sleeves covered the backs of her hands, making her long white fingers appear stark.

"She may accompany me to the shops to view the merchandise. But I'll have the last say."

"It wouldn't be appropriate for me to make any decisions for your daughter's room," Teresa said, standing. "Maybe we could take a short walk today."

"I don't like walks. Jose will drive us wherever we go." Isabella thought a moment. "He still works here, doesn't he?"

"Yes. Do you wish to meet the staff? You may even

wish to have your meals served in the dining room," Luis suggested.

"Your mother was very uncomfortable at table when I was present." Isabella hunched her shoulders and knitted her brow.

"Mother is gone. There would only be you and I. And perhaps Teresa would care to join us."

Both turned to her, their eagerness not to be alone with each other written clearly on their faces.

"I would be honored to dine with both of you. Shall I inform Gaspar and Señora Toledo of the plans?"

Luis and his aunt gratefully agreed, but refused to allow her to rush away. The three sat for several minutes, not saying anything until Isabella complained of the cold. Luis volunteered to start a fire, but Isabella didn't want to waste the wood.

"We have plenty, Aunt. Jose makes sure the box is kept filled."

"What of the furniture?"

"The furniture?"

"Yes." Isabella ran a finger across the large desk. She had chosen the chair behind the desk because she remembered her brother sitting in the exact place. "If it becomes too hot, won't the wood swell?"

"But if you're cold, Aunt . . ."

"I'm not all that delicate. Although I could use a wrap."

Teresa stood and offered to retrieve a shawl from upstairs. Isabella quickly sent her off. Exiting the library, Teresa heard Luis's audible sigh.

Upon her return, she noticed Isabella had moved to the settee, which was much closer to Luis's chair. They sat with heads bent close, whispering. Teresa almost decided to step away when Luis spied her and invited her into the library.

"I've brought the shawl," Teresa said, laying it over Isabella's shoulders.

"We were talking about you." Isabella's low voice forced Teresa to sit down on the settee. "Was your family Jewish?"

"Aunt, I told you she's an orphan. Please don't pry."

"Didn't the nuns know anything about your mother?" Isabella persisted.

"My mother didn't want me to know my family history."

"How strange. I plan on telling Catrin all my secrets. We'll talk for hours. It will take months before she'll be able to move from my side."

"Your daughter is lucky, Isabella. I wish my mother would have seen fit to leave a hint of where I came from."

"You came from inside her belly," Isabella said, reaching out a hand to touch Teresa's stomach, making the young woman laugh.

Teresa missed breakfast, had a light lunch, but dinner was a feast. Fearing she would make a wrong move, she consistently followed the lead of her dinner companions. Even though conversation was sparse, a certain warmth pervaded the room. Gaspar served the food, Hilaria carrying the various trays and platters. For a brief moment she looked up into Gaspar's face as he laid a serving of the venison on her plate. He didn't flinch, and he gave no indication of his churlishness. Hilaria, on the other hand, kept staring at Teresa with lips held in a tight line.

Señora Toledo had been enthusiastic about the dinner. It had been a long time since she had used her skills on a number of courses. Her efforts proved to be exceptional. Even Isabella commented on how well the dinner had been planned and prepared, delighting the cook so much she spent the rest of the night chuckling to herself.

Over the next two days Isabella did go for walks with Teresa. She even picked fresh bouquets and took her shoes off near the pond to dangle her feet in the water for a while. But when twilight darkened the sky, Isabella returned to her brother's grave. She would not permit a cross to be placed at the head of the grave; instead the ground was marked with a large stone on which she attempted to carve out her brother's name and the dates of his birth and death. Luis promised a larger, engraved stone, but Isabella wouldn't hear of it.

"No, the simple stone will do," she had said, shining the rock with the skirt of her dress.

Luis almost insisted until Teresa caught his eye, and he accepted the arrangements as they were.

Teresa now took breakfast and dinner with the family, attempting to ease the strained relationship between Luis and his aunt. At times the house came close to feeling lighthearted again, even with Gaspar's haughty swagger and Hilaria's sour face. Juana and the cook worked well together in the kitchen, and Teresa had hope that the girl might be able to stay after all.

Finally the grand day came when Teresa and Isabella took the coach into the city. Isabella sat amazed at the sights. She played with the linen curtains on the windows of the coach and giggled to herself, only rarely sharing the humor with her companion.

"You needn't buy what you first see, Isabella. Many of the merchants can be bargained down in price with time."

"Of course. I know."

Jose laid a hand on Teresa's forearm when they climbed out of the coach. "Watch her closely. Señor Roberto Velez never gave her much freedom. I don't believe she's ever bargained for anything in her life."

But Isabella became so confused by all the objects for sale she couldn't make any decisions and returned to the manse with only a small trinket for Señora Toledo.

One day Isabella suggested stopping at the convent where Teresa had grown up. She wanted to meet the women who had raised such a sweet, helpful girl. With trepidation Teresa agreed. Teresa had not been to the convent since Sister Agatha had talked her out of leaving the Velez manse.

Isabella madly went through her closets, most of which held old clothes that had not been in fashion in years. She wanted something simple, something that would make her look "virginal." She insisted on sweeping out white dresses that were much too large for her thin frame.

"Will they be able to see the sins on my soul?" Isabella

asked.

"No," Teresa answered. "Only God knows your deepest secrets. I think you should wear the black satin dress since the sisters will be aware that you are still in mourning."

"I'll look matronly. They'll think I'm an old spinster." When Teresa frowned, Isabella became sad. "I am an old spinster. I've never married, but I did have a child. But the nuns wouldn't approve, would they? I'm so confused. What kind of an impression am I supposed to give?"

"Just be yourself, Isabella."

"Who am I, Teresa? I never knew. Only Roberto knew who I was, and now he can't tell me."

"You are Isabella. That's all you need to be."

Isabella sighed but agreed to wear the black satin dress.

As the coach drew near the convent, Teresa could see Isabella worrying her bottom lip and tapping her ragged fingernails on the velvet seat.

Should she ask Jose to turn back for the manse? Teresa wondered. She didn't feel comfortable bringing the elderly woman to the convent. The woman had committed truly mortal sins. *Did she belong within these sacred walls?*

"I'm not wearing a crucifix!" Isabella suddenly shouted out. "Will they think I'm a heretic?"

"Not everyone wears a crucifix, Isabella, but if you're uncomfortable . . ."

"No. You say they are pleasant, and maybe they can help."

Teresa caught her breath. Of course, she thought,

the woman wants to request assistance in freeing Catrin from the Inquisition. This trip had nothing to do with meeting Teresa's so-called family.

The coach stopped in front of the door, and Jose quickly jumped down to assist the two women descending from the coach. The convent door opened, and Sister Agatha stood smiling, her arms opened wide to capture Teresa.

"I've brought Señor Roberto Velez's sister with me."

Sister Agatha released Teresa and acknowledged the elderly woman who hung back shyly.

"I'm a *converso*," Isabella suddenly blurted out.

"Yes, I know. I'm glad you are able to visit with us, and we are all very sorry to hear of your brother's death. Please come in and have some sherry and a bite to eat. Sister Roberta has made Teresa's favorite dessert."

Inside, Isabella almost wandered off into a small hallway leading to the private section where the nuns resided. Teresa linked arms with the elderly woman while talking to Sister Agatha, who gave an understanding smile. Isabella reached for her food as soon as she was taken to the table, not from hunger, but to feed the nervous butterflies in her stomach. Teresa moved to stop her, but Sister Agatha held Teresa back, muttering a quick thanks to God under her breath.

A small squeal flew from Isabella's mouth.

"Is something wrong?" Teresa asked.

"That man is all bloody." Isabella pointed to a large crucifix attached to the far wall. A realistic figure of Christ hung from the crucifix, blood sluicing down His side and sprinkling His forehead and cheeks.

"It's an image of Christ, our Lord," Teresa explained.

"How horrible. Why do you have it where you eat? Doesn't it make you sick and ruin your appetite?" Isabella looked directly at Sister Agatha.

"We don't actually take our meals in this room. It is meant for guests. The crucifix in our own dining room is much more dramatic. It is meant to remind us what God suffered for our sins."

"What did you women do?"

Sister Agatha raised a hand to her mouth to hide a smile before answering.

"He died for the sins of all mankind, Señora Velez, not just because of our sins."

"Would He do that for me, too?"

"He already has."

Isabella began playing with her food.

"He died like that because of the things I did?"

"He wanted to show His love for us."

"He did that and we kept on sinning?" Isabella looked at Teresa. "No wonder God wants the Inquisition."

"Oh, the Inquisition isn't a matter of revenge, Señora Velez. No, the Church has many reasons for the Inquisition, but God never demanded it because of the pain His Son suffered."

Isabella looked up from the table, her eyes alert.

"God's Son was crucified, not God?"

"It's complicated, but yes."

"Then He knows how much it hurts for me to have

Catrin imprisoned by His people. Can you help me? My daughter might be suffering torture as we sit here, and if she doesn't give the answers the Inquisitor wants, he may have her burned at the stake. I'd never be able to survive that, watching my baby in such bitter agony."

"God will give strength to you and your child, Señora Velez."

"I don't want strength. I want my child back. I want her whole and happy." Isabella stood, knocking over the chair on which she had been seated. "You think I could bear watching a babe that had come from my flesh suffering the way His Son did? God should have torn the men who did that apart. He should have roasted the flesh of anyone involved. No one deserves to die like that." Isabella's voice rose higher as she spoke, and she spat saliva into the air.

Teresa rose to put her arms around the elderly woman.

"Let's go home, Isabella."

"No!" she shouted, shrugging away. Isabella walked quickly around the table, and Sister Agatha rose to meet her. "You must promise to help Catrin," Isabella continued. "Tell the Inquisitor I haven't seen her since she was a babe. Now is my only chance to know her before I die. I've lived locked up inside the manse ever since she was taken away from me. I thought I had already died when she came back. When Roberto took her back. Even then I couldn't speak to her because I'd frighten her. Roberto said I would overwhelm her and cause her to run away. Instead I smuggled peeks of her when she'd be cleaning or helping the cook. I'd watch from her nursery when she stepped out to go to the barn for milk. Oh, she was so beautiful, her skin fairer and smoother than mine ever was. Her features were a perfect match for Roberto and myself. I love her, Sister, please send her back to me." Tears tumbled from her eyes, and Sister Agatha used a piece of her garment to wipe Isabella's cheeks.

"I'm sorry, Sister Agatha. I didn't know this would happen," Teresa apologized.

"We live in a time of hatred and hypocrisy. No mother should have to beg for her babe's life. No sweetheart should have to keep secrets from her beloved. No child should be forced to betray a parent. Friend indicts friend to spare his own life. The air is foul with revenge, ripe with evil, and it sickens me." Sister Agatha reached out and took Isabella into her arms. The embrace lasted a long time. Neither women seemed to want to let go, and when they did, Isabella shyly hurried back to Teresa's side.

The women left without any promises from Sister Agatha. Teresa knew the convent held no power with the Inquisition, and Isabella, too weak and tired to protest anymore, left quietly.

Upon arriving home, Isabella took to her room and refused her evening meal. She didn't even wander out of the house to enter the graveyard. Roberto slept in the cold earth, reviled by his sister for what he had done to their child.

chapter 55

THE WINDS BLEW STRONG IN THE MORNING, causing the house to whistle and the trees to rustle. The barn animals became noisy and restless, the horses kicking at their stalls. Manuel sulked in the kitchen while Hilaria grumbled about having to serve the bastard from the convent. Gaspar made a point of shutting all the windows, ordering the servants around more belligerently than usual. Jose didn't bother to linger in the kitchen after breakfast, and Señora Toledo banged pots and dishes loudly in the kitchen. Manuel eventually managed to stay out of everyone's way, crouching in the barn near the horses to keep himself warm. Only Juana managed to carry on with her tasks without the glumness that enveloped the rest of the house.

Even Teresa suffered a dark mood, delaying the time when she would go up and speak to Isabella. The elderly woman had slept late, not appearing for breakfast. Luis and Teresa thought it better to allow this little luxury. Late in the morning Teresa wrapped herself tightly in a wool shawl against the chill invading the house and climbed the stairs to Isabella's bedroom.

Isabella had a small bed put into the nursery for herself. The cradle had been banished to the cellar, but all the rest of the furnishings remained. Teresa knocked gently on the door and waited a few moments before turning the knob to push the door open.

Isabella lay on the bed, her body spread across the linens, arms wrapped around the porcelain doll. Her naked, slender feet peeked out from under the covers. Her wild, white hair lay spread across the pillow surrounding her aged face. As Teresa moved into the room, she noticed how peaceful Isabella's face looked. She looked younger with her face relaxed, the lines less pronounced. The late morning sun peeked from behind the clouds and washed her flesh free of the weight of age. Teresa hesitated to wake the woman. She had spent so many wakeful nights, thought Teresa; maybe she deserved to sleep the day away this once. Teresa brought a chair near the bed and sat, took the rosary from around her neck, and prayed.

A spray of lightning lit up the sky, followed by the bold clap which filled the room with a frosty chill. Teresa shivered and drew closer to the bed to cover Isabella's feet. But at that moment the elderly woman sat up, wide-eyed, hugging the doll tightly to her breasts. Her body shook, and tears filled her eyes.

"Pray for me, Teresa. Please pray for me."

Teresa sat down on the bed and pulled the covers around the elderly woman's shoulders.

"The lightning must have given you a fright, Isabella. You are safe at home in the nursery. Don't you recognize this place?"

"But God will come for me. He'll hurt me."

"No, no, Isabella." Teresa hugged the woman. "God loves us all. He doesn't want you to suffer."

"I . . . I . . . have to pay for my sins. The bishop, he'll see to it."

The bishop. Teresa's own heart beat fast remembering Señor Roberto Velez's burial. The past few days had made her forget, but now the vision reappeared inside her mind.

"Let me get you something to eat. The weather today is dreadful, but we can find some things to do in the house. Perhaps we should begin to remove some of the toys from this room. There are many poor children who would enjoy having these beautiful treasures."

Isabella clung even harder to the porcelain doll.

"I didn't mean the doll, Isabella. She is quite beautiful and would be decorative in Catrin's bedroom."

Isabella smiled, looking down at the doll in her arms. Her fingers drew light circles on the doll's cheeks.

A loud rap came to the front door, and Teresa heard a flurry of activity in the house. Gaspar dared to open the nursery door without knocking. He stood at full height, his breath calm, his eyes hard, and upon his lips rested a chilling smirk.

"Bring her down now!" someone yelled from the bottom of the stairs.

"Who is there, Gaspar? Who do they want?"

Isabella wailed loudly, carrying the doll up to her face. Teresa stood.

"What are you doing here? You're upsetting Señora Velez."

Two guards appeared directly behind Gaspar. They wore the insignia of the Inquisition.

"Where's Señor Luis Velez?" she asked.

"Downstairs, attempting to bargain with the Inquisition's representative," Gaspar said. "I've been told to bring Señora Velez downstairs."

"By whom? Certainly not by her nephew."

"No, but I don't believe he will have a choice. Get her dressed, Teresa."

Teresa moved to the door, hoping to go downstairs to assist Luis.

"If you don't get her dressed, the guards will take her as she is. This is one mercy we can allow her, don't you think?"

"Then close the door. We will be out in a few minutes."

Gaspar backed out, and the two guards took their places on either side of the door while Gaspar shuttered the women inside the room.

Uncontrollable, Isabella flailed her arms about, driving Teresa back several times.

"You must dress. Don't give them the pleasure of dragging you out of this room in your bedclothes. Please listen."

"But they want to hurt me like they hurt God's Son." Her wailing had quieted into a whimper.

"Your nephew will help us, Isabella." Teresa hated her lie. No one could stop the Inquisition's hunger for more souls.

"You'll take care of her for me," Isabella said, presenting the doll to Teresa. "I want Catrin to have it."

"Of course. I'll put it back on the shelf and make sure she's dusted every day."

As Isabella dressed, she asked whether the soldiers might simply be taking her to meet with Catrin. "Do you think Sister Agatha may have entreated the Inquisitor to allow me to visit my daughter? Maybe she said some prayers that reached up high to God's ears."

"Here, Isabella, wear the heavy dress. The day is cold."

"But it's not my prettiest."

"Catrin wouldn't want you to be ill. And wrap yourself in the thick shawl."

"Are you dressing me for the dungeon, Teresa?"

"I'm making sure that you'll stay warm. Look how hard it's raining."

Isabella looked out the window.

"Why is it so dark?"

"The sun is behind the clouds. After the rain, you'll see the sun."

"Will I ever see the sun again, Teresa? Will Catrin?"

Another knock. This time the person did not presume to barge into the room. Must be one of the guards, Teresa thought, combing out Isabella's hair. "We'll be out in a minute," she called.

Finally the women entered the hall. Before descending the staircase, Isabella took Teresa's arm. The soldiers followed behind the two women; the sound of their heavy footsteps beat out like a morose drumroll. Luis stood at the bottom of the stairs, waiting to take his aunt's hand in his.

"Listen to me, Aunt Isabella. I will immediately go to the bishop and obtain his assistance in this matter. I'm sure he'll agree that it's a mistake. You were distraught at my father's burial and didn't know what you were doing."

"I spat on the bishop's damn cross."

Teresa saw Luis's hand tighten around the elderly woman's.

"But you didn't mean to."

"Must I tell the truth?" Isabella asked.

"Torquemada will make sure you do," said the Inquisitor's representative.

The soldiers grabbed Isabella's arms and jerked her away from Luis.

When the door closed behind his aunt and the soldiers, Luis took the steps two at a time, rushing to collect his rain gear for his journey to the bishop's residence.

Teresa followed as quickly as she could, but Luis had already disappeared inside his room by the time she made the landing. She waited, pacing for several moments until he came out, carrying his cloak with him.

"Do you wish for me to travel with you? Perhaps I can speak to the Inquisitor and tell him that she meant no harm."

"Thank you, Teresa, but you'll only slow me down.

Every second is important. My aunt is old and will not last long in Torquemada's hovel."

She watched him run down the stairs. Gaspar held the front door open, letting it slam shut behind Luis. He looked up the stairs at Teresa and smiled.

"You gain nothing if this house falls!" she shouted at him. *Nothing but a hostile satisfaction that benefits no one.*

chapter 56

"But he is ill, Señor Velez. He hasn't been out of bed at all today." The bishop's servant rudely kept Luis waiting at the door, the rain sweeping against his back.

"He will see me, or his pet project will go unfunded."

The servant's eyes opened wide, and she swallowed words she had prepared. This threat could not be taken lightly.

"Let me speak with him again. If you could keep your visit short, perhaps he might be strong enough to see you." Her eyes pleaded for a compromise.

"I am soaking wet, woman. I'm not about to bargain with a servant for a bit of courtesy."

Blushing, she opened the door wider and invited Luis in.

"There is a fire in the salon. I'll take your outerwear."

Luis walked into a toasty room, the fire swelling to full strength. On one table he noticed the port with which he had gifted the bishop, along with a half-full crystal glass. "Not been out of bed," Luis muttered to himself. He walked around the room, trying to piece together what he would say in his aunt's defense, but the most relevant excuse he could make was based on her madness, well known to the bishop. *Why else would he have lowered the crucifix to her face?*

He heard the tapping of a cane against the marble floor of the hallway and prepared himself for the role the bishop would play. The servant opened the double doors to the room and stood aside to allow the bishop to pass. The cleric swayed a bit at the doorway as if reclaiming his balance before stepping across the threshold onto the Persian carpet. The cane was silver-handled and the burled wood expensive.

"Oh, Luis, these rainy days cause havoc to my poor bones." The bishop limped dramatically over to the settee. "Could you give me a hand? On my own I will simply tumble onto the floor." He reached out his ring hand. Luis was sure the cleric purposefully chose that hand to make a point. *Remember, I am a man of the Church.* The bishop grasped his hand, slowly lowering himself onto the settee. "I've told my servant to bring us some tea. You don't mind, do you?"

"I suppose after the port you need something to clear your head for our talk."

"Port?"

Luis pointed to the bottle and glass on the round table next to the bishop's favorite chair.

"Must be from last night. My housekeeper, Bettina, becomes more careless each day. I think she takes advantage of my ill health. Please don't stand over me, Luis. Sit." He swept the room with his hand. A number of chairs stood vacant.

Luis chose to sit next to the cleric on the settee.

"I need to speak with you about my aunt."

"Is the poor woman babbling again? I am sorry for your burden."

The servant interrupted them briefly to serve the tea. Neither man spoke, each rehearsing poorly planned sentences. When the doors closed behind the servant, Luis returned his cup to the table.

"The Inquisition's soldiers came for Aunt Isabella this morning."

The cleric looked shocked.

"Would you mind setting my cup next to yours, Luis?" He folded his free hands together. "We should pray for her."

"I didn't come here to pray, Bishop. I want your help in getting her released. They now have two members of my family."

"Two?"

"You know Catrin is my half sister. You probably assisted my father in finding a home for her when she was born."

"My life is as vulnerable as anyone else's. Torquemada will damn priests as well as the laity."

"Is that why you reported back what my aunt did at the funeral? No one missed your holding the crucifix up high, Bishop."

"I wanted to give comfort to your aunt, but she re-fused it."

"Don't lie."

"Most family members are pleased if I lower the cru-cifix for them to kiss. Not your aunt. No, she is a heretic. Yes, she was baptized because your brother insisted, but she never believed. And unlike the heathens, she had the education available to her. I tutored her personally before baptizing her."

"The woman is mad. Growing up I saw her mainly as a malevolent harpy, but since my father died, and with . . ." Luis almost mentioned Teresa's name, "I've seen her in a different light. She has quiet, graceful moments. It is the burden of what she has had to bear during her lifetime which has driven her to her madness."

"Let her tell Torquemada her sad story. If she is con-trite, she has nothing to fear."

"He will torture her. Her life . . ."

"Her life has run its course, Luis. Now she must an-swer for her sins." The bishop took hold of his cane.

"I'm not finished yet. If you want the money for your abbey, or whatever it is, you will see to it that Isabella and Catrin are freed. Catrin has already paid a heavy price."

"Your father and I were close friends. Sometimes we engaged in acts of . . . what some would call depravity. We had hungers of the flesh, the same as any man. We craved the warm flesh of women. We had the expensive tastes for fine wines and foods. We liked our luxuries, as you see from this room. I sit in a fine house with exquisite carpets, beautiful crystal, silver and gold ornaments to touch and admire. Plenty of wood to keep me warm."

"All based on donations," Luis said with spite in his voice.

"Yes, but should I live on bread and water before a few twigs just because I'm a religious man?"

"Many of your people do."

"Fools. There is no reason to be poor if one doesn't have to be. Should I deny people like you the chance to share, to be charitable? Charity is a true virtue. And now I will be charitable, too, Luis. Take whatever you can. Liquidate as much of your wealth as quickly as you can and leave Spain. This is no place for *conversos*, especially for those who do not truly believe in the Holy Mother Church. I gently managed to tame Torquemada while your father lived, but I cannot continue to do so. He has been eyeing your family for the past six months. We spoke of your father's illness, and Torquemada was willing to let your father die in peace. But the tide has turned, and there is no hope for you now."

"I will not leave without Catrin and Isabella."

"You put their lives in danger by staying."

"And if I left?"

"I cannot promise you anything. They may still be sacrificed."

"I will not abandon my family, Bishop. You must think me a coward to believe I would."

"No. I would think you wise if you turned your back on them. Who are they? One is old, not long for this world. Her mind is soft, and she drifts in her own world far away from reality. The other is a woman, a child who should have never been born."

"Everyone has a right to life, no matter what the circumstances of their birth. If you really believe what you said, you should pray. Pray for your own soul."

Luis stood and walked over to the table on which the crystal glass rested. He lifted the glass in his hand.

"And, Bishop. You should pray for forgiveness for all the lies you've told." Luis downed what remained in the glass and called for the servant to bring his rain gear.

chapter 57

TERESA SAT BUNDLED IN HER SHAWL AT THE
foot of the stairs, waiting for Luis to return. Hilaria and
Señora Toledo came from the kitchen occasionally to ask
whether Señor Velez had returned. Every time she shook
her head, the two women moaned and made the sign of
the cross. Gaspar and Juana carried on with their day as
if nothing had happened. This was typical of Juana, Teresa thought; the girl always put on blinders when trouble
arrived. Sylvia had been away for two days. Finally arriving home, she prattled on about the weather and the
terrible condition of the roads.

"I nearly bumped myself on the head each time the
coach driver hit a hole in the road. And I'm sure he didn't
miss a single one." Finally she quieted, noting the dreari-
ness of the house. "Has someone else died? Is it Señora
Isabella Velez?"

"She has been taken by the Inquisition," Teresa replied.

With a gasp Sylvia rushed to sit beside Teresa.

"When?"

"This morning."

"And Señor Velez?"

"He is at the bishop's residence, pleading for his aunt."

"Do you think we'll all be called to the Inquisitor?"

"Why should we?" Teresa looked at Sylvia. The woman's frightened eyes glittered in the poorly lit hall. Her soaked clothes smelled, and her hair drooped unattractively into her face.

"You'll be leaving soon, I imagine," Sylvia said.

Teresa hadn't given any thought to returning to the convent since she had agreed to stay and care for Isabella. Certainly Isabella needed her more now than ever, but where would she do the most good, here in the manse or at the convent, where she might enlist the help of Sister Agatha?

"I may leave myself. I visited with a distant relative. She offered to let me work in her tavern. I know, it isn't the kind of job you'd expect me to have, but it may be far safer than this house."

"You've already made your decision," Teresa said, sure Sylvia would see to her own preservation.

Surprised, Sylvia looked at Teresa.

"Yes, I have. I'll be informing Señor Velez when . . ." She thought for a few moments. "Perhaps this would not be the right time. I can wait a few days, but no longer. Have you already set the date you'll be leaving?"

"I haven't made any plans as yet. I don't want to abandon Señor Velez in the midst of his troubles."

"Admirable. Just don't join him in the Inquisitor's

prison." Sylvia rose, lifting her bag from the marble floor. "I'm going to my room. I don't care to be here when Señor Velez returns. I don't imagine he'll have anything positive to say. Good evening."

Teresa listened to Sylvia's fading footsteps, her eyes dreamy and distant. At the convent she had nurtured many of the poor and watched children as well as adults succumb to life's miseries. She prayed with and for them, but never had she felt their pain as dramatically as she did for Luis, a wealthy man who now drowned in the political and religious whirlpool that Spain had become. He never went without a meal, yet she sensed he starved for emotional support.

The front door flew open, and Luis tracked the bad weather into the manse. Teresa quickly stood, surprising him.

"What are you doing here?"

"I wanted to wait for you. What did the bishop say?" She had little hope, but needed to hear the words.

"He refuses to help."

Gaspar removed Luis's wet garments, his demeanor passive, professional. *What horrible thoughts are going through Gaspar's mind?* Teresa wondered.

"Shall I tell Cook to begin preparing the dinner, Señor?" asked Gaspar.

"Dinner?" Luis looked at Teresa.

"Perhaps something light. Soup and bread with a bit of wine," Teresa suggested.

"Yes, that would be good. Please see to it, Gaspar."

"I assume Teresa will be joining you." Gaspar never turned to acknowledge her presence.

"I'd like that," Luis said.

Teresa nodded her head in agreement.

After Gaspar left, Luis invited Teresa into the library. He sat behind the desk, opening and closing drawers. She quietly took her place on the settee.

"I'm looking for the paperwork for the bishop's project. I mean to cut the funds off."

"You don't want to anger him at this time, Señor Velez."

"Anger him? He has flatly refused to help me and suggested I should leave my home to live in a foreign country."

"It may be an honest warning." Teresa pulled her shawl closer around herself. The evening chill grew worse, and Gaspar hadn't bothered to set a fire in the library.

Luis looked over at her, his dark eyes burning from the conversation he had had with the bishop. His hands mindlessly fumbled with the papers on his desk.

"I shall visit Torquemada tomorrow, Teresa. I cannot run away."

"What will you say to him?"

"By tomorrow morning I should be calm and able to speak in a rational tone. Obviously Catrin has nothing to say, and poor Isabella is totally insane. She couldn't describe the Jewish rites to him. Our family has never been religious, but you must know that by now. I'm sure my father didn't believe in an afterlife, which is the reason he so feared death."

"I think he had doubts, Señor Velez."

"Yes, I suppose lying on one's deathbed can alter one's faith."

"I can return to the convent and ask the nuns for help. I'm not sure they'll be able to do anything."

"Stay here, please, Teresa. I may need your advice on how to approach this Church of yours."

"A start would be to accept the truths of the Church, Señor Velez."

"I want only to coexist peacefully with the Catholic Church. I'm not proselytizing for any religion. My own Jewish faith is almost as foreign to me as the Church's is. But my father and I worked hard for the wealth we enjoy. We didn't accrue the money on the highway as bandits. Why should I now be forced to leave our home and lands, even the country in which I was born?"

"But Torquemada will never agree with your plea, Señor Velez. He believes in only one Church, and thinks he is saving souls with the measures he takes."

"What of those he condemns to be burned at the stake? He believes those flames are a mere hint of the pains the poor victims will suffer in hell. Those 'heretics,' as he calls them, are hastened to their eternal damnation."

Teresa had no answers to his arguments. She herself always thought the penalties the Inquisition imposed were hateful and not truly the will of God.

chapter 58

THE HUNCHBACK, HUGO, OPENED THE DOOR. A small smile spread his lips when he recognized Luis. His deformed feet inched closer to his visitor, taking in a whiff of Luis while obviously scanning the rich clothes the man wore.

"I need to see Father Torquemada."

"You have no appointment," Hugo said, twisting his head to the side to stare up at Luis.

"I must speak to him about my . . ." Luis had decided to admit that Catrin was his sister, but still he hesitated. His father was now out of the Inquisition's reach. "My sister and my aunt."

"Sister?"

"Catrin."

"And her mother?"

"My father kept that secret." Admitting Catrin and Isabella were mother and daughter would only seal their fate.

"The Grand Inquisitor doesn't usually see anyone

without an appointment. However, I believe he may have some questions for you. Come in." Hugo stood back. The dimly lit hall made Luis search the shadows for another presence.

"Sit." Hugo pointed to an ornately carved bench standing against a wall. He didn't wait to see whether Luis followed his order. Instead, he limped deeper into the shadows until he came to a door, which he opened slowly, allowing some sunlight to creep through the doorway into the hall.

Luis noticed several religious paintings, but had difficulty making out the subject matter because of the dark colors used. He wasn't positive, but he thought he heard laughter; given the circumstances, the sound sent a chill up his spine.

The door at the farther end of the hall opened again, and Torquemada stepped out, followed by his scribe, Hugo.

"Forgive me for not sending regrets about your father's death. I meant for Hugo to carry my condolences this very afternoon."

"Thank you, Father. I'm afraid we are doubly grieved in our home."

"Ah, let us go into the library and discuss the other matter." Torquemada led the way, with the hunchback unctuously bowing to Luis to follow. Hugo carried his writing materials into the library and sat at the great desk before the window.

"You've come about your aunt."

"Yes, and my sister, Catrin."

"Her mother has been demanding to visit with Catrin."

Of course, thought Luis, his aunt wouldn't have the sense to remain still about her familial connection.

"If you've spoken with my aunt, you know she is not well."

"Excuse me?"

"Her mind. She often lives in an unreal fantasy world."

"Are you saying she is not Catrin's mother?"

"No. But Isabella means no harm. She certainly isn't a heretic. I suspect she doesn't have the intelligence to understand the mystery of God."

"Please sit, my son." Torquemada chose two chairs close to the scribe. "Señora Velez has much to say. She speaks of her own brother as being the father of her child. And Hugo says you've owned up to Catrin being your sister. Is that true?"

"Yes. I make no defense for them, but it certainly does not make them heretics. Sinners, yes."

"When offered consolation by the bishop, Señora Velez spat on the crucifix."

"My aunt was disoriented. Distraught."

"She's done the same in her prison cell." Torquemada lowered his voice, forcing Luis to lean forward.

"She doesn't understand the significance of the cross."

"What is there to understand? Our Lord died on the cross for our sins. Spitting on the cross is like spitting in our Lord's face."

"Her mind is innocent like a toddler's. She may do something bad, but it's not meant to cause serious harm.

She doesn't understand the limits."

"Perhaps the fact she has conspired with the devil has wasted her mind."

"That's nonsense!" Luis heard the hunchback scribble a few words. "May I speak with her?"

"She is undergoing questioning and cannot have any contact with the outside world."

"Has she been harmed?"

"If she cooperates, there will be no physical action taken against her."

"What do you want her to say?"

"Only the truth, my son. Is there someone who may have influenced her?"

The Inquisitor wanted Luis to testify against others to save his own family. He wouldn't exchange another family to these terrors. *But what has Isabella said of those living in the manse?*

"I would be greatly indebted to you if I at least was allowed a few moments with my family, Father."

"I may appear too harsh, but I have a heavy burden. The royal family has requested that I hunt out heretics, especially those who would put on a false face of belief while their souls are black from their sins of worshiping false gods."

"You already questioned Catrin and allowed me to see her before. Can I not at least have some time with her?"

"Her mother has incriminated her, and she will need to be requestioned."

"She doesn't even have a tongue to speak."

"There are other ways of communicating, my son."

Luis became aware of his breath. He attempted to slow the pace to quiet his mind, to enable his mind to think clearly. He couldn't push too hard, or matters might be made worse for his family.

"When may I see them?"

"I can't say. It is most unusual to allow family members inside the prison. In your case, the bishop came to me, requesting a favor. Now he is contrite and understands the danger these women pose to the souls of others."

"My aunt hardly leaves the house, Father."

"She's been seen in the city quite a bit the past several days."

"We have tried to get her out of the manse because of her brother's death. We didn't want her to fall into a dark fugue."

"I'm sure your intentions were good, my son, but she has admitted to performing many harmful acts."

"Such as?"

"You know we refuse to give out that kind of information." Torquemada took a moment to think. "However, perhaps I should share one of her heinous acts. She evidently had a witch as a nursemaid when she was a child and was taught all the secret herbs of witchcraft. She used such a potion to slowly murder your mother."

Luis grabbed the armrests tightly, swallowing down the sob he felt caught in his throat. No one understood his mother's illness, and he remembered his aunt spending evenings fawning over his mother while she lay in bed. Even as a child, he couldn't understand what drew the two women together. Neither liked the other, but for some reason they needed each other.

"I take it that you were not aware of this, my son."

"My aunt is not sane."

Torquemada leaned forward in his chair. "Satan has driven her mad. He has worked his devilry through her hands and used her tongue to profane all that belongs to God. Have you not felt the heat of hell when you walked into her room? The child doesn't belong to your father. No, she is the devil's spawn, and her mother would teach her all the demon's tricks. Even now she calls out to Catrin. She fouls the cellar with her curses and fills her child's mind with dreams of revenge. You are blessed because I keep you from such a spiritual plague as she would pass on. Hugo and I are forced to listen to the devil's hellish threats and temptations, but we are capable of casting his words aside. You, my son, are vulnerable. You give them the opportunity to attack your mind with their vile words."

"You insult me with your ravings, Father."

"No. You are weak, Señor Velez. You think you come here out of strength. No, you are being manipulated by the devil."

"I'll go to Rome, make a plea to the pope."

"The pope has granted broad powers to King Ferdinand and Queen Isabella. Once I was Queen Isabella's confessor. She is the one who requested I be made Grand Inquisitor. Are you also going to flee to the royal court to make your request?"

Luis stared into Torquemada's cold eyes until a hand nudged him. Hugo offered him a small glass of sherry.

"No. I want nothing from you except my family." Luis rose, and the hunchback stood back, his loping movements an irritant to Luis's anger.

Luis turned from the Grand Inquisitor and headed for the hall, the hunchback sweeping his bare feet against the carpet behind him.

"Wait, Señor Velez."

Luis stopped, and Hugo moved around him to exit first.

"In two weeks there will be an *auto da fe*. Unfortunately the royal family will not be able to attend, but I believe the situation is such that we cannot wait."

A storm of anger propelled Luis into the hall, where Hugo stood with the front door already open. The hunchback bowed as Luis passed.

chapter 59

THE BISHOP TOOK TO HIS BED, AND NO AMOUNT of cajoling could cause him to meet with Luis. Luis wanted to go personally to Rome, but knew he would never be in time to stop the *auto da fe*. Teresa watched as he refused meals and frantically wrote letters meant to stop the Grand Inquisitor. Instead of sleeping, he roamed the manse, muttering to himself, spending hours standing in front of his mother's portrait. His ill temper drove even Spider away. The dog whimpered and cried outside the rooms in which Luis would lock himself. Manuel and Jose took the dog on walks and cared for him as their own.

Sylvia never did confront Luis about her leaving; she simply informed Gaspar and left the same day, warning Teresa against staying too long in the manse.

Late one evening Teresa found Luis standing in front of his father's grave. She purposefully crunched the debris on the ground with her sandals, not wanting to surprise him, but he remained still.

"Señor Velez," she whispered in order not to alarm

him or wake anyone in the manse. She moved closer, the night chill causing goose bumps to pepper her flesh. "Señor Velez, may I speak with you?"

"What is it, Teresa? Why are you still awake?"

"I visited the convent this afternoon."

He looked up at the dark trees, which shivered in the breezes. His eyes searched the wood.

"I asked for their help."

"And they refused."

"No." She stood, ashamed of the meager offer Sister Agatha had made. "They will pray for your sister and aunt."

His laugh stung her.

"I begged them to speak with the bishop. And Sister Agatha plans on visiting him tomorrow."

"Ah, but he is terribly ill, I hear."

"He is her confessor and agreed to meet with her."

"And what do you think that will accomplish?"

They stood in silence, each knowing the answer.

"I am so sorry, Señor Velez." She reached out to touch him but stopped herself, knowing that it would be improper.

He turned and reached his hand out. She took a small step back, staring at the pale hand beneath the half moon. Slowly she took hold of his hand, feeling the chill of his flesh and the strength of his body as his hand closed around hers.

"I don't know how to pray, Teresa. Teach me."

She came to his side and began the Our Father, her voice soft with the crackle of emotion cutting into her words. He joined her in the Amen.

"Must I watch my family die?" he then asked.

"We need to pray that the Grand Inquisitor has mercy on Isabella and Catrin. Perhaps they will ask for mercy and be granted freedom with only the penitent's garb as their punishment."

"My aunt will die. There is only hope for Catrin."

chapter 60

THE STREETS OF THE CITY WERE FILLED WITH people. Peasants from the surrounding villages clamored into the city, their children with them. Toddlers sat astride their father's shoulders, giggling and pointing at trinkets being sold. Mothers carried food in baskets for their families' lunches, while merchants tempted them with fresh produce and even rotten fruits and vegetables to be thrown at the penitents. The strong heat of the sun enticed most people out of their homes to catch an occasional breeze.

The royal couple would not make an appearance, but they sent members of the court to observe and condone the *auto da fe* that was to take place. Wealthy nobles spent their coin and drank their full in honor of the festive occasion. The din of the crowd frightened animals; they tried to flee but were secured by heavy ropes.

On the outskirts of the city, the *Tablada*, or stone stage, had been decorated with statuaries symbolizing the prophets, and strips of cloth hung with the colors of the Inquisition. Instead of wooden pillars, the *quemader*, or burning place, was set with stone pillars that could be reused, since this area of Spain apparently was infested with heretics.

On horseback, Luis and Jose passed the *Tablada*. The stains on the stage reminded them of what would occur today.

"Teresa wanted to join us, Señor."

"There is nothing here for her to see. She is better off at the manse."

"I fear that Carmen and Hilaria might take flight. If your aunt should . . ." Jose stopped speaking and sighed.

"If she should burn, I expect that you and the rest of the servants will leave."

"No, Señor. Where would I go? Who would abide my clumsiness?"

Luis looked at Jose. "We both know you do exceptional work, and so do my neighbors. Any of them would accept you." Luis didn't wait for Jose to say anything else as he spurred his horse forward.

Soon the men dismounted, since the crowd was too thick for them to maneuver well on horseback. Neighbors glanced at Luis but did not acknowledge him; instead they managed to drift farther away from where he stood.

The church bell rang, announcing the procession that would pass through the city on the way to the *Tablada*. Excitedly people began to line the streets, pushing and shoving for the best place to stand. Children toward the front crawled in between their fathers' legs to better protect their view. In the back other children begged parents to lift them up and squeezed spoiled fruits and vegetables in their hands, the juices running down their arms, leaving a sticky trail. Hardly anything would be left of the produce by the time the procession passed. The children's aim often went astray, leaving stains on the adults' clothing. Infants lay nestled near their mothers' breasts, feeding, oblivious to the excitement around them.

Luis stood on the stone steps. Before he rode out to the *Tablada*, he wanted to be sure his sister and aunt were part of this procession. In but a few minutes he saw the Dominicans carrying high the Inquisition's banner. The sleeves of their black-and-white woolen cowls rose up their arms, their flesh pale, feathered with dark hair. Like Hugo, they all walked barefoot. Behind them came the local magistrates, dressed in high style for the festivities. The first of the halberdiers, the guards, followed, their axes at the ready to prevent any of the prisoners from escaping. All the heretics who could be seen wore *sambenitos*, yellow gowns symbolizing their shame, a large red cross appearing on the front and back of each garment. Some carried devotional candles; some wore nooses around their necks; several wore conical hats. All the men were barefoot. The halberdiers surrounded the heretics, making it difficult not only for the rotten fruits and vegetables to hit their targets, but also blocking the clear view Luis had hoped for. A rise in the voices of the crowd brought Luis's attention to the last of the heretics. His aunt and Catrin walked naked, causing vile comments and laughter to issue forth from the crowd. He almost rushed to cover them, but Jose grabbed his arm and reminded him that he'd never be able to get past the halberdiers.

"We must go to the *Tablada*." Jose squeezed his master's arm, his voice controlled, even, without emotion.

At the *Tablada*, a few people had chosen to await the procession rather than following it, but Luis and Jose found room for themselves close to the stage. A disgust for the surrounding crowd rose inside Luis as he watched the people picnic; by their feet they had placed baskets filled with cheese, fruit, and wine. The crowd's breath and sweat filled the air with pungent and foul odors. He wanted to spit in their faces, send them sprawling against the cobbled streets.

Soon, from a distance the kettledrums sounded, and the crowd quieted in anticipation of the heretics' arrival. From his position near the stage, Luis could see Torquemada leading the procession; behind came Hugo, his body jerking as his limp slowed him down. He carried the parchment that listed the heretics' offenses. Franciscan friars dressed in their brown robes began circulating in the crowd, admonishing people to repent and reconcile with the Church before the flames of hell condemned their souls to eternal torture.

The heretics climbed the steps of the stage slowly, each bruised and weary, some almost catatonic in their suffering. At the end of the line, Isabella and Catrin shuddered from the cold and their fear. Anger overtook Isabella as she attempted to spit at the crowd, bumping into the halberdiers, who flung her backward. Several times she lost her footing, fell, and needed to be picked up. Fiercely she tried to undo the ropes that tied her wrists together, only causing her skin to break open. Luis watched the blood drip to the stage, the ropes becoming sodden.

Catrin stood quietly, not looking at the crowd crowing with insane mockery. The swelling on one side of her face was a rainbow of colors. When she opened her mouth, Luis saw several front teeth were missing. He stood beyond prayer, filled with hatred and frustration, while the enlarging crowd shoved forward, pushing him almost flat against the *Tablada*.

Torquemada began his sermon, the words spilling into the unruly crowd. He raised his hands calling for order, a bit of silence for his scribe, who would read out the accusations and condemnations.

Only Isabella and Catrin were to be "relaxed." Luis knew this meant they would burn at the stake. Parishioners, promised indulgences for their participation, brought forth the necessary faggots for the fire. Torquemada faced the women and asked if they had repented and wanted to be reconciled with the Church. Catrin, who could not speak, fell immediately to her knees and kissed the Grand Inquisitor's feet.

Luis shut his eyes. Her plea for forgiveness meant she would be garroted before the fire reached her flesh. A slight mercy for one who had suffered so much.

Isabella attempted to drag her daughter to her feet, and when Torquemada stooped to pull her away, she spat in his eyes. Hugo limped forward with a piece of linen to wipe the Grand Inquisitor's face clean. Both women were taken to the stake and tied. A guard slipped a rope around Catrin's neck in preparation for her strangulation. Isabella would not be blessed with such generosity.

Quickly the parishioners lay the faggots around the women. After they had finished, a proud-looking man came forward with a lighted torch and set the wood ablaze. The flames shot upward with the roar of the crowd. Additional lit faggots were thrown at the women. Isabella used her arms to push them away, and sparks stung her flesh, spotting it with reddish-black spots.

"What is he waiting for?" Luis asked out loud.

The man holding the rope around Catrin's throat waited till the last moment to pull the rope tightly into a death grip. But he had waited too long. Luis watched as suddenly flames licked the man's hands; frightened and in pain, the man dropped the rope into the fire. Feeling the rope drop from her neck, Catrin attempted to scream. Horrid noises issued from her mouth. Even in this most intense pain, she wouldn't be able to voice her agony.

Luis lurched forward, his stomach roiling from the smell of burning flesh and the ravings of his aunt. Vomit spewed from him, covering the garments of a woman standing too close. He looked at her and saw Teresa's tear-filled eyes. Her sobs vibrated against his chest as she held him in her arms.

The chaos around him swirled into a mindless blackness.

chapter 61

LUIS OPENED HIS EYES TO HIS OWN DARKENED bedroom. The covers were wrapped around him, his body swaddled in tight cloth like a baby. Immediately he stretched out his arms to free himself. He heard a rustle of fabric and looked up to see Teresa. She brushed his hair back off his face.

"My aunt and sister?" he asked.

"It's over. They're at peace."

The awful nausea overwhelmed him again. He took deep breaths and swallowed several times.

"That horrendous smell," he muttered more to himself than to Teresa. "I'll never forget it. And the screams. Worse, the sounds that came from Catrin's open, tongueless mouth."

"The doctor gave Jose some medicine for you to take," she said, reaching for a bottle on the side table. She hoped he would take it without a fuss. Oblivion would be the best healing remedy right now. "He said you should take half the bottle." She began to undo the plug, but Luis brushed it out of her hands.

"Is that the same lousy elixir with which he drugged my father?"

"You need to find some peace."

Luis sat up in the bed, the covers falling to his waist. The room looked different to him. Empty, he thought. Empty and vile, full of the memories he wanted to forget.

"What did they do with the ashes?"

"The Church is burying them in unconsecrated ground." Teresa paused, remembering her last look at the dying women covered in blackened flesh, the skin bubbling up into waves of fat that sizzled in the fire. "The Church will not return their remains to you."

"And Jose?"

She hesitated but couldn't lie.

"He is taking Señora Toledo and Hilaria into the city. They have left for good. Gaspar and Juana remain. I don't think they have anyone to turn to right now. Jose, of course, is coming back. None of us have seen Manuel for a while." Teresa had caught a glimpse of the boy at the burning. *Would he return? Better that he didn't.*

"How did you manage to get to the city?" he asked.

"I was determined. I started to walk, but a neighbor saw me and offered a ride."

"You have been very kind to me, Teresa. I should send you back to the convent, but . . ." The words didn't come.

"You have need of me right now, Señor Velez."

"My name is Luis, Teresa. This formality between us is ridiculous."

"Would you like something to eat?" she asked.

He grew pale just considering the question. Not bothering to answer, he thought a while about how much he owed her.

"Teresa, for your entire life, a secret has been kept from you. I've learned how secrets can tear one's life apart. I know who your mother was. The woman who cared for Fernando's dead body did the same for your mother." He heard her intake of breath. She backed away slightly from the bed, perhaps afraid of the truth.

"She is dead, then," she whispered. "I always thought someday she would reappear. I would touch her face, hear the sound of her voice."

"Your mother was Susanna Diego."

"The skull above the lintel?"

"Yes, that is hers."

Teresa didn't cry. She walked back to her chair and sat staring into the past, searching for clues that would either prove him right or wrong; but the nuns had done a fine job of keeping the secret.

"All these years she has been shamed. Ridiculed by passersby. Pointed at by children who saw her as an evil ghost, haunting their nightmares. Even I . . ."

The room filled with silence.

"Teresa, I want to give your mother back to you."

She looked at him, not understanding the meaning of his words.

"I will steal the skull and bury it in our consecrated cemetery behind the house. Then you will know she is finally at rest."

"You mustn't. If someone should see you . . ."

"I will be careful, Teresa. I don't want to die at the stake."

"But the Inquisition's soldiers might be watching you."

"I can't right what Torquemada did to my family, but I can at least see that your mother has a proper burial."

A soft knock came to the door.

"Come in," Luis commanded.

Jose pushed the door open. "Look who I found lost on the road."

"Manuel!" shouted Teresa, rushing to take the boy into her arms.

"I told him to stay at home, but he wouldn't listen. I found him shivering in some bushes, his face all scratched from the twigs and thorns."

"Let me wash your face for you." Teresa led the boy out of the room.

"Was it wise to bring him back here?"

"He is in shock, Señor Velez. Besides, he has nowhere else to go."

Luis nodded his approval.

"Juana is downstairs, dusting. She acts as if nothing has happened. The girl is not very clever, I fear."

"When she is frightened, she cleans, Jose. Just as she did when Gaspar terrorized her. I understand he hasn't left."

"I would be wary of him, Señor. He is too quiet."

"I'm sure I couldn't find anyone to replace him right now. Jose, there is something I must accomplish and may need your help."

"Of course."

"There may be some danger, although I will do the act myself, but if you should be implicated . . ."

"You are speaking of the Inquisition?"

"Yes. Say no and I will not hold it against you."

"But it is my duty to keep you out of trouble. What is this lunacy you plan?"

After Luis explained how he would steal the skull of Susanna Diego, Jose stood silent for a prolonged period of time. He walked over to the chair Teresa had abandoned and sat, his features contorted into complex thought.

"Señor Velez, I can't imagine what you would do with such a thing."

"It's a private matter, Jose, and involves someone else. I can't reveal the reason for the theft."

Jose nodded. "I don't ask you to share a confidence with me, but you do know there is a curse on the skull."

"By the Church?"

Jose shrugged. "People never touch it. Children are warned away, told that Susanna Diego will visit them in the night if they throw anything at the skull. It has set on the lintel for several years, Señor. The Grand Inquisitor himself threatened the flames of hell for anyone who would attempt to retrieve the skull. Many people refuse to even look at it. One of the Inquisition's soldiers lights the lantern every evening just before dusk. People clear the streets in anticipation of his arrival. Best to remain invisible to anyone involved with the Inquisition."

"I must do it, but . . ."

"No, Señor, I have not refused to help. I only want you to understand the magnitude of what you are about to do. This could mean death for you."

"I'll be careful, Jose. I recently walked down that street and found it to be deserted. There is no guard."

"No, Torquemada doesn't believe it is necessary to watch over the skull. The flames of hell he talked about were not necessarily those surrounding the stake. He meant in the afterlife. But my faith is not strong, Señor, and even when it was, I never believed in hell. How can I be of help to you?"

chapter 62

THE PITCH DARKNESS OF *LA CALLE DE LA MUERTE* made the night feel colder than it really was. Jose waited at the end of the street, his shoulders hunched, stamping his feet against the ground. Dressed in old black clothes, Luis strode down the street, his step certain, his manner that of a man who lived in one of the houses on the street. The hour was late, but not late enough to draw suspicion. He could have spent too long at a tavern. He wore a hat low over his face. As he passed one house, he noticed a child peering from the window. A candle set on the sill illuminated the child's face, whose sleepy eyes barely registered the sight of the passing man. Luis took no chances, bowing his head lower and swaying a bit as if he had had too much to drink. Most of the homes were dark; a stray dog skulked along close to the buildings, avoiding Luis.

A hundred yards away, Luis saw the light of a lantern. As he neared, the skull came into view. Rain-washed and sun-bleached, the skull's crown shone under the lantern's glow. There would be no difficulty in reaching the skull. Seeing its precarious position so close to the edge, he thought it strange it had not fallen long ago. *Could the skull be attached in some way?*

He looked over both his shoulders. There was no one walking up or down the street. The caterwaul of a cat and the sharp piercing squeak of a rat made him jump. *Grab it quickly. The longer you wait, the more likely someone will open a door or glance out a window.*

He stepped forward, reached high, and felt the cold bone chill his fingertips. It had not been attached to the sill. It came down easily. But the flame in the lantern flickered several times before dying. A strong wind blew his cape about his body. He almost dropped the skull when a large beetle crawled out from an eye socket onto the back of his hand. He flicked it away, watching it fall to the ground near the toe of his boot. He stepped backward, and with difficulty he managed to slip the skull within the folds of his cape.

"What are you doing there?"

Instinctively Luis looked up and saw the face of the man he had met on this street the last time he was here.

"It's you again. Your aunt was just burned at the stake. There's talk your father will be next."

"He is already dead."

"That won't stop the Grand Inquisitor. Don't you know they dig up the dead heretics and burn their remains at the stake?"

"A waste of good firewood."

"Yes, yes it is. My daughter-in-law and the children could use that firewood. What do you have under your cloak?"

Luis backed away from the man, wanting to run but afraid the man would yell out after him, waking others and perhaps calling their presence to the attention of a guard.

The man looked around until he noticed the lantern sat dark. He moved closer, trying to spy the skull.

"You've taken it. What for? I remember last time we met, you were curious about it. What will you do with it?"

"See that it is properly buried," Luis answered.

The man nodded. "About time. But the Inquisitor will find you. The skull is cursed by his very hands and tongue. Some think he can watch us through her eyes."

"They are empty and will never see again."

"People think Torquemada's magic lives within the skull. Otherwise someone would have taken mercy on Susanna Diego before this and buried her."

"I'm not superstitious, Señor."

"If I don't see you burned at the stake, I shan't be superstitious ever again. Go, and bless you."

Luis almost ran but remembered the caution he must use. Once he turned, but the man had gone, and the street lay empty. Perhaps he had met no one. Perhaps it was a trick of his mind. Or . . . maybe the skull did have magical powers.

chapter 63

LUIS AWOKE TERESA, AND SHE QUICKLY DRESSED before allowing him into her room. He carried an oriental box of black lacquer with gold trim on the corners and a complex lock on the center of the lid.

"What . . .?"

He stopped her from speaking with a gentle touch of his fingers.

"Sit, Teresa."

She swept the cover over the sheet and sat. He knelt before her, raising the box up to the level of her lap. With one hand he balanced the box, and with the other he undid the latch.

"Open it, Teresa." Her name felt soothing on his lips.

Her hands shook as she lifted the lid. The skull looked back at her, the empty eye sockets dark but shiny from the velvet beneath the skull.

"Do I look like she did, I wonder?"

"If so, then she was beautiful."

Teresa looked at his earnest face and knew he would

do anything for her.

"I love you, Teresa."

"Don't say that. Your father would have preferred you love a lady, not a bastard child of a sinner."

"Your mother loved the wrong man. That was no sin."

"Stupid. Foolish. Naïve. There are many names for bad relationships."

"But look what their love gave me."

The room felt far too warm for Teresa.

"Can we bury her now?"

"I've already dug her grave."

"What shall we bury her in? We can't use this expensive box."

"Let this box be my gift to your mother, Teresa." He slowly closed the lid, stood, and gave Teresa his hand, lifting her to her feet.

Outdoors the winds had died down. Teresa and Luis intruded upon the stillness of the cemetery. The small grave lay open toward the back of the cemetery. A shovel lay by a mound of dirt, and Luis had collected some flowers, dropping them inside the grave as a bed of petals for Susanna's long-awaited rest.

"I must look upon her once more," Teresa said, lifting the lid. Her hands reached inside and cradled the skull in her palms. She bowed her head to place a kiss on her mother's forehead. "I've missed you all my life," Teresa whispered.

"But at last you've finally come to know who she was."

Teresa looked up at Luis, his intense dark eyes staring down at the skull she held. His features, shaded by the night, looked careworn and much too old for his age. He loved her, she thought; the idea made her heart beat faster, and her breath caught in her throat.

She returned the skull to the box and lowered the lid, fumbling with the latch. He assisted her, brushing her fingers with his own. Her cheeks flamed, and the smell of his body drew her closer to him. Lifting her chin, he kissed her forehead, her eyelids, the tip of her nose, and with hesitation he set his lips against hers. When she didn't pull away, he deepened the kiss.

"Thank you," she whispered when their lips parted.

"For the kiss?"

She smiled. "For finding my mother." She hesitated shyly for a moment. "And the kiss."

He helped her lower the box into the grave and waited while she said some prayers, watching her lips move silently. Her sleepy bed-tousled hair sprang out in wild waves around her face, highlighting her delicate features. When she had finished the prayers, Luis pronounced the final "Amen," and with surprise, she smiled at him.

"Why don't you go into the house and warm yourself? I'll finish here," he said.

"No. I want to stay until the end."

It didn't take long to fill in the grave. He held her hand as they walked back to the manse, but his gaze picked up a slight movement inside the manse. A curtain had just dropped back into place.

Probably Jose was still awake, wanting to be sure all had been accomplished. He hadn't told Jose to whom the skull had belonged, but he imagined Jose had figured it out. Now the poor man could get some sleep without worrying about what his master was up to.

chapter 64

ALL THAT NIGHT TERESA COULDN'T SLEEP. LUIS
had kissed her again when he had left her in front of the
door to her bedroom, and she had allowed his hands to roam
to places on her body that made her blush to think about.
Blush and . . . yearn for something, she knew not what.

She turned her face into the pillow, imagining his
lips pressed against hers, imagining his hands lingering
on her breasts and sliding down to touch the curve of her
bottom. Her groin pressed into the mattress, she felt a
wetness drip lightly onto her thighs. Moaning in pleasure, confusion, and frustration, Teresa ached to join Luis
in his bed. Just to be able to touch his body the way he
had felt hers would have been a relief.

She sat up, remembering that she had just buried
her mother and should be praying for her soul instead
of indulging in this sin. She took the rosary from the
night table and began with the sign of the cross. Placing her finger on the first bead, she tried praying, but her
thoughts kept slipping back to Luis.

At the convent she had suffered no such temptations. Her days had been filled with activities, and by nightfall she would fall asleep as soon as her head touched the pillow. She was a happy child ... But that was the problem. She had been a child far too long there, never giving any thought to her future. Did she want to dedicate her life to the sick? Certainly she took joy from what she did. Seeing a child overcome a high fever. Helping with the birth of a baby. Keeping men from climbing out of bed too soon after an accident. Occasionally there would be some she could not nurse back to health, but then she prayed with them, holding their hands until the end. The families showed their gratitude by gifting the convent with what little food they could spare or with garments or bed linens.

What would she say to Luis in the morning? How would she even be able to eat, sitting across from him? She'd go back to eating in the kitchen. Juana had already taken over the task of preparing the meals, and if she were anything like Señora Toledo, she'd not allow anyone else to interfere.

Teresa had thought she would stay and help Luis to accept the fate of his family, but now she didn't think that would be a good idea. They lingered too long when they touched. She couldn't help but take sly glances at him when he entered a room.

She placed the rosary around her neck and got out of bed. After dressing, she bundled the few belongings she had and softly opened her door. Jose's room was the last one at the end of the hall. Creeping slowly down past Juana's room, she hugged her bundle tightly against her chest. Jose had left his door slightly open, and when she knocked, it opened farther into the room.

Jose muttered unintelligible words; quickly she spoke his name.

"Be there in a second," he called.

He was buttoning his shirt when he entered the hallway.

"Is there something wrong?" He looked worried, squinting at her in the dim candlelight.

"I want to go back to the convent."

He rubbed his head, messing his hair up even more than it had already been.

"When?"

"Now. Before the others are up."

"What has happened to bring this on? Has Gaspar said or done something?"

"No, he ignores me. That I can deal with."

"Oh, Señor Velez."

"What does that mean?"

"He has perhaps shown some sort of affection for you?"

She hated the sly smile on his face. "He doesn't need me anymore. His father, aunt, and sister are all dead."

"Those may be the reasons why he would need you now, Teresa. He can use a bit of support from all of us at this time."

She shook her head.

"He must make his own decisions about what to do. His father feared the Inquisition would want the house and land. There is a better life for him far from here, I'm sure."

"And you think your leaving will drive him away?"

"Jose, you were at the *auto da fe*. Torquemada has gone mad with his obsession with *conversos*. See that Señor Velez leaves. Go with him, keep him safe."

"Stay, Teresa. Speak to him yourself."

"He might want . . ." Her lips trembled.

"Why not wait and see what happens? You are both young and have no other obligations. Perhaps you are denying yourself love."

"I belong back at the convent, serving the Lord. If you don't take me now, I will start walking."

"Teresa, the last time you did that, the roads were heavy with people going to the city for the *auto da fe*. At this hour, you'd only find drunks and villains."

Teresa turned to walk away, but Jose grabbed her arm.

"I will take you. Señor Velez will not be happy, but he'd be angrier still if I allowed you to go alone."

By dawn Teresa and Jose found themselves in front of the convent. Teresa liked the morning chill alerting her senses, clearing her mind.

"They may be asleep," Jose said, preparing himself for a wait.

"No. They are in the chapel, but someone always listens in case a poor soul needs assistance."

"And this morning you are that 'poor soul.'"

She smiled at Jose, hugging him and kissing him on his tanned cheek.

"I'll wait to make sure you get in all right."

She knocked rapidly at the door, eager to see the sisters once again, positive she belonged here. Sister Roberta answered, her chubby round face looking like a cherub's with the big smile she wore. Both women begged Jose to come in for a bite to eat or for at least a cup of something warm, but he waved them off and climbed back atop the coach.

chapter 65

WHEN JOSE EXPLAINED WHAT HE HAD DONE, LUIS initially became angry, although he didn't quite know where to direct the anger. Jose had made sure Teresa hadn't foolishly left on her own. She could be foolhardy; obstinate, even. What was she fleeing? Him. He had acted on his emotions instead of giving her back her mother without the confusion of how he felt.

It showed how ignorant he could be. A woman born and raised inside a convent didn't know about sexual love. The nuns were married to their God. And even though Teresa had not taken vows, she acted and thought like a nun. She had probably never even flirted with a man before. He laughed, thinking about how he had wanted to go back to her room and make love to her in that small bed. Her screams at the suggestion would have brought Jose and Gaspar running.

"Señor Velez, are you all right?"

"Ah, Jose, you wonder why I am laughing. Simply because both you and Teresa did the right thing. I'm the oaf."

"I don't understand."

"I have given my blessing for everyone else to leave. A few of you have chosen to stay. I never thought of freeing Teresa. In my selfishness I intended to keep her near. Maybe hold hands with her on the way to the stake. What do you think, Jose?"

"I think you love her. Holding hands while walking down the aisle in a church would be more appropriate."

"But less likely."

"You haven't asked yet."

"I'm not going to. What do I have to offer? Be my bride. We'll honeymoon in the Inquisition's dungeon. Let us lie down on the rack together for the short time that we have."

"You are wrong to think your life is over. There is much you can do; if not here, then elsewhere. You've traveled much and know a number of well-connected merchants who can assist in finding a new home for you."

"I don't want a new home, Jose!" He heard himself shout and stopped to breathe before continuing. "No one should be driven from their home because they worship a different God or have a different way of praying. The Catholic Church wants to destroy my people. They've already killed two members of my family. Someone told me he had heard the Inquisition wants my father's body to burn. They can't even let the dead rest in peace. The bishop would walk into our home, eat at our table, sit with my father until late at night, talking. Where will he be when the Inquisition's soldiers come to dig up my father's grave?

I will be here, Jose, with a weapon in my hand."

"Señor Velez, your death will not prevent them from burning your father's remains. He is no longer inside his old, withered body. The only way your family will prevail is if you survive."

Luis's eyes hardened. *How dare this servant speak so freely?* But then, they had always told each other clearly what they thought.

"I know my aunt's clothes are old, Jose, but take them to the convent to be given to the poor. Most of the clothes have hardly been worn. Tell them my father's clothes will follow." Luis lifted his breakfast from the table, held it over the carpet, and turned the plate over. Spider rushed to feed on the treat while Luis walked out of the dining room.

Late in the afternoon, inside the convent Jose sat at a table drinking sherry with Sister Agatha and Teresa. He had allowed them to fill his glass several times, and Teresa sensed this was to build courage.

"Tell Señor Luis we appreciate the clothes. As for them being out of date, it does not matter; most of the poor women have excellent sewing skills and can alter the dresses easily." Sister Agatha held up the bottle of sherry and Jose enthusiastically nodded.

"Señor Velez is not doing well. He insists upon staying in this region. If he were wise . . ."

"You must change his mind," Teresa said. "Shouldn't he, Sister Agatha?"

"Jose is employed by Señor Velez, Teresa. It is not Jose's job to tell his master how to live."

"But if he stays, the Inquisitor will arrest Luis. I mean Señor Velez."

Sister Agatha folded her hands on the table and sat taller in her chair.

"Teresa, you should never use the familiar name of Señor Velez. People would misunderstand. I know it to be harmless, but those who do not know you well might question your relationship with him."

"They care for each other, Sister." Jose had almost taken another sip of the sherry but stopped when he heard what Sister Agatha had to say. He set the glass back on the table. "I am here to ask Teresa to reconsider her decision to leave the manse."

"Señor Velez no longer has any need of Teresa's services. I understand the staff has dwindled considerably, but Teresa is not a household servant. Today we spoke of her taking vows."

"She's a bastard child," Jose said.

"Teresa is baptized. The circumstances of her birth can be overlooked."

Jose turned to Teresa. "Tell her how you love Señor Velez."

Teresa shook her head. "I pity him and wish him well. God has tried him sorely. Señor Velez will have a good life if he leaves for another country. Perhaps Portugal. He mentioned doing some business there."

"You are lying to yourself because you don't know how to live outside these damn walls."

"Enough!" Sister Agatha's harsh voice made Teresa

cringe. "It is time for you to leave, Jose. We have prayers in ten minutes and must go to the chapel."

"Pray your life away, Sister, but let Teresa go."

"Teresa, please go to the chapel and light the candles." When Teresa didn't move, Sister Agatha tapped her on the arm. Immediately Teresa stood, bowing her head to Jose before leaving the room.

"Jose, I believe Gaspar and Juana are still employed at the manse. I would prefer one of them to bring the rest of the clothes."

"Why keep Teresa under lock and key? Let her make up her own mind."

"She has. She entreated for the honor to take her vows."

chapter 66

Days had passed since Teresa had left the manse, and Luis had kept himself busy planning his next business venture. One evening he rode his horse to the fanciest whorehouse in the city. He planned on paying for the services of two women. The manse didn't need his attention for a day or two, and he could afford to drown himself in the most indecent of debaucheries. He had his choice of the best women in service. A feast had been set on the bedroom's table, and abundant alcohol filled the room. But he noticed a different smell about the place. A rancid odor of bodily fluids, expensive perfume, and overspiced food. It sickened him. Most of all, the women's attentions intruded upon his somber mood. He was there to relax, he reminded himself, reaching out to wrap his palm around one woman's naked breast. She pushed against him, her tongue licking the side of his throat before nibbling on his flesh. Instead of flaming his desire, the bite hurt. It annoyed him as the sting of a bee would. Abruptly he threw a handful of *maravedies* on the bed and left.

On an overcast day, Luis took Spider for a walk. It had been raining the previous two days, and his boots frequently stuck in the mud, making the walk far more exercise than he had planned. The dog bounded through the high grass, bringing back twigs for Luis to toss.

They were not far from the manse when Luis sighted the Inquisition's soldiers approaching the front door. He ran in their direction, thinking they had come to take his father's body away.

He stopped short, out of breath, when he saw Gaspar point in his direction. The soldiers met Luis part of the way.

Catching his breath, he stood tall, ready to deny them what they had come for.

"Señor Velez?" The man asking knew well who he was. He was the same man who had come for his aunt.

"You know me. What do you want now? My father's corpse?"

"We are not here for a dead man, Señor. The Grand Inquisitor wishes to speak with you."

"Am I to be his guest in the dungeon?"

Jose came running from the barn. "This is a mistake, I am sure! The bishop dines with Señor Velez. He has given generously from his pantry and wealth!" Jose shouted in the leader's ear. His excitement earned a backhanded slap.

"Leave him be. He is a servant, not a member of this family. He is Christian. I am not."

The hunchback greeted Luis and the soldiers at the door. Only Luis was allowed to enter. Hugo bowed deeply, beckoning Luis into the library.

"Señor Velez, I'm glad they found you at home. I feared you may have taken leave of Spain by now."

"I am a Spaniard, Father. Why would I flee my homeland?"

"But you are also a Jew, aren't you?" Torquemada's robe brushed against Luis as the cleric walked to a shelf of books. "I have a book you could translate for me."

Luis took the volume and recognized the Hebrew writing on it.

"I don't know this language."

Torquemada looked surprised.

"My father never taught me Hebrew. He gave greater weight to my Spanish."

He heard a knock, and the Inquisitor waited in silence until Hugo came into the room. He carried the laquer box in which Susanna Diego's skull had been buried.

"They found a fresh grave and dug this up, Father." The hunchback unlatched the lid and opened the box. The skull still rested inside.

"Susanna Diego's skull. Why would you steal this and bury it in consecrated ground?"

"Because after all these years, she deserved a decent burial."

"Her father was a heretic. He burned at the stake. The Church had mercy on her because she was with child. A mistake."

"She can do no harm now. Let her bones mingle with the earth."

"They will after we burn her remains. The ashes will be thrown into a common grave with the rest of the heretics. She will not be lonely in hell."

Torquemada picked up a white cloth on the desk and carefully reached for the skull, taking care that his own flesh would not come into contact with it. He held it up for Luis to see.

"I have heard she was an attractive woman. It no longer matters. Her beauty has been robbed, as has her soul. Lucifer possesses that. She burns in hell, suffering the loss of God, wishing to see His face at least once. An eternity of pain and longing. Do you wish that for yourself?"

Luis refused to answer; seeing the wild gleam in the cleric's eyes, he understood his fate.

"Hugo, have a guard take Señor Velez to his new living quarters."

"As I recall, Father, those quarters are more for dying than living." Without protest Luis followed the hunchback.

The guard led Luis to the cell where Catrin had been kept. The familiar smell of waste filled his nostrils. The hay hadn't been changed, and when he rearranged the stack for sitting, he found the shawl he had given to Catrin. The sight made him stagger back. The image of the flames seeking her flesh to feed its hunger forced him to close his eyes.

"Catrin, I wish we had known the truth from the start."

A few steps and he picked up the shawl, holding it to his nose. Could her scent have survived over the miasma filling this cell? He believed he caught a hint, an illusion perhaps.

"Thank God," he said, relieved to know Teresa had returned to the convent.

chapter 67

"Are you sure you want to take your vows, Teresa?" Sister Roberta assisted with the laundry, her sleeves rolled up and her hands dripping with water.

"Yes. Sister Agatha said the bishop should give his approval within the next few weeks." She twisted the wet clothes tightly, wringing out as much of the water as she could.

"You aren't laughing the way you used to, before Sister Agatha sent you to care for Señor Velez. I think you miss living at the manse."

"It wasn't so grand. No one bothered to care for the house. The expensive furniture was badly used, and some rooms were left empty."

"I don't mean to suggest you liked the wealth. But often you are preoccupied."

"The manse is a very sad place. You know the problems the family has suffered."

"Why not continue working here without taking vows?"

"Because I want to dedicate myself to God."

"Secretly I've had doubts."

Teresa looked over at the nun who stood without moving.

"I never speak of them with anyone except my confessor. He has given me some harsh penances for thoughts I have had. I was but sixteen when I took vows. My family wasn't sure they ever would marry me off. Feeling ashamed, I entered the convent."

"But you love God. I can see it when you pray."

"What does loving God have to do with being a nun? My mother loved God, and she married and had seven children. Only four of us survived, and we are a comfort to her now. Who will I have when I'm too old to get out of bed?"

"The sisters will care for you."

"Because they must, not out of love."

"That is silly, Sister Roberta. Here we are part of the same family." Teresa dropped the wet clothing she had been wringing onto a pile of clean, wet clothes. "Help me hang these outside, Sister Roberta."

The two women lugged the clean clothes to the backyard.

"When you were a baby, I loved holding you. Your warm little body snuggled in my arms, sleeping so peacefully. You trusted us."

"I'm safe here. I always have been."

"Is that all you want from life?"

The women set the bundle down on a rock and shook the clothes out one by one to hang on the line.

"Sister Agatha thinks you were contaminated at the manse. She hopes you came back a virgin," said Sister Roberta.

"Of course I did."

"Señor Velez is a handsome man. Were you not tempted?" Sister Roberta's face peeked out from under her veil.

"Yes. He can also be kind." Teresa thought back to the lacquer box, remembering the box's contents. "He did something very brave for me. I'll always be indebted." *And in love with him*, she silently thought.

A young novitiate of not more than seventeen rushed into the yard.

"The servant from the manse is here. He asked for Teresa, but don't tell Sister Agatha I told you. She is trying to send him away."

Fearing something wrong, Teresa immediately went into the house. Hearing the sound of her sandals on the tile floor, Jose rushed to meet her.

"Teresa, it is awful. I don't know what to do."

Sister Agatha came up behind him, reaching out with her right hand to turn him around. He tried to push her hand away.

"You've not been invited into this convent. I shall . . ."

"What?" he shouted, facing her. "Tell my master! Go ahead. Maybe you can obtain permission to enter Torquemada's filthy pit!"

"Torquemada?" Teresa held her breath. *No.* The Grand Inquisitor couldn't have acted so quickly. "Luis has been arrested?"

"Teresa!" Sister Agatha attempted to place herself between Jose and Teresa but failed.

"Yes. They came digging around in the cemetery. At first I thought they wanted to dig up Señor Roberto Velez's remains, but they found what they wanted in a far corner of the cemetery."

"A black lacquer box?"

"Yes, Teresa. I believe it is the skull of Susanna Diego."

"God have mercy on him," Sister Agatha said.

"I told him not to steal the skull, but he insisted. He said he owed someone."

"This has nothing to do with you, Teresa. It must be some sort of a cruel joke or wager."

"You know that isn't true, Sister Agatha."

"What else could it be?"

Teresa stared into the nun's eyes, never wavering, begging the nun to admit the truth. Embarrassed, the nun couldn't hold the stare; she looked down at the floor.

"Susanna Diego is my mother, Jose."

"God forgive me, I didn't know. If I had, I wouldn't have come. There is nothing you can do to help."

"But I can go to the Grand Inquisitor and explain why Luis stole the skull."

"No, Teresa." Jose backed away from her. "It would bring the Church's wrath down on your head. They will accuse you of bewitching Señor Velez."

"I must take that chance."

"Teresa, listen." Sister Agatha stepped past Jose.

"Your mother made a great effort to have you birthed inside this convent. She pleaded with us to take her in. While here she insisted upon doing as much work as possible, even though we warned her to be careful. At your birth she took your little bloody body into her arms and cried. She kissed you tenderly, and we had to drag you out of her arms to clean you. She feared if the Inquisition found you, they'd burn you the same way they did all heretics, to punish her for the many sins she had committed. For a time, even after your mother left, we kept you hidden inside these walls. Only when rumor spread that Susanna had miscarried did we take you into the sun. Many looked askance at us, thinking one of us could be your mother. We didn't care. Our joy was seeing you survive during these cruel times. Too many people have sacrificed for you, Teresa, for you to hand yourself over to the Inquisitor."

Teresa lowered herself onto the cold tile floor and sat cross-legged.

"Sister Agatha is telling the truth. Señor Velez gave you the gift of knowledge. He wanted you to be able to be at peace about your birth. Don't throw his gift back into his face. Stay here. I will make a plea to the bishop for his help. Señor Roberto Velez did many favors for the bishop. Now it is time to pay a dead man back." Jose fled the convent.

The two women heard the horse he rode galloping away. Teresa listened to the thudding of her heart, sure that it would break.

Sister Roberta moved slowly into the hall where the two women were. She walked over to where Teresa sat and clumsily settled her body down on the tiles. Her arms encircled the young woman.

"Teresa, what does your heart tell you to do?" Sister Roberta's hands tightened around Teresa's arms, and they looked at each other.

"I love him." Teresa watched the nun nod her head. "I can't let him die for me without trying to save him. If it is my time to meet the Lord, I will accept that."

"Teresa, that's foolish talk. Didn't you hear Señor Velez's own servant? Señor Velez would never want you to die in his place. He took a chance, and it gave the Grand Inquisitor the wherewithal to arrest him, but remember, Torquemada had been watching his family for some time. If it hadn't been the theft of the skull, it would have been something else. Torquemada would have invented something," said Sister Agatha.

"She is right, Teresa," Sister Roberta spoke in a low voice.

"If he had been arrested for coming to his aunt's aid, I would have tried to save him. He is my life. My mother and I may share loving the wrong man in common. We both may pay heavy prices for that."

chapter 68

TERESA FELT TINY, WAITING IN THE OUTER HALL of the Inquisitor's house. The hunchback had corralled her into sitting on a hard wooden bench. Filled with splinters, the rough wood pulled at her skirt when she made the slightest movement. A door opened at the end of the hall; a giant of a man appeared, his bare chest heaving from some heavy exertion. The beard on his face looked infested with lice, and his shaggy eyebrows threw shadows over his eyes. When he saw her, he rubbed his large hands together, the smile on his face reflecting his lurid thoughts. She turned her head, hoping the hunchback would quickly return. He had been gone much too long, and temptation to flee grew strong.

"What are you doing here?"

She recognized the hunchback's voice. A great sigh escaped her lips. When she looked in the direction of the voice, she saw the giant had disappeared.

"Come. Hurry! Father Torquemada will see you."

She clutched her skirt in her hands, stood, and followed the hunchback into an enormous room filled with nothing but a desk, a single chair, and a long table. Torquemada stood next to the desk, his hands folded together, the spray of hair circling his head sprinkled with gray.

"You have come to plead for Señor Velez. What do you know of him?"

"I took care of his father."

"Ah, the bastard child from the convent. He has chosen not to speak your name, but I believe the bishop mentioned the name Teresa."

"Yes, that is my name."

"Do you fear me?"

"I respect you, Father. You are doing God's work."

"Then why interfere, my child?"

"I am Susanna Diego's daughter. Señor Velez felt indebted to me for the care I had given his father. That is why he stole the skull and buried it. I am guilty of not discouraging him."

Torquemada went to Teresa and gently put his hands on her cheeks.

"Are you in love with Señor Luis Velez?" The mellifluous sound of his voice and tender, warm touch disarmed Teresa.

She nodded, unable to speak.

"Would you like to see him?"

"Please," she whispered, her eyes searching his for comfort.

He moved his hands from her cheeks to her hands and led her to the chair, which he pulled into the center of the room.

"Sit down, child. First I want you to tell me what happened at the Velez manse while you were caring for the senior Velez."

Teresa's mind became a jumble of scenes and words. How could she carefully pick and choose what to say?

"I cared for Señor Roberto Velez. I spent most of my time with him."

"Not all of your time, because you became enchanted by his son."

"He often visited with his father. I watched them together and observed the love they shared."

"And because of their love, you learned to love Señor Luis Velez?"

"He is kind. I told you he offered to bury my mother's skull."

"You knew I had condemned Susanna Diego, and part of her penance was the mortification of her skull after death."

"Everyone knows that."

"Why encourage him to steal it?"

"I just had learned she was my mother. I was confused."

"Confused or tempted?"

"Confused, Father."

"What did you know of Isabella Velez and Catrin?"

"I never met Catrin. She had been taken from the house before I arrived, and Señora Velez kept to herself."

"You are lying. Isabella told us of the conversations

she had with you. Does that spark a memory?"

"Señora Velez was not always coherent, Father."

"You certainly could understand the words she spoke. Why won't you share what she said? She is no longer able to take revenge. Are you trying to protect Señor Velez by protecting his aunt and sister? You do know Catrin was his sister?"

"I'm sorry, Father. I don't know what they have to do with the current charge against Señor Velez."

"The devil spins webs to ensnare souls, Teresa. You see, one blackened soul isn't enough. The devil wants more and more. He fills his hell to overflowing."

"Señor Velez has nothing to do with the devil. He tried to do a favor for me, and I was foolish enough to accept. Neither of us were party to the devil's mischief."

"Hugo, let's take Teresa down to see her ... would I be wrong to call him your lover, Teresa?"

"We hardly touched or kissed, Father, and we certainly never knew each other in the biblical sense."

Torquemada nodded, accepting her statement.

Slowly the threesome wended their way down the steep staircase to the dungeon. She recognized the giant of a man she had seen in the hall upstairs. He leered at her, forcing her to draw closer to the Inquisitor. They walked past cells filled with bodies half-dead, exhausted from the brutal treatment they consistently received.

"Here we are, Teresa." The Inquisitor made her stand in front of a heavily stained door while the giant undid the lock.

Initially when the door flew open, she saw only pitch darkness, but the smell wafting from the room made her take a step backward. Luis appeared out of the gloom, and she ran to him. Her hands touched his tattered shirt where bruises marred his body. The stubble of his beard prickled her cheek, but she wouldn't pull away from him.

"Why did you bring her here?"

"Like you, she had an interest in seeing our dungeon. She wanted to be sure you were all right."

"I came on my own to explain why you had taken the skull." Her voice wavered with subdued sobs.

"You've seen me. Now go." He pushed her away.

"But . . ." She looked from Luis to Torquemada. "You can't keep him. I explained . . . It is I who did wrong. I should have told him not to. Please, let him go. I can't stand to think he is here because of me."

"Although many may not believe me, I, too, have a soft spot in my heart for lovers. It is dreadful to see them parted." Torquemada stood back out of the doorway, and with a hand signal, the giant closed and locked the door, leaving Teresa and Luis reaching out to each other in the dark.

chapter 69

ALL NIGHT TERESA AND LUIS HELD EACH OTHER. No one bothered to bring them food or empty the waste from the pail. Teresa barely slept, listening instead to the screams, the crying, the torment of words flowing from the mouths of the dying. She gagged from the horrid odors enveloping them. But neither spoke in the unreality of the darkness. Words meant nothing; only a touch could comfort.

In the morning a new guard appeared, bringing bread, water, and a bit of tough flesh that vaguely resembled beef. The portion small, Luis wanted her to eat it all. Instead she ripped the bread into pieces and fed it to him with her own hands, his tongue lapping at her fingers, his lips kissing the back of her hand.

A key turned in the lock, and the door swung open.

"Come, the Grand Inquisitor wishes to speak with both of you."

In a few moments they found themselves inside a small, stuffy room. Torquemada sat at a table, Hugo beside him with pen poised. To the right of Torquemada stood two men in long brown robes. The hoods pulled over their faces had slits for their eyes.

"Take her back outside," Torquemada demanded.

Shoved back into the hall, the pressure of the guards' hands on her shoulders made her fall to the floor. She brought her knees to her chest, wrapped her arms around them, and waited. Thinking she heard the cry of a child, she tried to stand, but the guard kicked her feet out from under her, and she fell back down. The sound came closer, the wailing more uncontrolled and adamant. A guard dragging something came into view at the end of the hall. A woman's limp body skidded along the stone floor; her child, held in the arms of another guard, thrashed at his captor's face. No more than five years old, the child kept yelling for his mother. As they passed, Teresa instinctively caught onto the woman's hand, feeling for a pulse. A kick in Teresa's side sent her sprawling, bringing tears to her eyes and a sudden blindness that immediately cleared.

"Stay still!" the guard commanded through the din inside her head.

The door opened, and as soon as Luis spied Teresa on the floor, he attempted to go to her, but the two cloaked men overpowered him.

Teresa felt a hand lifting her up and mistook it for Luis's. Sorely disappointed when she recognized the guard, she almost sagged back down, but the guard's strength kept her standing. She leaned against the wall, smelling the guard's sweat. She closed her eyes and searched for a vision of the convent, something to bring a moment's peace.

In a few minutes she found herself in a dingy room lit by several lanterns. The hunchback sat at a small table, dipping his pen in ink, writing rapidly.

"Teresa, I'm sorry that it appears you had an accident." Torquemada appeared in front of her, his face a blur through the pain she experienced. He felt her face.

"Physician, could you have a look?"

Immediately a guard lifted Teresa and placed her on a table. She fought as he lifted her skirt and the doctor spread her legs to reach inside her.

"She is a virgin," the doctor pronounced.

Freed, she swept her skirt back down and sat up.

"You told the truth, Teresa. I must say you gave me cause to doubt you. Ah, Señor Luis, the woman did not need to entice you into committing sin. Or did she make promises not kept?"

She heard a muffled reply before seeing Luis strapped to a slanted board, his shirt ripped to shreds on the floor. Slipping off the table, she gradually made her way to him. Iron prongs kept his jaws open, and a linen cloth lay inside his mouth.

"What are you going to do?" she raged, facing Torquemada.

"Señor Velez has refused to testify to what occurred inside his home. We thought he might need encouragement."

"What do you want him to say? You've killed his aunt and sister. His father is dead. Luis has done nothing wrong except for aiding me."

"Only eight jugs of water. Let us start with the first jug." Torquemada spoke to one of the robed guards, who brought forth a filled vessel. "Commence."

Holding the jug above Luis's mouth, the robed man tipped the container and began pouring. Water tumbled into Luis's mouth, making the linen fall back against his throat. Teresa heard the gurgling noise and the choking gulps Luis was forced to take.

"Stop! I'll tell you everything. Please, don't harm him."

With a slight hand movement, Torquemada stopped the guard.

"What you have to say would be of use, Teresa. Hugo is prepared to listen. He will transcribe. Can you write?" She nodded. "You will sign the testimony?"

Again she nodded, exhaustion overtaking her.

chapter 70

She spoke of her own sins of lust, of anger, of petty disputes. None of it satisfied the Grand Inquisitor. He wanted more from her, but would not give her a clue as to what the magic sentences would be. Slowly she revealed what Isabella had told her, knowing the dead woman no longer experienced earthly pain. But what of Señor Roberto Velez? the Inquisitor asked. She hesitated, and another jug of water was poured into Luis's mouth.

Sliding ever so slowly into revealing confidences she never meant to speak, she began to feel numb. Until one day the dead, decaying body of the older man lay in front of her. Torquemada's men had dug up Roberto Velez's coffin.

She and Luis had been allowed only one night together. The only time she saw Luis was when he was either on the slanted board or tied naked to the rack, his body gradually shrinking before her, emaciation and disease claiming his once-healthy physique.

"You'll have Luis in a casket like this one," she said in a monotone, staring down at the deceased elder Velez.

"That is not our intent, child." Torquemada touched her hair, but he pulled away when he saw the lice crawling through the curls.

"Shear her," he said in disgust.

Already on her knees, she waited like an animal to be stripped of her pride. Snippets of hair fell onto the face of the corpse, the vermin scurrying across the blackening flesh.

"Are you a witch?" Torquemada asked.

"A witch?" She looked up at the Inquisitor, confusion obvious on her face. "I was raised inside a convent. I prayed every day. My confessions were heartfelt."

"But are you a witch?"

"No. Bring my mother's skull here and I will swear on it."

"Woman, the skull is worthless. It is linked with the devil, not God."

Torquemada pulled her to her feet and dragged her to the fire stoked by a robed man. Grabbing her hands, Torquemada held them to the fire, her screams echoing off the walls, causing other prisoners to flex and moan in their own terror.

From that day on, a guard's dirty fingers pushed food into her mouth and held cups for her to drink out of, as her own hands were swollen and blistered.

As days passed, she learned to pray for death. Luis no longer recognized her. One of his broken bones protruded out of his flesh. The physician rebroke the bone, stitching the flesh back together without relief of brandy.

One day, evening, night, she no longer knew, a guard came to her cell carrying the yellow *sambenito*. She didn't bother to cover her flesh where the great rips in her clothes revealed a good deal of her body. Too much had passed for her to retain that kind of dignity.

"You had better pray hard tonight, for tomorrow will be the *auto da fe.*" The guard threw the *sambenito* on the floor. "In the morning take off those rags and put on your penitent's garb."

"Will I see a confessor tonight?"

"You'll have the opportunity to repent on the *Tablada.*" He closed and locked the door behind him.

Teresa raised herself up onto her knees. Torquemada had allowed her to keep the rosary Sister Agatha had given her, and she attempted to remove it from around her neck. Her palms, covered with open wounds, ached, but she forced the beads into her hands and prayed. Prayed for death to come quickly. Prayed for Luis, who didn't acknowledge her anymore. His somber face never changed its expression. Through pain he maintained stoic silence. His eyes at times bulged, unwanted tears rushed from his eyes, but no sob broke his lips.

She touched her head, recalling how clean shaven it now was. She wished they would give her something to cover her head, but quickly she felt shame for the prideful thought. Lifting the *sambenito*, she noticed the flames painted onto the bottom of the garment, the orange-and-black paint meant to remind the wearer of the hell to which he or she was headed.

"Our Father, who art in heaven . . ."

She prayed through the night until she heard the screams and fights coming from outside the cell. A few of the prisoners got in line without any argument. She slipped the rosary over her head and dressed in the *sambenito*, knowing that if she didn't, the guard would rip what little clothes she wore off and pull the *sambenito* over her head for her. There were no choices to be made. This was the smallest dignity allowed.

When the cell door opened, she stood, lightly bringing her palms together while she mouthed her prayers. Already a long line of heretics stood just beyond their cells. The guards pushed them forward, up the stairs and into the blinding dawn. She covered her face, but a guard forced her hands down by her side.

Once accustomed to the light, she searched for Luis. First she saw Señor Roberto Velez's coffin, carried by volunteers who were promised plenary indulgences for their assistance. A short man with a pocked face and long dark hair walked slowly nearby, carrying her mother's skull. A crude effigy of a woman tied to a pole led the group. Teresa tried to turn to look behind her, but the halberdiers with their axes threatened.

"Luis," she said, wanting to see him one last time before the fires snuffed out her life.

A brute bumped into her, and she turned slightly to see the face of Gaspar. But the haughtiness had disappeared. Instead, fear raged in his left eye, his face covered with bruises, his right eye missing. She had heard that the vise on the rack could be used in such a way as to cause eyes to pop out of their sockets.

"Gaspar," she said.

The fear in his eye quickly changed to hate.

"Whore," he charged. "Whore!" His voice rose. He kept shouting that one word at her. She moved away from him closer to the front of the line, the defeated people surrounding her easily pushed out of the way.

"Don't rush so fast to the stake. We have to warm up the fire!" yelled a guard in her direction. The observing crowd laughed uproariously.

"Burn! Burn!" began the chant from the crowd, a chaotic mass of people lacking any humanity.

chapter 71

ON THE STAGE, LUIS RECOGNIZED HIS FATHER'S coffin. One of the guards ripped the lid off, and the smell of decaying flesh momentarily made the front row of the audience take a step back. But the crowd surged forward, not wanting to miss a single moment, pushing those in the front against the stage.

An ugly little man pranced across the stage, holding Susanna Diego's skull high, once in a while lowering it toward the crowd where many in the audience spat on it. Luis jerked forward, wanting to throw the bastard off the platform, but his broken arm pierced his mind with pain, bringing back the caution of reason.

After a prolonged sermon by Torquemada, a Dominican priest began to call off the names of the heretics, stating their crimes and the punishment for each. He knew his name would be at the end with those who would burn at the stake.

When Teresa's name was called, he watched as she stepped to the front. His heart broke to see how she had been shorn of her glorious hair. He remembered how soft her locks had been, how comforting it was to feel them in the darkness of their prison cell the first night she had been taken prisoner.

"Burn!" someone shouted from the crowd.

Luis closed his eyes and found a few words of a prayer on his lips.

"And you will make a pilgrimage to . . ."

His eyes opened. "A pilgrimage," the man had said. Teresa would not die here at the stake. His lips shaped into a long-forgotten smile. At least she had been saved. He watched her walk from the stage into the arms of the bishop. He heard a chuckle deep in his throat. *The old pervert came through. The nuns must have a special influence after all.*

He hadn't heard his name called, but it must have been, because a guard roughly dragged him to the center of the stage. He didn't bother to listen to the lies the Dominican spewed about him. It no longer mattered. Teresa would be safe in the arms of the bishop. The nuns would take her back into the convent.

His eyes caught sight of the men holding the faggots for the fire, and his thick tongue tried to press saliva onto his lips, but his dry mouth failed him. He would not kneel in front of the Grand Inquisitor. He would not beg for mercy. Instead he would burn alive with the remains of his dead father. He would suffer the same fate as poor Catrin and his mad aunt. But then he was being moved to the end of the stage, pushed off the platform by a large oaf with hands so rough they scraped Luis's tender flesh.

"Come, Luis, quickly." The bishop's voice was eager, resolute, but Luis couldn't stand, his numb legs and feet unable to feel the ground under him.

The bishop called to someone, and Jose suddenly arrived, his strong arms practically lifting his master off the ground. Shuffling forward, Luis saw his coach; Teresa sat inside, peering out the open door.

"Hurry, get him in. He must be gone before Torquemada changes his mind." The bishop's hot breath was close to Luis's face.

Jose handed him up to Teresa, and only Spider took the time to lap happily at Luis's cheek.

"What happened?" Luis asked.

"We managed to place the blame on Gaspar. Juana swore the most horrible things about him. She hated him more than I did. Possibly slightly less than his own cousin," the bishop explained.

"And where is she now?"

The bishop shrugged. "It doesn't matter anymore. Gaspar will burn today, and if Juana is wise, she will already be gone from this region."

"I must do something to help Gaspar." Luis stretched his body to descend from the coach.

"Don't be a fool. Who do you think testified against you, Luis? Gaspar watched you and Teresa bury that lacquer box. He remembered Teresa kissing the skull. No, he doesn't deserve anyone's help. The Inquisitor has agreed to burn your father as a heretic in your place. I promised you would leave Spain immediately. Go now. Don't make it look like I deceived Torquemada, for then we all would burn."

"Jose and Manuel will be taking us away," Teresa said, her arms holding on to Luis tightly.

"Manuel?"

"Yes, he'll be riding up top with me. The boy has no home. I didn't think you would mind." Jose stole a cautious look at Luis.

"Of course, I don't mind, but will he be safe with us?"

"Luis, you must listen," the bishop said. "Jose will be taking you out of Spain to Portugal. I know you and your father made business contacts there. This is what little money I can spare." The bishop handed him a small sack full of coins. "The manse and your lands now belong to the Church and the state. You have Teresa to think about now."

Rage almost took over, except when Luis looked at Teresa, thin, vulnerable, frightened; he suppressed his rage, knowing the bishop spoke the truth.

"Never come back. Never contact me or the sisters," the bishop said, his gaze straying over to Teresa. They nodded their agreement. The bishop slammed the door closed and motioned for Jose to take his place.

"Why?" Louis asked.

The bishop smiled. "Your father and I lost count of the number of times we had done favors for each other. I think now I am ahead. Perhaps he'll intercede with the Lord for me."

The coach pulled forward, and pain spread through Luis's body, but he knew he'd heal. Alerted by his grimace, Teresa looked worried and wanted to stop the coach, but Luis wrapped an arm around her, bringing her close, kissing the barren top of her head. Again she would have those beautiful dark curls, and he would regain the strength he needed to make a decent home for them in their new country.

SIREN'S CALL
MARY ANN MITCHELL

Sirena is a beautiful young woman. By night she strips at Silky Femmes, enticing large tips from conventioneers and salesmen passing through the small Florida city where she lives.

Sirena is also a loyal and compassionate friend to the denizens of Silky Femmes. There's Chrissie, who is a fellow dancer as well as the boss's abused and beleaguered girlfriend. And Ross, the bartender, who spends a lot of time worrying about the petite, delicate, and lovely Sirena. Maybe too much time.

There's also Detective Williams. He's looking for a missing man and his investigation takes him to Silky's. Like so many others, he finds Sirena irresistible. But again, like so many others, he's underestimated Sirena.

Because Sirena has a hobby. Not just any hobby. From the stage she searches out men with the solid bone structure she requires. The ones she picks get to go home with her where she will perform one last private strip for them. They can't believe their luck. They simply don't realize it's just run out.

ISBN#9781932815160
Mass Market Paperback / Horror
US $6.99 / CDN $9.99
Available Now
www.maryann-mitchell.com

THE WITCH

mary ann mitchell

Deep in the basement a wooden box sits on a table. Demons that were called into the world are etched on the box. With tiny claws they writhe, push, and scratch at the wood, attempting to gain freedom. The forked tongues flick the air, bulbous noses scent, swollen cheeks pulse. Their icy determined voices vibrate the atmosphere with inaudible high-pitched screeches calling for revenge.

Five-year old Stephen's mother, Cathy, is dead. Her body was cremated, her ashes cast into the ocean. Yet her spirit hovers over Stephen. It urges him to go down to the basement. For Stephen is meant to be the demons' instrument. His innocence will be their mask, his love their weapon.

Because Stephen's father ended his affair with the babysitter too late. And Stephen's oppressive, demanding grandmother must pay for the pain she selfishly forced on her daughter.

With blue eyes and cherub smile, Stephen will set out to punish Mommy's persecutors.

ISBN#9781932815818
Mass Market Paperback / Horror
US $6.99 / CDN $9.99
Available Now
www.maryann-mitchell.com

The Vampire Shrink

LYNDA HILBURN

Denver psychologist Kismet Knight, Ph.D., doesn't believe in the paranormal. She especially doesn't believe in vampires. That is, until a new client introduces Kismet to the vampire underworld and a drop dead gorgeous, 800-year-old vampire named Devereux. Kismet isn't buying the vampire story, but can't explain why she has such odd reactions and feelings whenever Devereux is near. Kismet is soon forced to open her mind to other possibilities, however, when she is visited by two angry bloodsuckers who would like nothing better than to challenge Devereux by hurting Kismet.

To make life just a bit more complicated, one of Kismet's clients shows up in her office almost completely drained of blood, and Kismet finds herself immersed in an ongoing murder investigation. Enter handsome FBI profiler Alan Stevens who warns her that vampires are very real. And one is a murderer. A murderer who is after her.

In the midst of it all, Kismet realizes she has feelings for both the vampire and the profiler. But though she cares for each of the men, facing the reality that vampires exist is enough of a challenge . . . for now.

ISBN#9781933836232
US $15.95 / CDN $19.95
Trade Paperback / Paranormal
Now Available
www.LyndaHilburn.com

SOMETHING BAD

RICHARD SATTERLIE

Gabe Petersen can't cross the borders of his rural Tri-county area—even the thought triggers the erratic cardiac rhythm and breathing difficulty of a panic attack. And he doesn't know why. His memories stop at twelve years of age, his early years nonexistent.

But when a strange little man arrives in town, Gabe feels an unsettling sense of familiarity. Then families begin to die, all because of bizarre natural disasters, and the events trigger glimmers of memory for Gabe. Memories pointing to Thibideaux, the strange little man.

Returning memories open a door on rusty hinges in Gabe's mind. Behind the door is a catatonic Catholic priest who fled the area years ago after he was found sitting on the church altar surrounded by the slaughtered remains of several animals. And Gabe now remembers . . . he was there. Along with Thibideaux.

The past explodes, revealing Gabe's deepest fears. This time, his family is Thibideaux's prize. And Gabe's only weapon to defend them is his mind . . .

ISBN#9781933836133
US $6.99 / CDN $8.99
Mass Market Paperback / Horror
Now Available

THE DREAM THIEF

HELEN A. ROSBURG

Someone is murdering young, beautiful women in mid-sixteenth century Venice. Even the most formidable walls of the grandest villas cannot keep him out, for he steals into his victims' dreams. Holding his chosen prey captive in the night, he seduces them . . . to death.

Now Pina's cousin, Valeria, is found dead, her lovely body ravished. It is the final straw for Pina's overbearing fiance', Antonio, and he orders her confined within the walls of her mother's opulent villa on Venice's Grand Canal. It is a blow not only to Pina, but to the poor and downtrodden in the city's ghettos, to whom Pina has been an angel of charity and mercy. But Pina does not chafe long in her lavish prison, for soon she too begins to show symptoms of the midnight visitations; a waxen pallor and overwhelming lethargy.

Fearing for her daughter's life, Pina's mother removes her from the city to their estate in the country. Still, Pina is not safe. For Antonio's wealth and his family's power enable him to hide a deadly secret. And the murderer manages to find his intended victim. Not to steal into her dreams and steal away her life, however, but to save her. And to find his own salvation in the arms of the only woman who has ever shown him love.

ISBN#9781932815207
US $6.99 / CDN $9.99
Mass Market Paperback / Paranormal
Available Now
www.helenrosburg.com

For more information
about other great titles from
Medallion Press, visit

www.medallionpress.com